JORDAN DUGDALE

COURTING THE DRAGON MAGE

ROMANCING THE REALMS

COURTING THE DRAGON MAGE

JORDAN DUGDALE

Bookvault responsible person GSPR
Copytech (UK) Ltd, Trading as Printondemand-worldwide.com
9 Culley Court Orton Southgate
Peterborough Cambridgeshire, PE2 6WA
United Kingdom gpsr@podww.com
01733 237867

ALSO BY JORDAN DUGDALE

The Whispered Tales Series
The Tidings of Misfits
A Waltz Through Flames
A Song of Hope

The Feyrsia Chronicles
A Flower's Fatal Thorn
Courting the Dragon Mage

AUTHOR NOTE

This is an **adult romantasy** that may not be suitable for all audiences. It contains the following content that may not be suited for everyone: sexually explicit content (with two open door scenes), a curse that involves rot, fantasy violence, gore, death, ritualistic sacrifice, and some cult activity. Your mental health matters.

To all the girls who burn bright despite the world trying to stifle their flame

FEYRSIA
Floating Isles of Amea
VRONA
Hot Springs
Souross
Ravenspire
Silverdrift
KINGDOM OF BRACAEA
Oriawood
Farmere
Neferil's Court
Mesa
Elvira Forest
Eirwyn's Court
KINGDOM OF KAHL
Nusa
Kraeva
Brûnheim

JORDAN DUGDALE

COURTING THE DRAGON MAGE

ROMANCING THE REALMS

CHAPTER ONE

LYRA

My head slammed against the floor, and the shouting became distant.

Still, I'd never felt more alive.

Get up, Lyra.

"No one told me the Pit Viper was little more than a weedy little cunt. It's almost unfair, beating on a woman like that..." My opponent's words were invigorating as my anger sang through me like a numbing drug. The taste of copper was thick on my tongue as blood flowed through my mouth, and I spat it out as I forced myself to my feet. People surrounded me, shouting, though I could not discern their words. The man who had struck me waved his hands as if he had already won. I wanted to groan; the world swayed, but I refused to fall again as I launched myself at him. The people around me gasped, but I was quick and had my legs wrapped around his waist and my arm across his neck before he could turn to see me coming. I pulled my arm taut against his neck, crushing his windpipe, and he flung us around in a panic, scrambling with blunt fingers to pry me from his back. If I could just get him to pass out…

I cried out as he threw himself back. I hit the ground hard, and my vision went spotty as the air was ripped from my lungs. Gods, had he broken my rib? No, no, I could still breathe.

"Submit," I whispered, forcing my arm to tighten around his neck. I had managed to keep my arm across his neck by Nymera's miracle. My fingers locked around my wrist, and though he struggled, his thrashing was beginning to fade. I was lucky; they'd put me against someone suited to my size in this fight.

After a few tense moments, the man slumped against me, allowing my hold on him to lessen. The fighting rings of Kraeva were not to the death, and though my blood sang for violence, I yielded. I used what strength I possessed to push the man off of me, allowing the one in charge of enforcing fair fighting to drag me to my feet. My hearing was distorted; the crowd cheered as he lifted my arm, their screams distant and too loud all at once. Still, I smiled.

This was why I came down here.

"The Pit Viper takes another prey!"

"Thank *fuck*. I put a lot of sandyms down on her victory."

"Fucking bitch cheated!"

Their words surrounded me as my head thundered painfully. The headache I was about to have would be merciless, but I won, which was all that mattered.

"A small spitfire as always, my little viper." A man in noble silks approached with a large bag of sandyms. My head throbbed again, and the motion jarred against my swelling cheek. My tongue darted out, tasting blood on my lip, which had split on the right side. My opponent had done a number on me before I knocked him out.

"Some of us have to earn our suppers." The lie came to me quickly. I had more than enough sandyms to fill my belly, but the fewer underlings who recognized me, the better. The last thing I wanted was to get my father or brother involved with the fighting pits in the belly of Kraeva. Hence, I paid a local mage handsomely for a potion that would mask my features for a few hours.

The bag of sandyms in Faeva's plump hand was for potions I could only find in the lower districts, districts my father was too proud to purchase from, even if it was for medicine for his son.

The magic was beginning to wear off, though. It prickled against my skin, a warning that if I didn't hurry away, my cover would shatter.

I attempted to keep calm as I held my hand out, hoping, for once, that Faeva would be merciful and give me my dues with little trouble.

He was not.

"Come and speak with the others. They wish to celebrate your recent accomplishments. It's not common to have someone of your stature go undefeated in the rings." His eyes raked over me, and I suppressed the urge to shudder in disgust.

"I'm afraid I have other business to attend." Now that the fighting had won, my lust for the fight had diminished and slunk away to the hollow of my chest to slumber until it woke again and demanded blood. I had no time for the squabbles of nobles, no time to pretend to give a shit about their praises. I didn't do this for the validation. I did this to calm the ache in my chest. I did this to try to save my brother from the Blooming Dahlia, a plague that had swept through the streets of Kraeva in recent months. My brother had fallen ill with it a week or so ago, and my desire to seek his cure had consumed all of my efforts.

Faeva frowned but relented with little trouble, passing over the bag of sandyms and simply nodding. The weight felt good in my palm, and I made a mental note to stop by the bakery nearby in the morning to buy some warm gyras. They were my brother's favorite. He may be well enough tomorrow to eat one. His appetite came and went, and he hadn't been able to enjoy his favorite treat since before he got sick.

"Next time, then," Faeva said, and I agreed with a feigned smile. He said that every time. Sometimes, I indulged him, but not tonight. Not as my skin itched, and the magic began to liberate itself from my skin.

People murmured quietly around me as I made my way towards the door. Another fight was getting ready to happen, so most people paid me little mind, which I was grateful for. The room was small, and sweat collected on my brow from so many bodies pressed closely together.

The nape of my neck prickled like I was being watched. I glanced up from where my eyes had been trained mainly on the floor and met the gaze of a faerie.

She was of Eirwyn's Court. I knew that much. The fae from Neferíl's Court did not come here, not while they warred with the humans of the north. If the fae were here, it was from the Elven King of Southern Elvira, the forest of the fae.

She stared at me, her hair almost ethereal as it wove around her, embellished with intricate braids. Her eyes were cat-like, her ears as pointed as her canines when she flashed a wicked smile my way. It wasn't uncommon for the fair folk to attend these fights; they had a simple curiosity for human affairs and could only breach the forest's edge at night.

Another faerie stood next to her, a male. He was tall and lanky, with dark hair that was longer than hers and draped over his shoulders. He was pale, eerily so, his eyes dark voids of black.

I ducked my head, ignoring the anxious patter in my chest, and strode past him.

The male faerie said something, but I couldn't understand him. Some folk from Kraeva braved the faerie food and wine to understand the fae, diluting it to avoid the consequences of too much of its consumption. I was not one of those people, and I smiled apologetically as I met the faerie's gaze.

He didn't say anything else, and I barreled into someone in my eagerness to escape them.

"*Shit.* I'm sor—" My words died as the stranger flinched away from me in disgust.

It was the crowned prince, Nasir, someone I was all too familiar with during my time growing up in the castle. His hair was slicked back, and his dark eyes raked over me in disgust. Luckily, he didn't seem to recognize me. His attention turned towards the front of his shirt, now covered in ale. I must have knocked his glass from his grasp.

What was Prince Nasir doing at the fighting pits?

"Stupid cunt—these silks cost more than your worthless life. They could throw you back in the pits, you know—all it would take is a snap of my pretty little fingers." He raised his hand, his fingers poised at the ready. Like a snake, ready to strike. "Next time, I'll see you fight someone you cannot win against."

I sneered, but my words lodged in the back of my throat as my skin prickled again. *Last warning. I need to get out of here before the prince recognizes me.*

"My apologies, Your Royal Highness." I curtsied and then turned on my heel, fleeing before the prince could rebut.

I spilled out into the alleyway. The air, while warm, was a welcome relief against my aching skin as I pressed myself against the wall and sighed.

That was too close. I would time things better next time.

Still, the thrill of it all sang through me, and breathless laughter escaped my lips as I pressed a hand to my face. I clutched the bag of sandyms in my other hand as I hurried from the alley, eager to be home. The fighting pits were located in the lower districts of Kraeva, but I had learned which alleys and side roads to take to reach the royal districts more quickly as I tucked my sandyms inside my shirt, hiding the bag from wandering eyes. I knew better than to flash currency in the struggling parts of the city.

Wind trailed through the deserted streets as I stayed within shadows, hidden from anyone who might be out. Knights patrolled the city in their light leather armor and khopeshes, but I managed to stay out of their observant gaze as I hurried up the cliffs towards the Royal Keep.

A low whimper echoed to my right as I passed by an alley. It was so soft it could have been the wind, but as my eyes adjusted to the dark, I flinched and ducked away as a fist swung past my left shoulder.

"Beat it, little rat," a man hissed, his eyes glowing in the darkness. Fae, perhaps? I couldn't tell as I scrambled away, my heart a wild, untamed thing in my chest. I couldn't see well enough in the dark, but it looked like there were two of them, and one had someone pinned up against the wall further in the alley, their shirt wrapped around his fingers. "Before you end up in'a sit'a'tion you don' wanna be in."

"What did he do?" I asked, gesturing to the man pinned to the wall. "Because if there's something I hate, it's pricks that think they can beat on someone half their size."

The man who had nearly punched me growled and

lunged, his bald head gleaming in the moon's light. I swung out of the way just in time and then let go. Headache be damned.

The ache in my chest rekindled as it sang in excitement. I swept to the side and turned, instantly swinging out to grab the man's wrist as he lashed out at me with a curled fist.

Dodging the man's attack, I sank low. I needed to take him out quickly. I was already exhausted from my last fight.

He was quicker than I thought, though, and he laughed. "Tired, street rat?" His words were meant to poke at me, tug at my resolve, and make me reckless, but I had learned long ago that anger only led to mistakes and loss.

Somehow, I managed to get behind him as he darted past me.

Gotcha. Like the man from the pits, I latched myself onto the man's back, wrapped my legs around his waist, and slipped my arm across his windpipe. Tugging, I did not hold back as I had in the fighting pits. Here, there was no one telling me to show mercy.

The man struggled for several moments before he eventually gave up, his body slumping. I released him and managed to stay on my feet, my attention turning towards the others in the alley.

The other man cursed in a language I did not recognize and spit on the ground. "Not worth the trouble," he said in a heavily accented tone, pushing the man towards me and bolting.

Chest heaving, my legs gave out. I had borrowed too much time tonight and fought the odds stacked against me. The man they'd been bullying rushed over and knelt, his face swimming in my blurry vision. Oh gods, I was going to pass out. I couldn't pass out, not here. Not now. Someone would find me. Someone would…

"Breathe." The man's voice washed over me, and I inhaled sharply, forcing the darkness encroaching at my vision's edge to retreat. It was as if by magic, and I blinked rapidly as my eyes fell upon the stranger.

"Thank you for saving me," the stranger said, his eyes burning with the flourish of magic. It was otherworldly, and I immediately flushed as he smiled at me. The alley was too dark to reveal his features, but I knew he wasn't human. No human looked as he did now, with the soft glow of magic brushed against his skin.

"You shouldn't be out at night unless you know how to handle yourself. Or at least keep away from dark alleys. There's a fucking war going on," I scolded, but my voice was weak, wavering from exhaustion.

"Yes, well..." the stranger's thumb brushed against the sharp line of my jaw, and the tingle of magic returned. Suddenly, I didn't feel quite so weak, as if I could stand if I tried. Pain pulsed through my face, a reminder that I had taken quite the beating *before* I had fought the men in the alley. "They caught me off guard as I was leaving."

"What were they bothering you for anyway?" I trailed off, distracted by the man's thumb against my cheek.

He pulled away, adjusting his jacket as he rose and offered me a hand. "Wrong place, wrong time, I gather," he muttered as I allowed him to pull me to my feet. Yes, I could make it home now, and a startling clarity overcame me.

Not many knew how to wield magic, which meant this man was either a fae or a mage.

Both prospects made me uneasy, and I watched the man limp over and pick something up off the ground. A cane, one he leaned heavily against as he turned to meet my nervous gaze.

I shouldn't have been so frightened; I had seen him incapable of defending himself, but the idea of what he was capable of magically didn't sit right in my stomach, and I sidled towards the lip of the alley and cleared my throat.

"I'm glad I could help, but I should get home."

"Let me accompany you. As you said, it's dangerous at night."

I sneered, trying to tame the flurry of my racing heart in my chest. "And as you saw, I know how to care for myself. Good night…"

A low, breathy laughter escaped the man's lips. "Alistair."

I turned and fled the alley, sticking to the main roads towards my flower shop. The magic had worn from my face, freeing it from its disguise, and while I was usually one to stick to the shadows to avoid recognition, the whole night had left me rattled.

No one was out anyway. The warring kingdoms had left the streets of Kraeva silent; everyone was too fearful of Bracaea flying their dragons to lay waste to the cities and villages to dare brave the nightlife. No one knew of the sickness that festered in the belly of their city. Not yet. I knew it was only a matter of time, though. The Crown couldn't silence it forever.

Chilly sea air brushed my face as I rounded the corner, and my flower shop appeared. It was near the keep, which loomed high up on a cliffside edging the ocean, and relief overcame me. Everything that had transpired tonight left me rattled. It was becoming increasingly dangerous to travel the city at night.

A shadow blotted out the moon, and my blood ran cold as I looked up and met the sight of a dragon soaring overhead. It wasn't close enough to discern its size or what it looked like, but there was no mistaking it as it sailed over the city and bells began to sound, an alarm signaling that the city was under attack.

I quickened my pace and did not look up again as I found myself safely inside my shop, my heart thundering in my ears.

What the fuck was a dragon doing in Kraeva?

CHAPTER TWO

LYRA

The following day bred an uncomfortable sensation of peace.

Despite being up half the night with the sounds of guards on the streets and a thicker patrol of knights guarding our homes, I rose from bed in good spirits as I padded down the hallway towards Cade's room. He'd been asleep when I had returned, so I'd left him alone despite my burning desire to check on him.

I knocked lightly on the door. "Cade? Are you awake?" A cough, a soft, pathetic noise, answered me. I pushed into the room, ignoring my instincts, screaming at me to do the opposite. The Blooming Dahlia was a terrible plague, attacking the lungs of its victims and causing welts on the face and arms. There was no evidence indicating that it was contagious, but considerable uncertainty surrounded the plague and how it spread. Father had insisted we move Cade to the castle, but the king had forbidden it, fearing it would spread. He then demanded that my father remain close in case anyone in the keep should get it. Father, ever doting on the crown, had not even come to check on his son's health.

My chest ached with infected bitterness. I often harbored dark thoughts of my father and the useless man he was to his children. My mother, too. She was gone more than she was around, too concerned about sailing around the world and growing rich off her trading empire. Fuck the both of them, I had thought more than once. Cade was the only family I needed.

The room was thick with the scent of sickness as I trailed inside. The tonics father had sent did nothing but stave off the pain the plague caused. I had hung water faelies from the ceiling, hoping it would pull the toxins from the air, but it didn't seem to work. The long, white flowers were as vibrant as ever, kept alive by the magic that soaked the air in Kraeva, but Cade wasn't even strong enough to sit up on his own today.

"Let me help you," I whispered, careful to keep my voice down as I hurried to his side. Some would call me mad for being so near him, but he was my *brother*, the only one who had ever been there for me. I would do anything to keep him comfortable.

"Gods, Lyra, what the fuck happened to your face?" His voice was a ghost of its former self, lacking strength as I helped him up, his back pressed to pillows that I plumped between him and the bed's backboard. Sunlight trickled through the window to our right, bathing the space in a comfortable glow.

I laughed. My brother had never been one for tact or subtlety. His face was pinched with worry. I noticed a fresh batch of welts lining his forehead, but kept a neutral face as I checked him over. He was ten winters younger than I, but he shouldered enough stress for both of us. Anxiety had caused grey to tangle within the dark curls of his head. His eyes, unusually blue for a man of Kahl, pierced through me like they were trying to uncover the secret I harbored.

"It's nothing, Cade. Don't worry about me." Typically, I would have tended to the bruising on my face with salves, but the chaos caused by the dragon sighting the night before had left my thoughts elsewhere.

Cade tilted his head towards the window. "What was the kingdom up in arms about last night? With the alarm bell going off, I could scarcely sleep."

I lowered my voice as if anyone were around to hear me. "A dragon."

"No! I don't believe you. Since the kingdoms went to war, the dragons have all been called back to Bracaea and the Voiceless Mountains." Still, the liveliness in Cade's eyes made my chest hurt. I hadn't seen such life in his eyes since before he got sick.

"It's true. I saw it with my eyes when I slipped away to catch some fresh air. I couldn't tell what it looked like, but—"

"Some of the ladies of court have been whispering rumors that Alistair Sylverhorn is in town," Cade interrupted. "Many know him as the dragon mage, though."

I stilled. "That's the mage the king spoke about a fortnight ago, right?" I struggled to keep my emotions from showing on my face then. "I didn't know his name was Alistair."

"I only found out his name talking to Analys," Cade said. His face grew sheepish at the narrowness of my eyes. "I didn't see her, but we've been writing to each other for a while. It was in her last letter."

I recalled the man from the night before, the one I'd saved in the alleyway. Hadn't he introduced himself as Alistair? It couldn't be the same.

Could it?

Panic clawed its way into my throat and squeezed my lungs. He'd used magic on me. Oh *gods*.

I had run into Alistair Sylverhorn, a traitor of Bracaea and enemy of Kraeva. I had saved his life. Did that make me a traitor to my kingdom?

Cade covered his mouth as a violent coughing fit overcame him, and he pulled me from my spiral. Silence filled the air for several moments, and I left to snag a glass of water from the kitchen across the hall. When I returned, Cade's eyes shone, his face awash with the gleam of sweat. "I don't feel very well, Ly."

Setting the water on the table beside the bed, I squeezed Cade's hand. "I'll go and grab some medicine. It'll help you sleep, at the very least. If you're feeling up to it later, I'll grab us some fresh gyras from the market. I know you love those."

"Ly—please be careful. I know the Greenheart Festival is coming up soon. Please tell Father that I understand why he hasn't come and that I miss him terribly."

I stifled my anger and nodded stiffly. "I will. I know he has been busy. I'm sure he has his reasons."

"Ly, I know you and Father have your differences, but…" he trailed off, falling prey to another coughing fit, and I laid a gentle hand on his shoulder.

"Just rest, Cade. I'll go grab that medicine."

After feeding Cade the medicine and ensuring he was comfortable, I descended the stairs into the flower shop to attend to the morning chores before the shop opened. The shop was small but homely, pristine from my doting touch; there was not an inch of dust on the shelves and tiled floor, a light green and white diamond-shaped tile. Flames flickered in glass orbs that dotted the walls, casting a warm glow over the shop. Vibrantly colored pots or flowers, including dark roses, multi-colored tulips, and light brown sand lilies, occupied much of the shelves. I had even successfully grown some faerie wildflowers, small, brightly colored flowers native to the groves of Elvira Forest.

The bell on the door sounded, and I glanced up and exhaled sharply. Did I forget to lock the door when I returned last night?

"I'm sorry, we're not open—" The words died in my mouth as the stranger limped inside and quickly shut the door, his fingers twisting in an intricate pattern as magic danced over the door and the stained-glass, round windows that decorated each side. A commotion sounded outside, and my hands curled tightly around the broom handle as I approached. "Sir?"

The stranger's cane tapped against the floor as he turned. It was Alistair—the man from the alley.

Now that he was in the light of the shop and not the darkness of an alley, I could study his features. A faerie, though humanity clung to him like a second skin. It wasn't unusual; many human-faerie relationships had been popping up as of late, and the offspring of such intimacies had presented themselves in Kraeva. His skin was a dark golden brown, his chin and cheeks dusted by a faint beard, a rarity for anyone with fae blood. Curls tumbled over his face and shoulders, the point of his ears peeking out as he stood tall. His eyes, a swirl of gold and green, pinned me in place.

His skin glowed as he strode forward, his eyes burning with magic. It was otherworldly, and I immediately flushed as he grinned at me, the tips of his pointed canines drenched in golden caps. He wore expensive clothing made of exquisite silk, the dark green of his shirt embellished with threads of gold. His leanness was highlighted in the tightness of his dark pants, and he leaned heavily against a golden cane with a dragon's head as he pressed a finger to his lips, his gaze darting back over his shoulder.

"Did not mean to intrude," he whispered. "I'm afraid I'm being followed." He eyed me as if studying me for the first time, and his nostrils flared as his eyes widened. "Wait, you're the girl from the alley, the one that saved me."

I narrowed my eyes at him. "And *you're* Alistair Sylverhorn."

Alistair bowed as the commotion continued outside. "In the flesh." He had the arrogance to laugh as he glanced about. "What is the Pit Viper doing running a silly little flower shop?"

My gaze shot up towards the ceiling, where Cade rested, and I leaned forward to hiss between gritted teeth. "Quiet. My brother is resting upstairs and doesn't know about my…"

"Late-night hobbies?" Alistair suggested, his head tilting to the side. He lashed forward, pinning me up against the counter as he pressed his hand to cover my mouth. He was warm, almost unnaturally so, and I glared at him as he raised his head to listen.

"There are mages about, tucked behind illusions," he whispered, drawing his lips to my ear. "They're looking for your shop. I fear I may have involved you, but I needed somewhere to hide."

How dare you. I couldn't speak, so I thought the words instead, my brow furrowing in rage. If I kicked the leg Alistair limped with, there was a chance I could get out from beneath him and get to the door. If I turned him into the mages that sought him out, maybe they'd have an answer for Cade's sickness. Maybe…

"Quiet, little flower. Your heart is beating like a caged bird." Alistair pulled away slightly, then entirely.

I exhaled sharply, still clinging to the broom pressed

between us as if that would keep me safe from a *mage*. "Get out."

Alistair's curls fell into his face as he lowered his head, his lips pursed as he backed a respectable distance away. "Little flower—"

"Don't call me that. Give me one good reason why I shouldn't hail a guard right now. You're a wanted man, Alistair Sylverhorn."

Alistair's eyes darkened like a shadow curled against his gaze. "You shouldn't believe everything you hear." He straightened, his eyes cast about the dark room as his cane tapped against the tile of the floor. *Tap. Tap. Tap.* "The world is full of terrible liars. Some good ones, too."

"Well, yes, but how do I know you're not one of them?"

Alistair gestured to the point of his ear. "Faeries can't lie."

I scoffed. "No, but they can deceive. That shit doesn't work on me. Who are you hiding from?"

Alistair stared at me for a good, long moment. So long the heat of his stare beckoned me to draw closer, to kneel before him, to worship— "Good day, Miss A'mar."

I looked at him, broken from my daze, as he turned to leave. "Wait—"

But he was gone.

He was gone, and I was left standing in the middle of my flower shop, wondering what I'd done to piss off the gods and have Alistair Sylverhorn tangled up in my business.

"Nymera, give me strength," I muttered, hurrying over to check the door. Locked. I suppressed the urge to shudder and still my panicked mind. I had no time to think about it. Cade was right. The Greenheart Festival was just two days away. Due to his illness, I couldn't even open the shop to prepare. The crown depended on me to deliver enough flowers to decorate the royal gardens for the masquerade, and I was behind schedule.

Leaning the broom against the wall, I turned and rubbed my hands together.

I had no time to worry about Alistair Sylverhorn.

Time to get to work.

CHAPTER THREE

LYRA

*B*etween taking care of Cade and preparing the carts full of flowers to take to Kraeva's Keep for the Greenheart Festival, I barely got any sleep. Two days passed in a blur, and I was so busy I had little time to think about Alistair breaking in or the strange conversation I'd had with him.

Everyone in the city, human and faerie alike, was invited to attend the festival to thank the magic of Elvira for stretching across the deserted, tropical lands of Kahl and blessing it with life. By the evening of the festival, I was exhausted, drenched in sweat, and worried about Cade. Perhaps I would slip away to check on him before my expected attendance…

"You've done good work, Ly."

I tensed as my father approached, approval etched in his gaze.

He was the last person I wanted to see, though I'd expected to run into him eventually. He was right; the gardens looked spectacular, with vibrant tulips and roses arranged in neat bouquets and arrangements on pedestals. The gardens smelled divine, a blend of rain-soaked wood and the sharpness of cinnamon. Servants flurried about, getting everything prepped for the arrival of guests. Many filled trays with food and drink, or slipped around me with shears to tend to hedges and flowers already in the gardens. I recognized Maya, one of the kitchen girls I'd befriended growing up. I made a mental note to find her later to see if there was any other news on the dragon sighting as I forced my attention over to my father.

"Hello, Father." I struggled to keep the ire from my tone, but seeing him flounder in exquisite silks and expensive jewelry, gifts from the crown for his healing when his only son lay sick in bed outside the keep, was difficult. "It would have been better if Cade had been here."

"I hope he is well. I feel terrible that I haven't been able to slip away to visit him. The king forbade it—doesn't want anyone in the castle exposed..." My father trailed off, settling on the fading bruise on my face. "What happened?"

"Nothing."

Father's gaze was disapproving, but he said nothing. Like Cade, he knew better than to pry. My will was stronger than steel, and he knew I wouldn't tell him. A part of me suspected he knew what I got up to at night, but I was twenty-eight winters old. Long had been the days when he could command me to do anything.

"How *is* the royal family?" Desperate to change the subject, my skin crawled. I was eager to flee this conversation entirely, my eyes darting around as guests arrived in elegant silks, their faces covered by masks.

"The queen is abed." My father sighed, pulling away. He looked rugged, as if he hadn't slept well for quite some time. His beard, though kept, had new grey streaking through it, and dark circles etched the brown skin beneath his eyes. My father, ever the nurturing type, did not know when to stop caring for others to care for himself. "I fear she will be for quite some time until we figure out what ails her."

I gave him a sharp look. "Blooming Dahlia?"

Father's nose flared, and he glanced around and stepped closer to lower his voice. "We're not sure, but we don't think so. She doesn't have symptoms of the plague. Fever, chills, bouts of madness. We keep her asleep with Lily Milk most of the time."

The news was most troubling. It felt strange to be celebrating life when there was so much death in Kraeva. People were sick and dying on the streets in the lower districts, only to be ignored by those here for the sake of privilege and ignorance. It was sickening.

"Excuse me, Father," I said, moving away to attend to the last of the preparations. I'd need to hurry if I were going to leave to return to the flower shop before the festivities began. I wouldn't return if it weren't for Cade's need for more medicine.

I checked every flower decoration from top to bottom, weaving around guests dressed lavishly with goblets of wine in their hands. No one paid me any attention, not that they would. I was a mouse among cats and easily ignored.

"Hi, Maya." I sidled up to Maya as I wove around the golden pillars that held up the keep towards her, who had slipped away and returned, now in a pretty blue dress that complemented her dark hair, which she had styled into swirling curls.

"Great job on the flowers, Ly." Maya smiled, a dazzling gleam against her face as she took my arm and tugged me close. "Where's Cade?"

I chewed on my lower lip, wondering how truthful I could be with her. Father had insisted we keep Cade's illness a secret. It was a miracle I was allowed in the castle with my exposure, but I was the only florist they trusted with the job. The risk of sickness was worth it for pretty flowers in the royal family's eyes.

"He couldn't make it. We're busy at the shop, so he's handling business there." The lie came easily despite the guilt of lying to my friend, and I quickly changed the subject. "Do you have a dress I could borrow? I forgot one."

Maya squeezed my arm and smiled. "Of course."

Maya told me stories about the castle as we strolled through it. It had remained much the same as I remembered it, with too many rooms and winding hallways to disappear into. I'd loved it as a child; getting lost in the castle had saved me from many obligations my father had tried to drag me into. Now, the castle felt like a prison, like you could never escape it. The halls were relatively empty, though, and I listened idly as we drew close to the kitchen quarters, where Maya's room was.

"Here," she said, tugging a green dress off the hanger in her wardrobe. Maya's father was the head cook, so she was given the honor of her own room, small as it was.

"Thank you." I slipped into the dress quickly and looked over myself in her vanity; nothing could be done about my hair in such a short time, but I ran my fingers through it and sighed. It would have to do. It wasn't as if I was trying to impress anyone.

"Ly?" Maya's voice was meek, her expression sheepish as I turned. "Do you think you could talk to your father? I hate to ask…"

"What is it?"

Tears swelled in Maya's eyes. "Its Mother. She's fallen ill, and for whatever reason, Father is too afraid to speak to your father about it. He has my mother locked in her room and has told me not to speak with anyone about it."

My stomach plummeted. "I'll speak with Father about it right away." I did not want to worry her, but if the king got wind of her mother's illness inside the keep, it would not bode well for her.

I rushed forward, took Maya's hands in mine, and squeezed. "It's going to be okay," I said, loathing the empty promise. "We'll figure out what's going on."

Maya nodded, blinking through tear-stained lashes, and hugged me. She was warm, and I hugged her tightly before pulling back and wiping away her tears. "Thank you, Lyra. There's something strange going on, but I'm rarely able to leave the castle to understand why. I know there's a war going on, but it's never affected us like this before."

I frowned. Maya was ignorant in that regard. The war had left people suffering and forced them to depend on locally grown food. The cost of meat had grown so expensive that most were surviving on fruits and what could be grown out of the ground, and the Blooming Dahlia had infected much of the lower district. It was some miracle that the general public of the upper districts hadn't seen hints of it yet. Perhaps they had, and they chose to remain woefully ignorant.

"Did you hear about the dragon?" I asked. "I wonder if the war efforts are worsening."

Maya nodded. "I overheard some of the servants talking about it. The cup girl said the king was blaming Bracaea for something. I don't know what it was, though."

The plague, perhaps? A thought I'd considered but refused to entertain. It didn't matter where the plague had come from. All that mattered was finding a way to cure it before it took my brother.

"I think it was Alistair." Maya spoke in hushed tones as if, somehow, she'd be overheard. "Alistair Sylverhorn? The dragon mage? Some say he can turn into a dragon and that he hides out here to avoid the mages hunting him for treason."

I scoffed. I couldn't help it. It slipped out of my mouth before I could stop it, and my gaze softened as Maya flinched away, offended. "I'm sorry, Maya. Those are just silly rumors."

"But what if they aren't? Alistair is a monster. He eats people's hearts." The fear in my friend's eyes was just; these were frightening times, full of uncertainty. We knew little of mages; they were mainly northern folk, and the idea of them eating hearts and performing unsavory magic was not out of the realm of possibility. My mind whirled. What was Alistair capable of? I knew for certain he *was* in Kraeva, but I didn't believe he could turn into a dragon, nor that he ate people's hearts.

"Come, Maya. The festivities will keep your mind off things," I suggested, pulling her towards the door. "We'll both do well for the distraction."

Maya and I separated the moment we returned to the gardens, and I accepted a goblet of sparkling wine when it was offered. Maya didn't have an extra mask, and my face felt incredibly bare as I sought out my father.

"Look at what the cat dragged in…a *street rat*." I tensed and turned, meeting the eyes of the crowned prince. He sneered as he draped an arm over the shoulders of one of the court ladies—I didn't recall her name—her fingers pressed delicately against her bare chest. A necklace of diamonds dripped down her clavicle, and she smiled wickedly as Prince Nasir laughed.

"Oh shit, how unkind of me. You aren't so filthy to have grown up on the streets. *Castle rat* is a better term."

I forced a smile. The last thing I needed was the ire or attention of the king. Not when Cade suffered from the plague. Still, my chest burned with rage.

I bowed. "Your Highness. I hope you are enjoying the festival. If you'll excuse me, I need to go and find my father." I turned, only to flinch when the prince grabbed my arm.

Dragging me closer, his demeanor shifted. "I didn't dismiss you."

I forced my gaze to his, stunned. The prince had always taken to bullying me. We'd grown up together in the palace, and he never failed to make me feel small. He'd never touched me, though. Not until now.

"Let me go." Fear would have been better at this moment, but any anxiety I might have felt washed away, reforging into pure, raw anger. Fingers curled into a fist, and I tensed, ready to lash out should the prince try anything. Consequences be *damned...*

"Ah, Lyra, there you are. I've been looking everywhere for you." A sharp scent, a cross between smoke and the woods after it rained, filled the air around me as someone slumped their arm over my shoulders.

I knew it was Alistair before I looked up. His voice was deeper than I expected as I met his golden-green eyes. He was warm, heat soaking through my clothes, and I was too stunned by his sudden appearance to wonder how he'd learned my first name.

The disgust that flourished across the prince's face was nearly palpable, and Alistair shifted against me. "You wouldn't deny a princeling his plaything, would you?"

The court lady beside Nasir sneered, laughter dancing on her tongue as Alistair tightened his hold on me, as if he sensed my anger and desire to show Nasir I was not some meek girl to bully.

"Of course not, Your Highness, but dear Lyra here promised me a dance. I can return her after, if you'd like?"

Prince Nasir's eyes flashed angrily, but he remained silent as Alistair turned and led me away.

"How are you able to be out in public?" I asked quietly. "You're a wanted man."

Alistair laughed. "No thank you?" He pulled away and offered his arm, which I took if only to keep up appearances. "This is not the face most know me. Now…about that dance."

I shook my head. "I must go and find my father."

"One dance—I can sense the Prince's gaze. He won't leave you alone unless he grows bored of waiting."

I relented, knowing his words to be true. The last thing I needed was for the prince to find me again after I had offended him. That was a worry for later.

"Unless you wish to spite me; there are many men and women in attendance that would love to dance with me."

Godsdamn it.

CHAPTER FOUR

ALISTAIR

Rahfín rattled his cage of bones in my ribcage, causing my chest to ache. Something about the girl in my arms made him restless and drew me back to her side. It was likely the reason I had braved the festival in the first place, even knowing Soria was likely in attendance. It was most curious. I had never had a reaction like this from him before.

Calm down.

Rahfín's demanding presence swelled in my mind. *I cannot. She will be the cure.*

What do you mean?

I don't know yet, but we must keep her safe until we do.

Rahfín's cryptic nature was foul, but I did as he asked, knowing my days were numbered if I couldn't find a way to separate the dragon inside me from where he'd tangled against my soul.

My leg ached, but it wasn't so unbearable that I couldn't ignore it. Still, it reminded me that dragon sickness was ever-present. It manifested itself in my pain, in the fire that burned fiercely in my belly. Every time Rahfín clawed his way out of my skin, I felt myself slipping away.

Meeting the girl in my arms was the first time Rahfín had settled, and I had to know why.

"Lyra," I tested her name on my tongue, satisfied with the way her eyes darkened when she met mine. "Do you know how to dance?"

"Of course. One doesn't grow up in the castle and lack their fair share of dancing lessons." She wasn't lying, as her hands came to rest in my waiting palm and against my shoulder. She moved with fluidity and grace, the same as I had seen her fighting in the pits beneath the city.

The festival was in full swing. Some attendees wore flower crowns or grass-made masks, with court faeries and humans alike arriving to celebrate. It was always court faeries that joined; wild fae never left the safety of the forest beyond Kahl's borders, save for the occasional bard, like the satyr who played near the fountain, his hooves sinking into the sand. I would never grow used to seeing all the green growing out of desert sand. Even by mage standards, it shouldn't exist the way it did. Faerie magic willed it so. Eirwyn's magic willed it so.

As evening gave way to night, I was pleasantly surprised by how the flowers unfurled and glowed a beautiful, luminescent yellow from their petals. Lyra had truly outdone herself with the flowers.

"I would not have expected such a natural from someone who likes to spend her time bringing down men twice her size in the pits."

Lyra tensed, her anger sending a thrill through me. "Keep your voice down. And he was the same size as me."

"Not that one. The one from last week."

Lyra's eyes flashed, and I smirked at her. "Your name—Pit Viper. You've earned that title."

"How long have you been watching me?"

I shook my head. "Not long," I answered truthfully. I wasn't sure she believed me. Leaning down, I brushed my lip against the cup of her ear. "Don't worry, Lyra A'mar. Your secret is safe with me. I have no intention of telling anyone what you like to do after dark. We all have our...pleasures." She shuddered against my words, and I pulled away, smug at her eyes' heated expression.

She reached a hand up to cup my cheek. It was oddly intimate, her fingers calloused and rough as I leaned into her touch. Rahfín hummed against my heart, contented by her gentle touch.

"Good," she whispered as quietly as I'd had, her eyes shining. "Because you know what I'm capable of if you decide to betray me."

I found myself at a loss for words. Lyra was unlike any human I'd ever met.

I sensed Soria's presence the moment she arrived. It was difficult to ignore the way the grand-mage's magic demanded to be seen despite *knowing* she was an enemy of Kahl. She was like a beacon of light in a room of darkness, and I found my eyes flickering to her the moment she came down the steps into the gardens. She wore a different face, but I knew it was her. I *knew*.

She didn't seem to have noticed my being here, but I knew it was only a matter of time.

"Are you from Eirwyn's Court?"

Lyra's question caught me off guard, bringing my gaze back to her, and I slightly shook my head. "My father is of his court. My mother is from here."

Her eyes flashed in surprise. "But you are a mage."

I laughed loud enough to draw the attention of those nearby, and I felt the moment Soria's eyes settled on me. My stomach twisted, and the dragon nestled in my bones growled —a warning. I needed to leave. "Last I checked, I could wield the magics of this world, yes."

Lyra flushed, and another thrill sang through me. Something about riling her up…

"What are you doing in the south, then? There are those who deem you an enemy of my people. You are a sworn traitor of Bracaea."

I flashed a toothy smile, ignoring the latter statement. Lyra was right about that, but I was no spy. "Do you think me to be a spy, Lyra?"

She frowned, her grip tightening against me. "I don't know you at all, do I? You *could* be a spy for all I know."

I sobered, keeping my gaze on Lyra even as I sensed Soria approaching. "Do you want honesty? Or will you feel better with a lie? I'll keep your secret if you keep mine."

Her eyes were a lovely shade of brown; one could get lost in them if they weren't careful.

"The truth," she said, her eyes narrowing. "Since you cannot lie to me. Not with fae magic…"

I laughed, and I pressed close. I could have laid a kiss on Lyra's cheek if I wished. Instead, I moved to the cusp of her ear, my breath tickling the curl of her hair. "I find the women down here are much more to my tastes. The men too. Who am I to deny myself a bit of life's pleasures, even with a war going on?"

When I pulled away, Lyra's frown had deepened.

"Not what you expected me to say?"

Lyra shook her head.

"Consider my curiosity—your culture is rich and full. It's *my* culture, a culture I never got to know. The north has their dragons and magic, but Kahl? Kraeva has good relations with Eirwyn's court, has *skünchrs* that work for your royal guard. It's fascinating." All a half-lie; it wasn't the reason I'd fled south.

Soria's presence was a reminder that I'd tucked myself away in Elvira Forest to avoid fighting in a war I believed, no, I *knew* to be unjust.

"And the north? What is it like?"

"Cold."

Lyra didn't seem satisfied by that answer, and it drew another laugh from my lips. "In all reality, it's about what you'd expect. The mages watch over Vrona inside the wall at Ravenspire, and some of the little villages outside of the wall suffer from the wrath of Neferíl's Court. The wild fae have been busy, stealing children up north in retaliation of an old grudge. The Bracaean's blamed Neferíl. The people up there are hardy, though, and the dragons keep the royal family company in their mountainous keep."

"Do you believe the rumors?"

"That the princess of Bracaea was kidnapped?"

When Lyra nodded, I spared a moment to answer, swinging her around and pulling her back in. Her dress flowed around her body like water, and a wave of admiration ran through me. She looked good in it, which was conflicting. I hadn't come to Kraeva to dance with Lyra A'mar.

Quite the opposite, in fact.

"No, I don't. There's so much more going on than what it seems, Miss A'mar." I pulled away then, ignoring her curious expression. I wouldn't give her anymore. I couldn't, not as I sensed Soria's presence drawing closer. She'd found me.

"Thank you for the dance."

Lyra scoffed. "Oh, I'm not allowed to dismiss myself, but you're allowed to abandon me mid-dance? Typical." Her lip curled lightly over her teeth, and I grinned, tugging her closer. I drew my lips to her knuckles and pressed a soft kiss there.

"It only means we have unfinished business. Until next time, Lyra."

I did leave them, turned just as Soria pushed between two dancing bodies, her eyes darting over everyone's faces. Our eyes locked, but by the time she'd opened her mouth to command me to halt, I snapped my fingers. A magical glamour wove over my body, changing my features, and I disappeared into the stealth of mingling guests.

CHAPTER FIVE

LYRA

"That man you were dancing with, who was he?"

A daze had overcome me when Alistair left, as if the world was too bleak or cold. I stood amid swaying, dancing bodies, and the voice called me back from the swell of my thoughts. When I peered over at her, I stilled.

This woman was from the north. I knew because of her accent and the furs she wore, which stood out plainly against the silks and bare skin of the South. She was also drenched in magic; it sang in the air like a life of its own, coiled around her like a second skin. I had no magic, no fae blood in my ancestry to speak of, but I sensed the magic in the air all the same. Her dark hair was short and curled, pressed tightly to her head, and when she smiled, it was cold behind a golden mask. No one seemed to pay her any mind, but I saw her clear as day before me.

"I—what?" The woman spoke Kraevian very well, considering she was a northerner.

"That man. Do you know him?"

Something about her question was off-putting. If she were

a mage from the north, she likely was hunting Alistair. I should tell her the truth. It danced on the edge of my tongue, willing to speak itself into existence, but something kept it tucked behind the bars of my teeth. Something did not seem right.

"I'm sorry, miss, but I don't. He didn't tell me his name." I curtsied slightly and turned away. "I wish you the best. I think he went that way, though, if you wish to ask him yourself," I said, pointing in the opposite direction I'd seen Alistair leave.

The woman lashed out and curled a hand around my wrist as I tried to leave. I was so shocked by the motion that I attempted to flinch away, but her hold on me was like iron and did not relent.

"How plain." Her tongue clicked in disapproval, and I blanched as if she'd struck me. "Wonder what led him to you."

"Let me go." I carried all the weight of my anger in that last word. People danced around us as if we were in an unseen bubble they could not touch, and I looked around, trying to make eye contact with anyone who could help me.

The woman's eyes were a maelstrom of blue, a stormy sea grey that seemed to change shades the longer I stared beyond the golden mask she wore to hide her features. "You reek of him."

The skin where her fingers touched me tingled.

Something inside me withered and died.

"He has condemned you," she whispered, drawing close, pressing her lips to mine. I was too shocked to react, and when I blinked, she was gone. With her, the magic left, too, and someone bumped into me, launching me to the ground.

"I'm so sorry! I didn't see you." The person rambled, but I flinched away from their touch and fled the dance floor. Hurrying up the garden steps, I tried to still my heart, which the woman's words had rattled.

Father. I needed to find my father.

I took a moment as I rounded the corner of the keep, pressing my back against the cool wall and closing my eyes. That woman had been looking for Alistair and knew I had lied to her. I had no idea what she'd meant by her words, but I wanted to get as far from her as I could.

"It's getting out of hand, Hasam." A low voice spoke in the room to my left, and I froze. Hasam was my father's name. "I fear it has come to the point where we must force our hand."

"If you'll just give me more time—" My father's voice bordered on desperation, and I pressed more tightly against the wall, eager to hear but less eager at the prospect of getting caught.

"There is no more time. The Blooming Dahlia has infected some in the castle. The king must not know this; he already worries too much about his wife. If we are to contain this, we must act." That sounded like Kamír, one of the king's advisers and head of the royal guard. I'd admired him once when I thought I could grow up to be a knight, but age had opened my eyes to his cruelty and harsh views.

Silence passed for several moments before my father spoke again. "All I ask is that you spare my son. If I were to ask for any favors and lean on the fact that I am the royal healer, it is this. Don't kill my only heir. Lyra has no interest in taking my place when I die, but Cade does. Kill the others but spare a few for me to continue my work and spare my son."

"My loyalty is to the crown, Hasam. No one else. I cannot promise anything, but I will try..."

I slunk away before I heard anything else, my heart pounding again. My father and the adviser were speaking about killing Cade, killing everyone who suffered the plague. I needed to get Cade and leave the city. I couldn't trust the crown to uphold my father's wishes.

No one stopped me as I hurried across the gardens towards a gate that led out of the keep. Several people had strolled out to stone benches and leaned close, wine glasses in their hands, and the music from the satyr carried out over the gardens, cloaking the monstrosity being discussed about the city's poor districts. It left a sour taste in my mouth, and I overlooked Maya until she was at my side.

"Did you have a chance to speak to your father?"

Guilt twisted my belly. Kamír spoke as if he knew the plague had infected the keep, which meant Maya's mother was in danger. Maya had always been good to me, kind when no one else in the castle had.

"Maya, listen to me—you need to get your mother and get out of the city. Go to Nusa. You have an aunt there, right?"

Panic swelled in Maya's eyes. "What are you talking about?"

"I don't have time to explain. I need to get back to the shop, but…trust me. Do whatever you need to convince your father to get her out of the city. Maybe the healers in Nusa can cure her."

"You're frightening me, Ly."

I turned away from her, pushing open the gate. "I'm frightened, too. Go and find your father. Get out tonight if you can."

"Lyra," Maya called out, "be careful."

CHAPTER SIX

LYRA

*L*uckily, the walk home from the keep to the flower shop was short, just a few blocks from the gates. I did not take the same cautious care as I did in the lower districts, where the guards did not patrol the streets and the law did not exist. People were safe to walk at night in the upper districts, and I hurried back to the shop.

Get Cade. Grab enough food and water to get us to Nusa. Figure out a plan from there.

Perhaps I could get a letter to Mother. She was absent often, but with her wealth and travel, she could find a cure for Cade. She owed him that much.

A series of guards walked down the streets, and I slipped into an alley, sheathing myself in the shadows to avoid them. There were more guards out than I was used to, and while they had no reason to stop me, many knew me from my time at the castle. I couldn't afford the chance of being recognized. I peeked around the corner, watching the guards move towards the streets leading to the lower districts. The implications sent a chill running down my spine.

Trepidation sank in the air, and thankfully, the streets were quiet other than the guards. Most everyone living in this district would be at the festival, which wouldn't conclude until sunrise. I was thankful for it and returned to the flower shop without being stopped or running into other guards.

The shop windows were dark when I slipped the key into the lock and pushed the door open.

What should have provided a sense of comfort did the opposite. Every shadow and dark spot in the shop manifested dangers that weren't there, and I quickly locked the door behind me and turned on the light. I'd pack the food first, and then I'd get Cade.

The small kitchen on the shop floor bore little in the way of travel food, and we hadn't had meat available to us since the war started, so I packed what would last the longest — pieces of bread and cheese and what little jerky we had stored away. I piled it all into a bag and hefted it over my shoulder before ascending the stairs towards Cade's room.

"Cade?"

A whimper echoed out of the room as I pushed inside. It was cold, unnaturally so, and I peered over to see if his window was open. *Shut it*, I thought, my fingers trailing over the windowsill. "Cade? Are you awake?"

It took a moment for my eyes to adjust to the darkness as I hurried over to his bed, where he thrashed against his bed sheets, another whimper clawing its way out of his mouth. It unfurled, followed quickly by a scream, and he shot up quickly in bed as I grabbed his shoulders.

"It's me, it's Ly. You're safe. You're *safe*." Tugging him close, I struggled to swallow the lump of emotion in my throat as Cade continued to shake and weep. One of the side effects of Blooming Dahlia; the victim suffered terrible nightmares and hallucinations. Cade's had been infrequent but grew more common and stronger as the days passed. For the first time, I regretted not paying more attention to my father's occupation. If I were a better healer, I might have been able to devise something to help him.

The violent ache in my chest rattled.

"Lyra…there was so much blood… oh *gods*," Cade cried while clinging to me. "I don't want to go back to sleep." He shivered, and I wrapped the blanket around him. I was thankful for our horse at that moment, but I would need to come up with a plan to get past the guards at the gate. They would have been alerted about the sick.

"Cade, I need you to listen to me." I pulled away from him, ignoring the cough that rattled his lungs. "We're going to go to Nusa. I need you to find your strength and get dressed. I'm going to go mix up some things for the road and get Nalia ready for travel. We can take the cart too, to make it more comfortable for you."

"What? No—" He stilled, and for the first time, his eyes focused like he wasn't caught in the thralls of nightmares.

I cupped his head in my hands. "Listen to me. It's no longer safe to be here. I'll go and get your medicine, but then we need to go."

He must have sensed the urgency in my voice because he nodded. "Okay."

I brushed the hair from his eyes and gently kissed his sweat-stained forehead before standing. "Ten minutes." I felt terrible prying him from his bed when he was ill, but I knew they were going to come for him if I didn't act fast.

Something shifted out of the corner of my eye, a shadow that darkened and seemed to move on its own. My skin prickled, but nothing moved when I looked at the spot against the ceiling. Perhaps a trick of the light, or so I told myself as I hurried back down the stairs as Cade dragged himself out of bed.

"Hello, Lyra."

I halted at the bottom of the stairs, my blood growing cold. My fingers tingled as if infected by magic, and I turned towards the darkness of my flower shop to see the lights had woken and that I was too late.

The woman from the festival stood in the middle of the shop, surrounded by three knights from the keep. The metal of their pauldrons gleamed in the firelight, and I did not recognize them under the guise of their leathers and faces wrapped in silk.

I turned to bolt back up the stairs.

"Seize her."

I was quick but not quick enough as a knight grabbed me and tugged me back down the stairs. My instincts and all the times I'd been grabbed from behind in the fighting pits kicked in. He made the mistake of leaving my hands free, and I dug them into his exposed arm as I swung my head back and struck his nose.

"Fucking *cunt*!"

His cry of protest was accompanied by my release, and he dropped me. My knee slammed against the stairs, and I yelped in pain but ignored it, even as tears pricked the corner of my eyes. My knee screamed at me in pain as I scrambled up the stairs, but I wasn't quick enough as the knight lunged out and grabbed me again. It took all three of them to keep hold of me as the knight quickly threw me back towards the shop floor. I whimpered as my elbow struck the corner of a wall, and the two remaining guards restrained my arms, roughly tugging me back towards the woman.

"Her brother is upstairs. Remember—by orders of the Kamír, he is not to be killed like the others." The woman's words made my panic swarm like a colony of angry, buzzing bees. They would take Cade if I didn't do something, but the knights' hold on me was strong and left no room for movement.

"I can see that small mind of yours turning—one wrong move, and I'll kill your brother right here and paint it an accident," the woman warned, sensing my tension as the knight released me.

"What do you want?" I snarled. I did as she asked, even as a different knight disappeared upstairs. "Just let us go. My father—"

"Your father is a smart man. He knows when to keep his mouth shut and follow orders. Now, you're going to be a good girl and help me find Alistair."

I trembled. Alistair? This was still about Alistair? "What? Can't find him yourself?"

The woman's eyes flashed dangerously, and her skin shifted like magic had washed over it. For a moment, her skin was bone pale, only to return to the golden warmth of my people, like it had been at the festival. "I know that his castle is somewhere beyond the Elviran border, but beyond that, I'm not sure. So you're going to do it for me."

I scoffed, my heart pounding as commotion sounded upstairs. A soft cry echoed, and I turned on my heel, only to greet the face of the knight who had apprehended me. "Not a step closer."

I thought about how I might make him suffer when a hand came down to rest on my shoulder. I flinched away, turning and meeting the gaze of the woman. She had drawn close, and I shuddered as magic swept over me and prevented me from moving. At her touch, something woke inside of me, something dark and rotting. "I see the curse I laid in your skin has not manifested yet, but it will." When she laughed, it was a cold laugh. "The only way to cure it before it claims your life is to find Alistair. Pry his heart from his rib cage. Feast on it. Make sure he loves you when you do. Only then will you be free of this terrible darkness, Lyra A'mar."

My head swam with the implications, and I growled in frustration. "I don't *care*. Let Cade go. I'll go with you wherever you need me to, but let him go. He's sick! He needs help, not to be rounded up with everyone else and murdered."

"I'm afraid I can't do either of those things, Lyra A'mar." The woman sighed, drawing her finger delicately over my cheek. "I've been instructed to spare your brother, but if you don't get me what I want—and I *want* Alistair's head—then… well, accidents do happen."

I tugged against my invisible bonds. "You're a monster."

"There are monsters in us all, dear." She studied me for several moments and stared at the knight over my shoulder, nodding as if they were communicating. "If you're good at twisting Alistair around your little finger, you might be able to get a cure for your brother while you're at it," she told me. "Now, go and find him."

Before I made sense of her words, she struck my forehead with her palm, and everything went dark.

CHAPTER SEVEN

LYRA

I woke suddenly.

"Cade!" I called out blindly, only to realize I lay before the edge of Elvira, the ancient forest that made up Feyrsia and home to the faeries. The sand of my home was slowly replaced by earthy soil and trees, and I groaned as my injured knee throbbed.

My memories and what had transpired were slow to return, like a slow crawl through dense mud. Gingerly, I reached up and hissed at a sensitive point in my temple, and I slowly looked around to gather my bearings.

Cade.

It came to me all at once. Dancing with Alistair. The woman threatened me and then showed up again at my flower shop. The way she'd cursed me and told me the only way to cure it was to kill Alistair. Had that woman transported me here? Kraeva was but a shimmer in the distance, and the sun was high in the sky, indicating that morning had already arrived.

Heart pounding, I bolted to my feet and took off towards Kraeva. If I walked all day, I'd make it back before dark.

A minute out, however, I halted, the woman's words coming back to me. She'd threatened to kill Cade if I came back without Alistair.

A frustrated cry caught on the edges of my lips. Fighting was in my blood; it made my bones sing, but I wasn't a killer. How was I expected to find one of the best mages on the island and kill him? Especially if he was somewhere inside Elvira. The forest was dark and vast, and rumor had it that it was easy to lose one's way once one stepped inside. Half-lies, as I'd been in there several times to gather plants and flowers for the shop, but ancient magic wove through the trees. If one wasn't careful, a faerie would find them. Wild fae were kind, so long as you offered them trinkets or some other kinds of gifts, and I'd made many friends in the fae that way. Perhaps one of them could help me find Alistair.

I laid my hand against the trunk of a nearby tree, trying to gather my courage. Almost immediately, the trunk of the tree I touched blackened and began to decay. I pulled my hand away quickly. Gods, had I done that? The woman's words were still fresh in my head: *Find Alistair. Pry his heart from his rib cage. Feast on it. Make sure he loves you when you do. Only then will you be free of this terrible darkness, Lyra A'mar.*

A low sound echoed throughout the forest —a fast, clicking sound that was haunting and mournful. Fear struck me so quickly that I froze, my heart thundering in my ears. What was that?

I straightened and found my courage. There wasn't any time for fear. No time to falter. I needed to find Alistair — I couldn't convince him to love me quickly enough to cure my hands and save Cade myself, but perhaps I could convince *him* to help me save him.

Curling my fingers into fists, I took greater care not to touch anything as I took my first step into the forest. I always expected something otherworldly to happen, a wash of magic or the pull towards the fae, but there was nothing. It was as if this were simply a typical forest, not one that was woven into another world. The greenery was dense, the trees expanding as far as the eye could see, and I knew it would only get thicker and the trees larger the further in I went.

Okay, Ly. You've got this.

Hefting the pack on my shoulder, I wove through the trees.

I managed to find a safe place to rest in a small hole carved between a small root system, and I stayed there until the next morning after realizing I had not slept for some time due to the Greenheart Festival and caring for Cade. My fear for his safety made it difficult to sleep, but exhaustion finally forced me. I took care to tuck my hands against myself in fear that my curse would cause decay in my sleep, but I was relieved to find no damage done to the earth around me when I woke.

Slipping the pack from my back, I pulled out a piece of bread and, without thinking, took a bite.

Immediately, I was plagued by a foul taste, as if the bread had gone rotten. I spit out the bread in my mouth and looked down at the piece I held, horrified to see mold flourishing across the food. I tossed it away with a soft yelp, my heart hammering against my rib cage, and then stared down at the pack. It didn't seem my curse affected the pack, not immediately anyway, so I took greater care, using the cloth to grab the cheese I'd packed and raising it to my lips. It was more challenging to eat, but I managed, trying not to despair at my situation.

After breakfast, I set out again. The forest was beautiful, with sunlight peeking through the trees and the soft noise of humming bugs echoing in the distance. The ground was soft as I walked, weighed down by moss and grass. There was a sharp scent in the air, like that of magic mingled with fresh rain. At one point, a twig snapped, but when I sought out the source of the noise, I found nothing.

I traveled for a better part of the day without running into any fae, wild or court alike, which I thought strange. Daylight tended to keep the fae away, but traveling through Elvira without seeing one? I had hoped to run into one, thinking it might know where Alistair's castle was located, but the forest was oddly quiet. At one point, I noticed a glimmer of a mushroom, its red caps a sharp color against the backdrop of green. Perhaps it was a nemalyn cap used to teleport into the fae realm. I had heard Father speak of them as if they could do anything. Maybe they could cure my hands, and I could abandon this attempt to locate Alistair. Cade needed me.

My face fell as I drew close. It wasn't a nemalyn cap at all, just a simple mushroom that was far too small to be what I was looking for.

Eventually, I grew so thirsty that I knelt beside a bumbling creek and sank my cupped palms into the water, raising them to my lips to drink.

It wasn't until the sun began its descent below the tree line that I stumbled upon something, a soft whimper that was so faint, I nearly didn't hear it. I blinked through the growing shadows of the trees. Exhaustion made me stumble over roots and rocks as I approached the source of the noise.

It was a fox, otherworldly in nature. Its fur gleamed white, so white it glowed, etched with a bio-luminescent blue that dashed across its fur, and it sported three tails. My breath lodged in my throat; it was easily the most beautiful creature

I'd ever seen. And it was trapped beneath a series of roots, entangled in their grasp and unable to break free.

"Hold on," I whispered, reaching forward tentatively. I did not want to see what would happen if I touched the fox, so I brushed my fingers against the roots away from where they curled around the fox's body, and I watched with some sick amazement as the roots decayed and sank away to naught but crumbled dust.

"Are you—wait, no!" I called out as the fox shook the dirt free of its fur and then bolted. Frustrated tears pricked the corner of my eyes, and I sank to the ground, wrapping my arms around myself. At this rate, I would never find Alistair's castle. I was drowning beneath the sea of the forest, with no idea in which direction salvation lay. Cade was going to die because I was too weak.

Panic swelled in my chest. The world slanted.

I couldn't breathe. I couldn't *breathe*…

A small light danced against the trees in the distance, accompanied by the soft lull of music. It pried me from my anxiety, and I stilled as tears continued to trail down my cheeks. The music was entrancing, as the bard's music had been back at the Greenheart Festival, and I rose to my feet. Fae? Perhaps they could help. Maybe they would know where Alistair was. I had nothing else, nowhere else to look.

The music was a gentle noise that beckoned me closer, so I followed, weaving through the darkness until I came upon a lit clearing.

Three faeries drank and danced about a small fire. One lounged delicately upon a large rock, their head tossed back to down whatever was in their goblet. Two females swayed as a creature, a satyr with deer legs and dark, reddish-brown hair, blew into a wooden pan flute.

One of the faeries noticed me almost immediately. She was

tall and curvy, golden-brown skin flecked with something that made it glimmer and sparkle. She spoke softly to the other faeries, and they all glanced over at me, their eyes imploring. Something in the back of my head screamed at me to flee and that I was in danger, but my body didn't want to listen, content with the idea of sidling up next to the fire and dancing until my feet bled.

"Come...join us..." the male that draped across the rock gestured to me, his eyes glowing in the darkness. How did I understand him? The water I'd drank from the creek earlier that day, perhaps? There was a sharpness to his face, and he was beautiful in a way all fae were. It reminded me just how different they were from humans, how much the forest had changed them. He'd been human once. That's what the scholars spoke of, anyway. Once human, then turned into visages of the forest.

"I need to find Alistair. Do...do you know him?" My voice sounded far off and meek. I took a step forward and then another. No, I couldn't. I knew if I joined them, I would never leave.

Their laughter was soft, like the trickling of a small stream or the distant song of bells. "Come...sit with us a while...we'll find Alistair after."

A flickering shadow danced at the edge of my vision. I blinked and then stilled.

Not a shadow. A dash of gleaming, white fur.

There, then gone again. It's almost as if I'd imagined it.

"What is your name?"

"Lyra," I said, almost as if the choice were not my own. My eyes met those of the male, and his smile turned wicked.

One of the female faeries trailed closer, her hand outstretched to take mine. I fought against my very instinct to reach out, but it was a moot point. Dizziness took hold, my vision slanting as my fingers threaded through the faerie's as she led me closer to the fire. The music overcame anything else the male faerie might have said, a pretty song that compelled me to sway and twirl with the female fae. She laughed, and the noise mingled with the music, bled into the sky, and made me dance until my legs ached. My heart was pounding in my chest; I wanted to sleep and dance simultaneously. I had forgotten what I was doing, what I'd come here for, what…

Lyra.

Something said my name and broke the trance. Reality crashed down upon me so hard I gasped for air and shuddered, even as my legs carried me in an eternal dance around the flame. *Stop*, I thought, but I did not, the faeries around me a blur as I twisted and twirled. *STOP*, I demanded more fiercely, and this time it worked. I blinked, and suddenly, there was no fae. I was alone in the forest. Even the fire was gone, its absence leaving a chill rolling down my spine.

I collapsed, my knees kissing the ground, and let out a shaky sob as my legs ached as if I'd been running for hours. Gods, that was a close one. I needed to be way more careful. I was such a fool to think that I would be able to navigate these woods, that I'd be able to find someone who could help me with this curse.

Foolish, foolish girl.

The fox appeared, darting around me, and then launched itself into the air. I blinked; it had transformed itself into a small wisp, a vibrant blue ball with tendrils that floated through the air as if suspended in water. The blue pulsated like the wisp was a flame, and it edged forward curiously.

I stared at it, entranced. Was that the fox that I'd saved? "Can you take me to Alistair?" A favor for a favor. Such was the fae way. Help them, and they will help you. That's what I'd learned about the wild fae in my earlier ventures into the forest. Bring them sugared milk, and they'll lead you to fields overflowing with beautiful flowers.

The wisp bobbed as if nodding and then darted into the woods.

This might be foolish, I thought as I stumbled to my feet to follow.

But what choice do I have?

CHAPTER EIGHT

LYRA

The longer I walked, the more my chest ached, that violent, untamed thing inside me begging for bloodshed. Who did I piss off to deserve this fate? I wrung my hands together, desperate to keep them from touching anything, and my anger simmered beneath my skin. Perhaps I'd simply go back to Kraeva, find the woman that cursed me, lay my hands across her skin, watch it peel away, watch her *pay* for cursing me…

"Are you sure you're leading me in the right direction?" I asked, forcing my dark, burdensome thoughts back into the shadow of my mind where they could not be entertained.

The wisp didn't respond. I did not expect it to.

Elvira was ancient, thick with old magic, and I had to be vigilant not to fall under its spell again. I halted when the wind brushed my face, beckoning me to follow it instead.

The wisp bounced some feet away before weaving around a tree as if impatient of my hesitant nature. *Come*, it seemed to say, but I was rooted in place. A slow chill clawed down my back, sinking cold fingers into my spine as I attempted to peer through the thick tree line.

The back of my neck prickled like I was being watched.

I turned.

No one.

I shivered despite the forest's warmth. I should have brought something to protect myself with; even my shears would have done the trick.

As if right on cue, a bush nearby shuffled, and a petite pixie shot out. She was small, no larger than a songbird; her wings were transparent, and her hair glowed. She left a trail of pollen as she flew by, and she was naked, her eyes large and imploring.

"Hello," I whispered as she drew close. I was familiar with pixies; they were the most sociable of the wild faeries of the wood and often accompanied me on my harvesting when I was able to brave the forest.

She smiled, the sharp gleam of her teeth radiant against her skin, and she came to rest on my shoulder, her fingers trailing through my hair. I knew that if I left her to it, she'd be gentle with me, so I continued after the wisp as the pixie sat down next to the curve of my neck.

At one point during the day, I tumbled, my foot kicking a rock that refused to budge, and I hit the ground hard as the pixie flew from my shoulder and chattered in ire and distress. My hands sank into the soft moss to break my fall, and I groaned, my foot throbbing painfully. The pain was forgotten as the moss below my fingers withered and died, and I scrambled to pry my hands away.

Luckily, the death did not spread far, not once I freed my hands, but the sight sickened me to my core.

What was I to do? Without my hands, who was I? Would my curse harm others, or was it simply plant life that suffered their wrath? I drew my hands over my arms and hugged myself, attempting to will away the panic that strangled me. I didn't seem to hurt *myself*, a blessing, but it provided little comfort.

Oh, Cade. Hold on. I'm coming.

"Just give me a moment," I snapped when the wisp drew close, unafraid of the destruction I had just wrought on the forest. The pixie had long since disappeared. Rain had begun to fall, a chilly, cold rain full of large, plump raindrops, and I shivered, unamused with nature's joy at my recent misery. The sharp, floral scent in the air nearly made me dizzy, like the wood was tempting me to relinquish control to it.

The wisp darted at me again, the luminescence of its blue body growing more vibrant as the rain darkened the world around us.

"For the last time—" My words were lost as I blinked, and suddenly, we stood before a tall castle, so unlike in design to the sandy, round buildings of Kraeva. Stone and sylver metal, a faerie-mined metal, embellished the walls, and tall spires reached up beyond the trees. Vines crawled up the stone, tucking it behind a small sea of green, and I forgot how cold and wet I was as I stared up at it in awe.

There was no way this wasn't Alistair's. Seeing it now sent a thrill of excitement and fear through me, but I wasn't yet courageous enough to step forward. The castle was massive— the longer I looked, the larger it seemed to grow, with a sylver-clad fence protecting it from outside dangers.

"I don't think I can get inside," I told the wisp as it led me up to a gate. I tried to pry it open to no avail; no matter how much I tugged, the gate would not open. Perhaps I could find another way in…

A soft exhale followed by the tinkling of bells echoed throughout the forest as the wisp dashed forward and seemed to explode against the lock. The gate swung open on its own accord as the wisp appeared on the other side, and it bounced as if it were entirely too pleased with itself.

"Don't leave me behind," I said, laughing as the wisp shot off towards the front door of the castle. I hesitated at the gate, a low hum echoing through the clearing. It sang through my blood and echoed in the hollow of my bones. When I reached my hand out past the gate, it was as if lightning ran through my fingers, and when I pulled away, it stopped.

A ward, perhaps. When I stepped through, I shuddered as the magic washed over me. The castle grounds were unattended but must have been beautiful once, with the corpses of flowers and bushes littering the edges of the castle. A long-forgotten fountain sat in the middle of a cobbled, half-circle pathway, and I approached it, enamored with its design. A dragon curled around a tree and raised its head towards the pool of the fountain; its mouth was likely where the water had once emerged. Now, it was overgrown with moss, and the water had long gone, replaced with old, rotten leaves.

I didn't know where the wisp had gone as I hurried across the front lawn of the estate. I rushed up the front stairs of the tall and imposing estate and knocked on the door.

"Alistair!" The name was ripped from my lungs and carried away by the yowling wind, ferried off into the dark forest beyond the wall of fae metal. "Please, let me in!" I would tear the entire estate down to find him if I had to. My rage grew inside me, an ugly and terrible beast that breathed fire through the blood in my veins. It rattled, an ache against the prison of my chest, and I slipped my hand around the door handle and tugged on the door.

To my surprise, it opened. Darkness met me, a sliver of it from what I could see beyond the crack in the door, but it was better than where I'd come from, better than the threat of faeries beyond the safety of the wall. I sensed them, their eyes on me as I slipped into the house and shut the door behind me. Pressing my back to the door, I slid down to the ground, forcing my breathing to slow. My heart felt like it might burst from my chest, and I held my hands to my stomach, afraid to touch anything else.

But I did it. Despite all the odds, I had made it to Alistair's castle.

CHAPTER NINE

LYRA

Unlike the outside, which was in a state of decline, the inside was immaculate, kept pristine and clean by invisible hands. Little sweepers and fans strayed about, suspended on their own as they dusted small marble statues of dragons that lined the walls. The main room was massive, the ceiling depicting several dragons and their riders atop snowy mountains. A broom swept nearby on its own, and I wondered fleetingly if there was an invisible cleaner or if the broom moved on its own accord, animated by magic. The castle was decorated with vibrant green, gold, and pink-colored silks, as well as paintings of various dragons atop snow-capped mountains or faeries drawn in charcoal.

A fox appeared on the stoop of the stairs, three tails twitching as they swept against the stairs. It stared at me knowingly, the blue markings in its fur swirling around its eyes and over its nose. I blinked, and then it was a wisp, then a fae, a girl with piercing blue eyes and twigs in her hair. She held out a hand and gestured up to the stairs.

Follow. The word washed through me as if it had been

spoken out loud, and I shifted on my feet. *My name is Kalaea. I will lead you to your room.*

Her voice was soft and ethereal as if her very essence was drenched in magic. I hesitated, but Kalaea did not seem dangerous. Quite the contrary, I was sure she was the one who led me here.

I shivered, hugging my arms to my soaking body, and followed Kalaea up the stairs.

The halls were winding, decorated haphazardly and chaotically, with little order. It was as if a crow lived there, with all its trinkets and treasures. Small skulls and dead bugs littered the walls, held up in decorum by golden-dusted frames and embellished with mirrors or hand-drawn fae creatures I had never seen before: grumpy goblins, small wisps dancing behind shadow-cloaked trees, redcaps with sharp teeth. A door sat ajar to my left, the black stain of darkness lining the space between the door frame and the door. It was a strange sort of darkness, a darkness that beckoned my fear forward, and I tore my eyes away before my mind conjured up long, spindly fingers curling around the frame or luminescent eyes blinking in the inky black.

Kalaea stopped suddenly as I nearly barreled into her, my mind distracted as I told myself over and over not to look behind me. Something about the house was unsettling, as if it were alive all on its own, and I halted and jerked to the side to avoid touching the strange creature before me.

I blinked as Kalaea, a fox once more, touched her nose against the door. My name appeared in fancy letters, carved into the wood on its own as if willed to life by magic. I was not used to being around magic, and a chill rolled down my back as I braved a glance down the hallway. Kalaea blinked up at me.

Your room. Her voice in my head was disorienting.

I hesitated and then stepped into the room.

Ordinary, more so than I would have expected after coming from the main hall. There was a homely feeling about the room, with dark wooden walls and tall, cathedral-style windows. A massive bed was nestled on the wall to my right, and a door sat slightly ajar on the wall opposite it. The room was covered in plants, much like my room back home, and another chill pressed against my spine at the sight of them. They reminded me of the life that had been stolen from me, of the curse that marred my hands. I hugged myself and took care not to go anywhere near the plants here. Perhaps I could find some gloves. Perhaps it could keep me safe from my plague.

Kalaea disappeared before I could protest, the door clicking shut behind her. I stood in the middle of the room for several moments before I realized I was still drenched from the rain, and alarm coursed through me when I turned and saw no evidence of a dresser or clothes I could change into.

"Shit," I whispered, shivering violently as my cold, wet clothes shifted against my skin. To distract myself, I padded over to the window, where several long, thick pothos vines were strung across the glass. I was tempted to reach out and touch one of the leaves to see if it was real, but fear stayed my hand, my heart thundering in my throat. I couldn't bear to see it wither and die.

Exhaustion overcame me all at once, so I peeled my clothes off quickly, draping them over the overstuffed chair next to the window. I had to hope they would be dry in the morning.

Naked and in an environment I did not know, I hurried to the bed, frightened someone would suddenly open the door and see me. The comforter that lined the bed was thick and soft, and I sighed in relief and comfort as I burrowed beneath it.

I would have to figure out what I was going to do now that I had gotten inside Alistair's castle, but that was a problem for tomorrow.

Tonight, I would sleep.

CHAPTER TEN

LYRA

I woke with the uncomfortable sensation that someone was watching me.

The bed was so soft I nearly ignored the feeling and fell back into the blissful state of sleep, but then everything that had happened the day before came crashing down, and I sat straight up in bed, startled, as my eyes met those of Alistair's.

My hands immediately flew to my chest to trap the blanket there, and even then, I felt bare beneath it. I cursed myself for not trying harder to find dry clothes before I went to bed last night.

Alistair smirked as he leaned against the door frame of the room, his skin glowing lightly in the rays of the sun that darted through the window. "Curious how we keep bumping into each other, Lyra A'mar. How did you wander into my home? It's not the easiest to find…"

"A wisp led me here after I entered the forest. I was trying to find you and lost my way." I trembled, remembering the faeries I had stumbled upon. If the wisp hadn't found me, I'd likely be deep within Eirwyn's Court right now.

A strange expression crossed over Alistair's face as he drew near the bed. Tension thickened the air, him being here while I was naked beneath the blankets, but I held his stare as he stopped at the foot of the bed.

"Most curious, indeed. If a wisp brought you here, then it can only mean Kalaea went out to look for you."

"What is she?" I recalled the fox that had led me here.

A slow smile worked its way onto Alistair's lips. "A kitsune, a messenger of Nymera, the wolf goddess of the moon. Sometimes you may see her as a many-tailed fox, or sometimes she takes the form of a wisp. She has been my friend for a very long time, and keeps this place safe from wicked, wandering eyes."

A messenger of the gods? My head swam at the implications, and I tugged the blanket up to my chin. "I need your help."

Alistair's gaze flashed with an unknown emotion. "Seems there is not a lack of that these days."

I tilted my head, not understanding. "They took my brother. I need you to go and get him. He's not well, and I cannot leave until..." I knew I made little sense, but the words tumbled out of me anyway.

"Who took him?"

"The city guard of Kraeva. They're rounding up everyone who was sick. I think they're going to kill them in an attempt to contain the plague. I—" The words caught in my throat. I loathed the idea of begging, but I was out of options. "Please, Alistair. I need you to find him and bring him here. I'm not a healer like him or my father, but I need to know he's okay until I can find someone who can cure him." I didn't mention the curse in my own hands. Now that I was here, all the anger and panic that had swelled up inside me over the last few days began to spill over, and I watched Alistair like a predator might their prey.

Alistair swept over to me. He walked confidently, his cane thumping against the floor as he approached. The darkness of his pants was accentuated by a long, dark, silver-lined tunic that bore embroidered flowers and wisps across the design. His hair was damp as if he'd just come from a bath.

Kill him.

The mage's words echoed in my head like an unwanted fly. Anxiety prickled along my skin and filled my ears with a dull roar. If I were quick, perhaps I could find some weapon to sink into his neck. Perhaps…

"Lyra."

Do it.

Kill him.

KILL HIM.

Wait.

I met the burning in Alistair's eyes as I frowned, and the second half of the woman's words enveloped me all at once. *He must love you.*

I was in way over my head. Between finding someone to help Cade and my own curse, I was overwhelmed.

Heat rolled off him as he leaned close. "Let me see your hands." He spoke suddenly, turning his gaze down to where my hands were pressed against the blanket to keep it from falling. Oh gods, did he know I was naked beneath this blanket?

"Why?"

Alistair's nostrils flared. "I sense there is more to your story than you are telling me, Miss A'mar."

I didn't trust him, my heart thundering in my ears. What if the curse pried the life from his bones and left him naught more than dust? Without Alistair, I couldn't save Cade. Without Cade, what was the point?

Trust him. Kalaea's voice washed through me, and it felt like nothing I'd ever experienced. The fox's presence was all-encompassing, a swollen power and complete comfort that faded almost as quickly as it appeared. *You won't hurt him.*

Keeping one hand pressed to my chest, I offered him my left one. "Someone asked about you when you abandoned me at the Greenheart Festival."

His mouth twisted, suppressing a smile as he reached out to take my hand. Before his fingers could brush against mine, however, something strange happened. Alistair's hand recoiled as if something had struck it as my hand darkened and decayed, and the air surrounding my fingers was sapped of any warmth. I tugged my hand to my chest, but it had already begun to return to its normal state, devoid of any indication of the darkness that had been harnessed to my hands.

Alistair murmured something quietly under his breath, unintelligible even as I strained to listen, and then he stiffened. "You have been cursed."

"Don't suppose you happen to know how to break it?" Disgust twisted my words, and I shook my head. "It doesn't matter. We were talking about my brother."

"Curses—they have a habit of infecting the bearer." Ignoring me, he gestured to my hands. "That curse will destroy you if you let it, Lyra."

"Then I will figure out how to fix it *after* I save Cade!" Exasperation echoed throughout the room. "Please...he's all in the way of family that I have. The only one that I give a shit about, anyway."

Narrowed eyes met my desperate ones. "Did whoever

curse you tell you how to break it? There's always a way to break a curse."

Fear floundered in my belly, and I shook my head to lie. "She didn't."

Alistair hummed and looked as if he didn't believe me. For a beat, I wondered if he might kill me. "Come with me," Alistair said suddenly, moving towards the open door. "There is something I must show you."

Heat crawled up my neck and settled in my cheeks as I hesitated. I was still naked under these covers, and I wasn't certain if my clothes had dried overnight. My frustration over Alistair's cryptic nature made my limbs ache, and I sighed. Perhaps it had been foolish to come here. Maybe I should have returned to Kraeva and attempted to find Cade myself.

"I will find your brother," Alistair said, pulling me from my spiral. "But first, you must come with me."

Relief. It struck me so suddenly that it took my breath away. *Cade. We're coming.*

"I don't have any clothes to change into," I said, gesturing to the clothes draped over the side of the chair. "It was raining when I arrived last night."

My stomach plummeted when I met the intensity of Alistair's stare, and his gaze raked over the blanket that covered my naked form. *Gods, he was overwhelming. I'm in way over my head.* I'd thought court life might have prepared me for the task of seducing Alistair, but I was wrong. I had never met someone quite like him. Not even those among the fae.

His grin was wicked as he held up a hand, his long, slender fingers darting erratically as strings of golden magic trailed from the tips. They were a small golden light, strings sparkling like glitter as they darted towards me. I might have flinched had it not happened so fast. I was clothed in a small, barely concealing green nightgown when I glanced down beneath the blanket.

I frowned. "This is hardly appropriate. I told you not to do that."

Alistair's eyes were smoldering when I met them. "Next time, I'll let you stay naked, then. Gods know it would have been...a *delightful* sight." He practically purred, his tone lowering as he glanced again at the blanket covering my body before turning towards the door.

"If it's not to your tastes, I suppose you can find a change of clothes in the wardrobe."

"What wardro—" He'd already left, the door clicking shut behind him. I ground my teeth in frustration; suddenly, it wasn't becoming so difficult to imagine killing him. *Smug asshole.*

I could have sworn there was no wardrobe the night before, but my gaze sought one out, situated against the wall across from my bed. There was nothing extraordinary about it, with its light oak color and simple knobs, but its appearance made my head spin. This castle was strange.

The air was cold as it brushed against my bare skin, and I darted from the bed. I shivered as I tugged the doors open to the wardrobe and snatched the first pair of clothes I saw: a silky deep green shirt and black pants.

After pulling them on, I padded over to the vanity with the mirror and blanched at the sight before me. I looked like I hadn't slept well in days, with dark circles etched beneath my eyes, and my hair was a wild, untamed mess that thankfully cooperated when I brushed it out with a brush I found in one of the drawers.

I stilled for a moment to gather my courage. I was in the home of Alistair Sylverhorn. He'd agreed to help save my brother. The look in Cade's eyes when they'd ripped him from me would haunt me even after he returned to my side. A soft whimper of fear passed my lips. I would never forgive myself if something happened to him, but I needed to remember why I was here. Even if I managed to save my brother, my hands were cursed, and I couldn't cure them without killing Alistair.

Grabbing my wrist, I held my hands to my chest. I'd do what I had to. The fate of Cade's future, of my future, depended on it.

Padding over to the door, I took a deep breath and then pried it open. Meeting Alistair's gaze, I hesitated. "I don't know how the curse works. It affects certain things, such as plants and food, but not others. I—" My fear lodged itself in my throat. *I am afraid to touch anything.* I felt foolish for my fear. For displaying it so profoundly on my face. For letting Alistair see me like this.

Weak, I thought.

Alistair's face melted to understanding as he gestured me to his side. "Kalaea's wards *should* prevent your curse from manifesting here. I do not know why or how it did so back in the bedroom, but I assure you—so long as you're on my estate, you are safe from its wrath. It does not keep *you* safe from it forever, though. Please... come with me."

Eager to see more of the manor, I agreed, though I ignored Alistair's offered arm and kept my distance from him. It was difficult figuring out how to trick him into falling in love with me when I didn't trust him not to see right through me.

"Take care walking the halls of this place. Kalaea's magic has certain... side effects," Alistair said, dropping his arm to his side and leading us down the dim hallway.

"Oh?" I peered up at him as we made our way. People in Kraeva whispered about it—the haunted home of Alistair Sylverhorn—but I had never believed their stories. Still, I recalled how unsettled I had been last night, and I stuck close to Alistair's heels as we moved forward. The hallway was different from how it had been the night before; the door to my room had once been in the middle of the hall, surrounded by many other doors. Now? My door was nestled at the end of the hall, next to a small wooden chair and table in front of a window overlooking the estate's grounds.

"Is it haunted?" I found myself asking.

Alistair laughed, a hand reaching up to tangle in the curls at the nape of his neck. My cheeks heated in embarrassment. "In a sense," he said.

I wasn't sure what he meant by that, but I didn't dare to ask. Still, he didn't say no, and the unease from the night before returned, prickling at my spine. There was so much chaos with the way Alistair decorated the walls, so much order to it. Ornate, golden frames in various shapes and sizes lined the faded wallpaper, encompassing different things inside, and rarely was there space on the wall devoid of decoration. Would my cursed hands cause the wallpaper to peel? Could I pull this off before Cade...

"Did you always want to be a florist?"

The question caught me off guard, and my instinct was to pull away. Why *do you want to know?* But then I remembered I needed Alistair to trust me, so I gave a slight shake of my head.

"I wanted to be a knight."

I wasn't sure why I didn't lie; I had never told anyone that before. I couldn't seem to gain enough courage to look up at him to gauge his reaction, but that dream had burned fires in my chest since I had first seen the knights of Kahl strolling the royal keep. I hadn't stoked that flame in a while, but Alistair's question had kicked the embers to life, and I wrung my hands together.

"Whose idea was it to open a flower shop?"

My father's. "My brother's. He wants to take over my

father's job as the royal healer one day. A flower shop can couple as an apothecary, so here we are." I glanced up then to see Alistair already staring at me. A thrill sang through me. "Don't get me wrong, I love flowers. Being surrounded by the vibrant beauty of nature—there are worse things to have for a job." But it didn't soothe the ache in my chest. The violent, wild thing in my heart. I was not made for a life of idleness. Perhaps I got that from my mother. Maybe that's why I never truly hated her for always being gone.

Alistair hummed, acknowledging my words. "Sometimes the world tries to push us into boxes because it would be the simplest path for us. I think you know better than anyone that it's good to fight against that path."

"How so?"

He stopped at a large double door and smiled. "I'd ask you to look at your nighttime activities, *Pit Viper*." I flushed at my title, but before I could respond, he pushed the doors open and ushered me inside.

CHAPTER ELEVEN
LYRA

The doors opened to another long hallway, the walls made of cobbled stone mingled with thriving vines of leaves that snaked up through the edges, filling the space with a vibrant green. A winding staircase sat nestled at the end of the hallway, with two torchlights flickering on either side. A soft aroma wafted down the stairs, the faint scent of cinnamon mixed with honey. It was lovely, and I followed willingly, ignoring my instinct's uncertainty.

You cannot trust him.

"What is this place?" I asked as we ascended the stairs and stepped into what appeared to be a glass room high up in one corner of the castle. Outside, the forest spanned out as far as I could see, magnificent in its own right. The room was filled with magical equipment and books, nestled on bookshelves and floating endlessly close to the ceiling above me. I had never seen anything like it; vials with various, vibrant colors bubbled, clamped to some sort of metal contraption near what appeared to be a globe detailing not just Feyrsia but all of Baltoras. Various spots lit up in the world, but I was distracted as several metal birds flew past. They looked like they had been folded like I used to do with paper as a child, and it seemed that there was something new to observe everywhere I looked.

"My observatory, where I do most of my studies. A mage isn't a mage without their observatory, even one exiled such as I." Alistair padded gracefully over to the vials, and he pulled a blue one from its clamp, swirling the liquid within the vial as he studied it intently. "Breaking curses has been my field of study as of late."

"He isn't very good at it, though." A voice called down from the spiraling staircase that led even higher up in the room. I looked up to a woman leaning over the railing, a soft smile gracing her features. Hopping up onto the railing, she slid down and landed, her eyes flickering between Alistair and me. She was beautiful, about my age, with sharp cheekbones and a dimple that cratered her cheeks when she smiled. Her eyes were dark gold, and her hair was spun into a white-gold tangle, tugged back into a high ponytail. She moved elegantly, dressed in loose white and gold clothing, and several rings glinted in the light on her fingers. Heat rose to my cheeks as my eyes fell upon her. She was more than beautiful. She was *divine*. A low ache curled deep in my belly.

"Masterpieces take time, Val."

I looked between them as Alistair paused, a vial poised delicately between his fingers. The woman, Val, trailed over to me curiously. She looked vaguely familiar, like I'd met her long ago, but where had I seen her? I couldn't place it…

"I… did not know Alistair lived with someone," I said awkwardly, forcing my thoughts to settle. I had always assumed Alistair would be alone, as he ran from those who sought to return him home so he could answer for his crimes.

Val and Alistair exchanged looks, and then Alistair turned and gestured to the woman in front of me.

"Princess Valencia, of Bracaea."

The floor threatened to reach up and meet me as the room slanted, and I remembered how to breathe. "The *lost* princess of Bracaea?" Of course. That's where I recognized her. When I was young, before my tenth winter, the Bracaean royal family had come to visit Kraeva. Valencia and I had played together once as children, and when Nasir had come to tug my hair or pinch my arms, she had stood up for me. I'd only met her once, which was why I hadn't recognized her at first.

The world had been at peace at the time.

"Your Highness?" I scarcely recognized my voice and cleared my throat, shaking away my astonishment. It was not becoming, and I did not care to embarrass myself as I lowered myself into a slight bow. What was Alistair doing with the missing princess?

"In the flesh." Her voice was bitter, and she rested her hand on my shoulder. "Please do away with the formalities. I loathe them."

I had never been a fan of formalities either, but it had been ingrained in my blood since I was a child; it would be difficult to break the habit. Still, I straightened as Valencia wandered over to Alistair to study the vial in his hand.

"Think it'll work?" She asked, and Alistair sighed.

"No." His honesty had my curiosity burning.

"What is it?" I asked.

Alistair swirled it around in his hand and then offered it to me. "Something I've been working on for a while. A way to break curses. I've nearly got it, but I fear something is missing."

I took the vial from him and studied it, raising it to my nose to sniff. It smelled sharp, like all magic often did, mingled with the scent of a berry of some sort. It wasn't an unpleasant smell, but I offered it back to him, fearful I would drop it. "Anything healing should have some sort of green tint to the liquid, even if it's light. That's too blue and would likely poison whoever drinks it."

"Oh, that's right. You're the healer's daughter. I recall from when we were children," Valencia said.

Alistair turned, pressing the vial into the metal contraption that held it above an open flame. It began to bubble, the vibrant blue almost unnatural against the backdrop of other colors in the room. Yes, it was entirely too blue. I wasn't a healer by trade, but I'd been around my father enough to know a little.

"Something to ponder over while I go and figure out where they're holding your brother." His words sent a current of excitement through me, and I straightened.

"Let me come with you."

Alistair shook his head. "I move quicker on my own. Plus—I need you here." He eyed Valencia as he snapped his finger, and a coat appeared. He slipped into it, leaned over a desk, and scribbled something into a small notebook.

"Can you show her the library? Perhaps the two of you can find something on curses while I'm gone."

Conflicting emotions rang through me, my worry for my brother outweighing understanding as Alistair brushed past me towards the door. He moved fluidly despite the slight limp in his leg, and I reached out to stop him before I changed my mind and let my hand drop to my side.

"It's my fault he was taken. Please—let me come with you." I loathed the desperation in my voice. It was weak. Pathetic. The threat to Cade's safety crushed my guilt over it as Alistair paused at the door.

"I'm simply finding out where they took him. It will be

impossible to retrieve him just yet. Once I know more, we can discuss this further. Until then, stick tight. Stay with Valencia. Search for an answer to our cure. I'll be back as soon as I can." He spoke without turning, and then he was gone, leaving me to stand amid an observatory with the missing princess of Bracaea.

"Come, Lyra. It's best to traverse the halls when Alistair is still here. The castle grows restless and unsettling when he's gone," Valencia said finally, moving forward. My mind was a whirl of conflicting thoughts. What if Cade was dead? What if Alistair couldn't find where they'd taken him? What if I was alone? What if...

"Lyra?"

I shook my head as I tucked my panic away in my chest. If anyone was equipped to save my brother, it was one of the mages of Ravenspire. Even if he was exiled and wanted.

"He said there's a library?" I asked. He was right. If I couldn't focus on Cade, perhaps the library would have some sort of knowledge on curse-breaking. Or at least, how to kill a mage.

Valencia smiled. "Follow me."

CHAPTER TWELVE

LYRA

Valencia led me through the castle halls, explaining how they'd shift and change. "It's usually worse when Alistair is gone, but they almost always change at night. Alistair explained that Kalaea is taking the necessary steps to keep us safe in case someone manages to find the castle while we are sleeping."

It was fascinating. I'd met many of the wild fae from my times in the forest, but I'd never thought I'd meet one of Nymera's messengers. A few of the moska's back home depicted Nymera with her messengers, but I never held much faith and had never visited one of the holy buildings. Kalaea's ability to weave illusions and wards such as she did was incredible, and I marveled as I watched a hallway pop into existence as we walked by. It was long and dark, and I shuddered against the trepidation it wrought when I looked down. It was disorienting.

"How bad is it out there?" Valencia asked.

"I—what?" Distracted, I tore my gaze from the hallway to

Valencia. She seemed troubled, thin brows furrowed together as she hurried us down the hall.

"The war. How bad is it?"

I thought about lying to her. Spare her the gritty and grim details.

I couldn't. It wouldn't be right.

"Terrible. There's a plague spreading through the streets of Kraeva. They call it the Blooming Dahlia. Makes you sick, but also gives you horrible nightmares." I quieted. "And the queen is sick. I overheard the council talking—I believe they're blaming Bracaea." I sensed her tension mingled with her anger, and I quickly continued. "That was *after* Bracaea declared war on Kahl for murdering you." My gaze flickered over her face. "But I see now that the accusation was bred in falsehoods." How much bloodshed could be avoided if the princess would just go home?

"Why do you stay here?" My bluntness came across harsher than intended, the pain in Valencia's face causing my guilt to blossom. "You could leave, could end this war…"

"I cannot," she said before I could apologize. "I was cursed."

I desperately wanted to know more. My curiosity burned questions into my throat, but I dared not speak them. I wasn't comfortable sharing the circumstances of my own curse, my hands twisting together as if I could somehow wring the poison from my hands.

"I'm sorry," I said instead. "I am all too familiar with that suffering." My fingers tingled as if reminding me that though my curse was fended off by the wards, it remained. Alistair's words of warning hadn't quite sunk in yet, barred by my worry for Cade, but I was forced to acknowledge the cold numbness that was now plaguing the tips of my fingers.

"It is why we help Alistair where we can. He was the only

one who offered to help me. Turned his back on the people he swore to serve to help me."

"Is that why they hunt him?"

Valencia nodded, pausing at a large mahogany door inlaid with carvings of deer and butterflies. "He speaks little of it to me, but they wanted him to fight in the war, and he refused. This was before he had even found me, mind you." She gave me a sharp look, and I stood tall despite its intensity. "He is not the monster they say he is."

I had not seen it either. Many whispered of his monstrosity, of the beast that burrows deep inside him and comes out to eat the hearts of those he seduces. How coincidental that the strange woman who cursed me wanted me to do the same if I wanted to see the end to my curse.

Could I do it?

"Get ready," Valencia said, an amused smile perking on her lips. "I wasn't when he showed me the library for the first time." Pushing open the door, I followed her inside.

It was larger than feasible had Alistair not been a mage. I tilted my head up, unable to spot the ceiling beyond the swirling floors of bookshelves. Several books flitted about like birds, much like they had in the observatory. Woodland creatures I'd never seen, girls with twigs for hair and a green glow in their skin, dusted the books. Small, round creatures with large, bulbous noses and grey skin waddled about, slipping books into empty slots on the shelves. Cathedral-style windows lined the walls, decorated with colored glass that depicted dragons in the mountainside or faeries in fields of wildflowers.

I exhaled sharply. It was beautiful.

"Incredible," I breathed. I was never much of a reader; the flower shop had taken up too much of my time. It was impossible to ignore the pull of this library, though. Coziness oozed from each bookshelf and overstuffed chair.

One could go mad in this place.

"I'd live in here if I could," Valencia said as she led me through the library. "Each book holds its own sort of magic, if you're open to seeing it."

I shivered as one of the rock fae strolled past, chattering at me in strange tongues. "How do you navigate this place?"

Valencia laughed. "Alistair didn't explain, did he? He does that. I'm sure he's so used to it all that he doesn't think. I'm not sure how I know. I just…do? You'll grow used to it too. I know what rooms to stay away from."

She halted in front of a sitting area in the middle of the library. A bustling fire burned in a fireplace pressed inside a mantle against the wall.

"Rooms to stay away from?"

Valencia gave me an odd look. "I'm guessing you have not encountered one of the spirits that haunt this place."

I recalled the first night I'd arrived when Kalaea had led me to my room and the unsettling feeling I'd had. "No, but I will admit. This place is…strange."

Valencia nodded. "Strange indeed."

"Come and sit with me," she said, gesturing to a series of puffy, green armchairs. "Let us talk for a while. I have fond memories of you, Lyra A'mar, even if we only met once." My cheeks warmed as Valencia sat, folding her legs beneath her and sinking into a chair. She did so gracefully, and I envied her as I sat myself, keeping my hands firmly in my lap.

I watched the princess with mild curiosity now that we were alone. She had grown from the girl I'd met once. The northern family was a prideful bunch, full of regal and stoic beauty like their dragons. Valencia radiated the same regal stoicism, but something accompanied it —a sadness that tinged her expression. I only knew what it was because I saw it in myself whenever I looked in a mirror. She was hiding something, tucking herself away. Still, I stared, entranced by her beauty. I desired to run my fingers through the liquid starlight of her hair.

"You mentioned your brother earlier…at least, Alistair said he would look for him…" Valencia trailed off, but I sensed her unspoken question. *Where was he?*

I looked at my hands. My rough, blunt hands. Callouses thickened on my palm, and I pressed against one as I centered myself. No sense getting emotional now. "He has the plague I spoke of. It's still early, he hasn't been as sick as I've seen it, but the crown ordered the sickness to be purged from the city." My eyes flickered to meet Valencia's, and my expression was pointed. "The woman who cursed me was waiting for me with some guards. They took Cade, and she sent me to the forest to find Alistair."

Valencia frowned. "What did this woman look like?"

When I described her, Valencia looked to the fire. The flames danced in the gold of her eye, and I stared, mesmerized. "That doesn't *sound* like Soria, but it has to be her. She's the grand-mage. She taught Alistair everything he knew, and if they're after Alistair, she'll be leading the charge." Her gaze met mine, and her expression turned to distrust. "Why did she think you could find him?"

Fear squeezed my lungs. "I don't know. She saw us dancing at the Greenheart Festival. Perhaps she thought we were closer than we are." I laughed nervously. "I nearly got taken away by some fae, but Kalaea saved me and led me here."

Valencia's eyes softened, and the tension fell from my shoulders. The last thing I needed was Valencia's suspicions to prevent me from doing what needed to be done. After seeing Alistair's observatory, I was confident we could work around

Soria's words. Still, I needed to prepare myself for the idea that I'd have to kill Alistair to free my hands, and I didn't need Valencia in the way.

"Have you found anything in here on breaking curses?" I was eager to change the subject. "Alistair seemed pretty confident there was something here."

Sweeping her lap, Valencia leaned back to peer around the library. "I've been searching for the answers since Alistair brought me here. You said you thought something might be missing from the potion to make it work..." She trailed off and stood. "Do you have any idea what might be missing?"

"Likely a plant of some kind," I said. "Something to nullify any toxins in the potion. Could be something poisonous itself."

Valencia waved her hand, and a wisp appeared. It danced about Valencia before settling near the fire, where it bounced, suspended, a few inches off the ground.

"Hi," I cooed. Wisps were my favorite of the wild fae, their calm and curious nature often making them excellent companions when I was alone in the strange wood. They glowed, too, providing an ample light source when the shadows of the trees conjured up monsters.

The wisp grew closer, gurgling lowly. The innate magical energy that wafted from it left me dizzy, but I reached out a hand.

The wisp was warm as it settled over my palm, its tendrils draping over the side of my hand. The sensation was strange; it didn't feel altogether corporeal, like the coolness of water mingled with the resistance of magic at times. Still, it was a pleasant feeling, and I drew the wisp closer as it nestled against my skin. It was one of the first comforting things I'd felt since arriving at Alistair's castle.

"My people fear wisps, say they draw faeries near or lead

you down terrible fates," Valencia whispered, watching the wisp with a soft smile. "I've grown to love them, though. They've brought me nothing but a sense of safety and peace." She gestured to the library surrounding us. "They're also amazing navigators. I'm sure he'd be able to lead you wherever you needed to go in here."

"Do you know where there might be books on plants?" I asked it quietly, feeling somewhat foolish. I never knew if they would understand what I was saying.

The wisp danced out of my palm and hovered momentarily before shooting off and disappearing near a row of bookshelves. I glanced over at Valencia, who waved her hand. "Go. There's another section I might try. We can meet back here."

The room was brimming with a comforting presence, and the fae folk tending to the library paid me no attention as I moved away from Valencia to where the wisp had wandered off to. I walked tentatively as if I would wake some slumbering beast if I were too loud. There were so many things to look at; if there was an order to the plethora of books, I did not see it.

There was everything here—studies on fae magic coupled with the dragon magic of the north, the correlation between plants and their properties, and some riveting tale between a human and a fae prince. Anxiety settled low in my belly as I brushed my fingers along the spines, fearing they would crumble to dust. They looked as if they hadn't been touched for a long time, but they were pristine. There was no dust to speak of, and none of them fell to destruction beneath my touch.

Tucking the tome on plants under my arm, I returned to the chairs in the center of the room. Valencia had disappeared, but I paid that no mind as I settled back into one of the chairs.

I sighed against its comfort, and warmth seeped through me as I cracked open the book and studied the first page.

The words were a language I couldn't read—faerie, perhaps? —but beautifully illustrated, and I studied the paintings that covered the pages, trying to seek anything that spoke of diluting toxins.

I looked until my eyes hurt, and the sun descended below the tree line outside. Perhaps I could sleep here in the library, where it was safe. Valencia had returned shortly after I'd sat back down to tell me she was going to venture up a few floors and then left me again. I hadn't seen her since.

Yawning, I shut the book and stood, padding over the bookshelf I'd pulled it from. Now that it was dark, torches had been lit, and small wisps danced through the air, illuminating the library with a soft glow of blue light. Still, the darkness caused tension to thicken in the air, and I wrapped my arms around myself after shoving the book back in its spot. Now that I was alone, my mind conjured silly fears that I attempted to quell. *Don't look behind you. Don't look behind you. Don't look be—*

I looked behind me.

Nothing.

Nothing but the imposing length of endless bookshelves.

"Gods, Lyra. Get a grip," I scolded, as if chastising myself would help. A title on one of the spines caught my attention. *Fungi and their multiple properties.* Perhaps…

Something flickered in the corner of my eye, a shuffle of a shadow that slunk across the books.

I shuddered just as something grabbed me and tugged me around the corner. A scream lodged itself in my throat, stifled to silence when I noticed it was Valencia pulling me away. The ache in my fingers to punch her quieted as well.

"We must hide," she whispered.

What were we hiding from?

CHAPTER THIRTEEN
ALISTAIR

The forest was chilly as I left, but my mind was distracted by thoughts of Lyra. How had she stumbled upon my castle? She spoke as if Kalaea had led her here, but the kitsune was supposed to protect my home from strangers, not lead them to it.

My leg ached, and Rahfín stirred. *Let me out. I will get us to Kraeva more quickly than you walking.*

No, I told him. *I will make do.*

Rahfín's ire sank into my bones like a physical weight, and I grimaced.

Let me out.

His insistence was ignored until it wasn't, until his weight swelled against me so much that I could scarcely walk. It was as if he pressed beneath my skin and demanded room I could not give. I groaned, my hand drawing up to press heavily against my face. "*Fine*," I said out loud, rolling my shoulders back like it would make the aching disappear. "But just until we've reached the city. We do not need another incident where they see us."

Rumbling laughter echoed throughout my head as I shuddered and draconic wings liberated themselves from my back. A part of me cracked at the seams as the wings shook and settled, and I stretched them out, testing their reach. Rahfín rarely liked this form because it gave me control over our shared body. A talon hooked at the top of each wing, green scales drenched at the tips in gold. It had taken time at first to get used to them, but I'd been bonded to Rahfín long enough now to grow accustomed to stretching that muscle, and I took off, leaped into the air, and soared above the trees. I couldn't deny the freedom I felt, being high above the world, where its hurts could not touch me. The wind brushed against my face, and I took care to stay low against the top of the treeline; once I reached the forest's edge, I would be forced to walk. I'd let Rahfín take control a few nights previous, only to discover we'd been seen soaring over Kraeva, and the alarm bells had sounded. Dragons did not frequent these parts, a staple in Bracaean culture. With the two kingdoms being at war, it was understandable that any dragon sightings might signal danger.

Yes, Rahfín sighed against my lungs. *This is good*.

We flew until we'd reached a cluster of tropical trees near the city's edge, and I shuddered as Rahfín's wings sank back into my skin, where the dragon settled low in my belly. Granting him access to my body, no matter how small, had left my leg screaming, and I leaned heavily against my cane as I limped towards the eastern gate of Kraeva. This gate was far less traveled than the western gate, where the main road led out to Nusa and Elvira. I relished in the brush of coastal sea air on my face and how the earth had turned from soil to sand. No one accompanied me on this road, but when I got to the gate, I found it barred, with many more guards stationed there than I was accustomed to.

"Halt!" One of the guards moved forward to stop me several feet from the gate. "You cannot come this way. Either check in at the western gate or turn around."

"I have used this gate often. What seems to be the problem?"

"The lower districts are off limits until further notice. If you have an issue with it, feel free to take it up with the crown." The guard offered little explanation, but I didn't need him to. I knew what it was: the Blooming Dahlia, which had finally begun blooming in Kraeva. Lyra was convinced they were rounding the sick up to contain the plague, and I believed her. Kraeva was not known for loving its poor. Bracaea was the same, leaving their villages to face the wrath of the faerie queen in the north.

A dazzling smile brushed my face as my fingers twitched at my side, beckoning magic. I didn't have time to go all the way to the western side of the city when the place I needed to go was *right here.* "Don't you recognize me? The king is my cousin, and he asked me to check on things here." I leaned close, infecting my voice with illusion magic. "I have heard the Blooming Dahlia has returned."

The guard's eyes flashed and then dulled as the magic washed over him. I had never been much good at compulsion magic until Rahfín possessed me. Now, it felt almost criminal how easily minds bent to my will should I desire it. I didn't use it often, my guilt outweighing my desire to take the easy path, but I was in a hurry today and needed to get inside before night fell and the gates closed for the night.

"Of course. Come with me." The guard's words lacked warmth as he turned on his heel, and I followed him, ignoring the other guards as the one who led me explained who I was and why I was there. One of them eyed me suspiciously but said nothing, and soon, I was once more inside the walls of

Kraeva. It was nearing midday now, but the streets were empty, eerily so. There weren't even signs of the poor on the streets where there were usually quite a few, and a strange thickness had settled in the air like something bad had just happened.

"Where are the sick being taken to?" I asked, turning to the guard.

He rubbed his beard nervously and glanced back at the other guards. "Down by the docks. We're told to avoid it and keep other citizens away from the docks until further notice." I felt the slightest resistance from him; my magic pulled taut as it worked harder to keep the guard under my influence. The change seemed to come as I asked more about the sick. It was most curious, and I tucked that curiosity away as I smiled at the guard.

"Can you take me there?"

The guard hesitated. "I'm not supposed to abandon my post—"

I shielded my gaze beneath my eyelashes as I stepped forward and made my voice coy. "The king did not tell me where to go, only to see that I ensured things ran smoothly. Surely a big, strong soldier like yourself can handle the task?" I infected every word with a sultry tone, my voice low and hoarse as I toyed with the guard. "I'll have you back before anyone knows you're gone."

The guard's demeanor changed as he took a hard look at me. I felt the air shift as his composure cracked. "'Course I can."

"Thanks," I said, winking and urging my magic along the pathways of the guard's mind just to enforce my words. Seducing others had always come easily to me. Only now did I find it awfully... *boring*. My traitorous thoughts turned to

Lyra, and I wondered what I could say to her to get her to swoon beneath my words.

I wanted her, and I didn't even know why.

The streets were silent, save for us, our feet quiet on the sandy roads beneath us. Tall, round sandstone buildings made up each side of the road, some covered in cloth, while others were rundown and abandoned. It was also oddly silent as if the lower district was holding its breath.

"What's your name?" I asked in an attempt to peel back the layers of the guard and dissuade him from suspecting me as I lessened my magic. Rahfín had made me an infinitely stronger mage, but doing so did not spare me from the consequences should I overdo magical use. I did not want to risk tempting my heart to explode or experience a nosebleed.

The guard spared a glance my way, laughter etching his teeth. "Raülio." Beneath his leathers and silks, Raülio was young, younger than I thought would have made for a Kraevian guard, his brows thick and his stubble cut neatly at his chin and cheeks. He couldn't have been much older than Lyra, his eyes still full of hope. Nothing like the disdain and dull nature in some of the older guards' eyes. I wondered how long it would take for the hope to fade from Raülio's eyes, too. "Took the vows of the sword a few months ago. I'll be honest, I thought joining the guard would be way more exciting in the event of a war going on, but it's been bloody *dull*."

"Trust me, Raülio," I said, taking a moment to speak his name as if to savor it, "War is not the excitement you seek."

Raülio held his hands up, spluttering in embarrassment. "Of course not—it's not what I meant. Just didn't think I'd be on wall duty is all."

"Consider yourself lucky," I said, resting a genuine hand on his shoulder. "Those out there fighting the fight are dying for a lost cause." I recalled the moment I'd discovered Valencia in

Vrona. They'd barred her from entering the keep due to the nature of her curse, her faerie visage wicked in Bracaean eyes. Before they could sentence her to death, I had whisked her away, and my defying of orders had caused a price to be put on my head. I'd seen right through Valencia's curse, though. I knew if they'd killed her that day, the fate of humanity would have been sealed in her blood.

How wicked the gods were for instilling such a cruel fate. I fought against it every day.

"Lucky?" Raülio tugged away, the gentle nature of his expression hardening in denial. "I wish I could kill some Bracaean bastards." Spitting at the ground, he soured, and I cursed myself silently for my quip. "You're not a sympathizer, are you? The north wrongfully accused us of stealing their bitch of a princess. *We're* the victims."

Yes, I thought sullenly, *and so is everyone beneath the royal families, Bracaean or Kahlian.*

I feigned a smile and shook my head, offering peace. "No, of course not. I only hope to see an end to the war, either way." Quickly, I changed the subject. The point of this mission was not to change the mind of one Kraevian guard. "Maybe later, after your shift, I can come find you..." I trailed off, leaving the ending open-ended to inject tension into it, the curl of my smile tucked, nearly hidden, as I turned my face away.

Raülio coughed, and when I glanced at him, he was smiling. *Gotcha.* "Yeah, yeah, I think that can be arranged." He coughed again and signaled to a building as we approached. Water lapped up on shore as we walked the docks, the water crystal clear and a bright, vibrant blue. Kraeva's docks were the biggest in the kingdom, but the trade ships were mainly those from the island of Brûnheim. The people there were a hardy bunch, moon-stalkers and skin-changers, who provided the people of Kahl with furs and services in exchange for fruits and protection. A couple of longboats bumped against the docks, and I stared out longingly at sea as Rahfín's desires washed over me. There was nothing more freeing than flying over the open ocean. Sometimes, Rahfín tempted me with it, relinquishing control and letting him carry us across the water to the great beyond.

It was always a silly dream.

"I think I can take it from here, Raülio, but thank you for accompanying me," I said, offering Raülio a dazzling smile. "I'll come and find you later. When are you relieved?"

"Sundown is when the shift rotates. I'll wait for you at the Jeweled Emerald. You know it?"

The Jeweled Emerald was one of the taverns in the upper district of the city, where most guards frequented when they weren't on duty. It would be the last place I should be as a wanted man, but a part of me considered it. Raülio seemed like good company. Still, nothing mattered when Lyra and Valencia were back at the castle, waiting for my return. Indulging in such pleasures could come *after* I'd cured us of our ailments.

"I'll find you after I'm done here," I lied. "This was a pleasure." I fully released my magical hold on him, and he shook his head as if clearing a fog that had come over him. My fingers danced across his shoulder like a promise, and then I moved away, my thoughts already on the task ahead. I wouldn't be able to get Lyra's brother out yet, but I could return to her with the news of his survival. I'd heard whispers of the Blooming Dahlia in recent months, but I had yet to know what exactly it was or where it had come from. Plagues didn't just…appear. Not when faerie and dragon magic infected the world the way that it did.

The building Raülio had led me to was a large warehouse,

likely where goods were stored before they entered the city. The windows were dark as if they were abandoned or not in use, and I called shadows to myself, wrapping them around me like a second skin. It wouldn't hide me from the wandering eye but rather make them pass over me, someone forgettable; they wouldn't need to remember. It was merely a precaution; I saw no one as I walked towards the warehouse, no sailors or fishermen.

Something does not feel right, Rahfín said, his anxiety washing over me like a slow, crawling fog. *The stench of death permeates the air.*

He was right. Death had its own kind of feeling as it trailed through magic, and there was a magical sense of death in the air. Death magic was taboo, requiring too much to wield. To feel it here…

"Shit," I whispered, looking for a place to hide as a small unit of guards strolled down from the city towards the warehouse. They had someone by the arm, a woman with dirty hair and wild eyes, and I pressed myself into the dark of the warehouse as they came closer.

"Please," the girl cried, trails of tears rolling down her cheeks. "Where are you taking me?" A cough rattled her lungs, a violent cough that had the guards pulling away in disgust and fear. It manifested in their eyes and how they flinched away, only to draw back when she finished. She was extremely malnourished, her bones jutting harshly against the pull of her skin at her shoulders, her cheeks sunken, and she barely put up a fight as the guards led her roughly to the warehouse door. They did not answer her, and I waited with bated breath long after they'd gone. It didn't come as a surprise that they were taking people in broad daylight; this was the lower district, where people went missing all the time without causing a fuss from the upper district or the royal family.

It would be better to come back at nightfall, Rahfín mused.

I know, I snapped. *We aren't afforded the time.*

Why are we even here? For the human? For her?

You're the one who said she was different.

Rahfín shuffled his wings in the cusp of my mind, his presence swelling in amusement. *She is. Her brother, however, is not of concern to us.*

If we want her to like us, then yes, he is.

Rahfín snorted. *Humans are strange. If her brother was strong, he wouldn't have found himself in this situation in the first place.*

Sometimes, we find ourselves in situations we didn't ask to be in. In this case, he's sick. If we can help him, we should.

Rahfín's disagreement sang through me, but I ignored him. He was right; waiting until nightfall would be better than trying to find a way to sneak in undetected. There was no time, but what choice did I have?

____

The moment the sun slipped below the horizon, I made my move. Guards had come and gone several times during the day, always coming with sick people and always leaving alone. I hadn't realized how badly the plague had gotten, but the death magic that permeated the air was so thick that my skin crawled as I found a side door to slip into. I would need to be quick before someone realized I was not where I belonged.

The door opened into a small, open space with docks where small boats could pull in to unload goods, and water lapped against the wood of the docks. The air was stale and musty, but there was a hint of something else…the faint metallic taste of blood that hit my tongue.

Something wicked is going on here. Rahfín's swelling presence was tinged with curiosity, and I inched deeper into the warehouse, towards a door on the other side of the room. Pressing a palm against the grain of the wood, I leaned in to listen.

Silence.

Tentatively, I pushed the door open. The door spilled into the main room of the warehouse, full of trading supplies and dark oak barrels. The supplies were all sectioned off and pushed to the side, creating space for a ritual circle to be drawn in the middle.

My nostrils flared.

"What are you doing here? I don't recognize you." A voice called out from one of the halls, and I froze before forcing a smile on my face and turning. The mage before me was a young woman, her hair light and curled delicately around small features.

Get her alone. She'll know where the boy is, Rahfín said.

I tapped my cane against the ground and leaned against it, offering the woman a disarming smile. "I'm the king's cousin. He sent me down here to ensure everything was running… smoothly." The lie came easily and flowed through my lips with an accompanying flash of my teeth. Some used to argue with me about the dangers of lies involving those with immense power, but it seemed I was never one to learn.

"I didn't know the king had a cousin. My sister works in the kitchens, and she's never mentioned the king having any family outside of his wife and children."

Bend her will.

In my mind's eye, I frowned. *Too much, and someone will suspect us.*

She doesn't believe you, Rahfín put simply.

He was right. The girl stared at me, her eyes narrowing suspiciously before flickering over to one of the hallways like she might bolt at any moment. My heart leaped to my throat, and I reached out just as she took off, running towards the hallway.

Go after her, Rahfín cried out, but fear was a monstrous thing, breeding hesitation that froze me in place. Soria was here somewhere; I sensed her presence, and I loathed the little boy she had instilled in me, the child who was fearful that he would never belong anywhere or amount to any sort of greatness.

Alistair, Rahfín growled, his heat licking the underside of my bones, *still that silly heart of yours. I wouldn't have chosen your body to share had I not seen the courage you are capable of. We must find the boy. If we must fight, so be it. That is what I am here for.*

Let's hope it doesn't come to that, I said finally. *We can't have Soria know we're anywhere near Kahl's lands.*

You should have thought of that before sneaking around the one place she frequents in the south.

I frowned and promptly ignored Rahfín after that, turning a blind eye to his smugness as I used a bit of magic to silence my footsteps and pulled the shadows of the dark warehouse around my form. It wouldn't render me invisible, especially if there were any mages in the warehouse, but it would make it difficult for anyone to locate me in the dark corners of the room should I need to hide.

Mere moments later, several guards and that woman returned, her finger wagging erratically as she spoke. "He was here. I didn't recognize him, but he was claiming to be the king's cousin!"

The guards sauntered about the room as if they didn't entirely believe the woman. "This isn't the first time you cried wolf, Mae." One of the guards sighed, turning to give the woman—Mae—a disapproving stare. "Are you certain?"

"Yes!" Mae had a wild look in her eye, and I held my breath as her gaze fell upon my hiding spot in the corner. I dared not move, only exhaling when she turned away to face the guards. "He would be gone by now, but we should mandate a search. He could be here for any of the sacrifices."

Sacrifices? That news was new to me and troubling. What was Soria doing, sacrificing the sick people of Kraeva? Sacrifice was used only in taboo magic.

Mae waved her hands impatiently upon seeing the guards' hesitations. "I'll go straight to Soria then."

The guards both paled and shook their heads. "No, no, that won't be necessary. Come, Fyrs. We'll check with the guards outside and then locate one of the mages to conduct a search. They'll be far quicker at locating anyone who isn't supposed to be here."

I remained where I was as they continued to speak, disappearing out the door that led to the docks outside. I would have to be quick. The mage would be able to find me once they retrieved them for the search.

Sweat collected at my palms as I slunk down the hallway Mae had disappeared into earlier, noting the rooms that lined each side. With Rahfín's keen sense of smell and heightened hearing, the soft symphony of the sick sounded beyond the doors. Lucky for me, some were nothing more than lines of iron bars I could peer into. Lyra had described her brother to me, but no one I had come across fit his description, and my search grew increasingly desperate, driven by a need to escape before Soria discovered my presence.

I was about to lay my hand on a door with no window to peer into when a magical hum emitted from the wood forced me to pause. It was warded, which was strange, considering none of the other rooms had been. What were they hiding inside? I sensed something living beyond the door, their heartbeat fast and erratic, like the other sick here. Was this person special?

"That bitch fought me for quite a bit longer than I expected her to. She was surprisingly strong for being so sick." A voice caused me to pause, and I found a home in the shadows of a small room nearby as a guard and a woman walked down the hall.

I sensed Soria's presence and flinched, sinking deeper into the darkness. She would be able to feel me soon if she hadn't already.

"Regardless, you continue to do your job until the city has been purged. The king must not know what's happening here, or that we're using the healer's boy for leverage. If things go my way, we'll have Alistair's location within a fortnight, so stay vigilant and ensure the healer's boy doesn't die. We need him so that when his..." Her words cut off, and I refused to seek her out, my heart pounding in betrayal. I hated the fear she instilled in me.

"Miss?"

"I thought I felt...never mind. Have you—" As their voices trailed off, I returned to the door and slipped outside before Soria returned and found me. My heart was still a dull roar in my ear, my panic in my throat, and I limped away as quickly as I could. The healer's boy *had* to be Lyra's brother, but what did they mean to use him for?

Rahfín's presence washed over me as I gave myself over to him.

CHAPTER FOURTEEN

LYRA

*V*alencia rushed us down the rows of bookshelves as a low whisper brushed against my back, spoken in tongues I couldn't understand. A chill sauntered down my back, but before I could turn around and look, Valencia had pulled me into one of the rows and trapped me against one of the bookshelves. Her arms enveloped me on either side, fingers pressed into the shelves, and her breath tickled my cheek as she peered behind me through the books.

"Quiet," she whispered, and I did as she asked, fear thundering in my ears. The library had turned from its comforting solace to something of a dark nature. The faeries had all disappeared, and a low creaking echoed two rows away. Something moved down the row behind me, and I stared up at Valencia as she pulled away slightly, her fear stitched into her face. I had little to fear in this life, but spirits were something that had always frightened me. I couldn't fight a spirit. Not with my fists. Like I could do most things.

Somewhere off in the distance, a book fell from its shelf and hit the floor. A soft sigh passed through the library, and I blinked, refusing to stare anywhere other than Valencia. To calm myself, I memorized her face, the sharp slope of her cheeks, the small scars that marred one of her eyebrows, the speckles of brown in the gold of her eyes. How her beauty made my breath catch. How a low ache burrowed deep in my belly.

"I think it's gone," Valencia uttered after we'd been there for some time. The library had lightened, and the faeries had come out of their hiding spots to resume their duties once more. "Strange. The spirits do not usually come into the library."

"What was that?" I asked, shaking myself from my fear. I didn't realize I'd leaned forward to avoid pressing against the books, but my closeness to Valencia became the only thing I could focus on. She was slightly taller than I was, but not overwhelmingly so, and I met her gaze as my cheeks heated. It was difficult to deny how beautiful she was, but I wasn't here to seduce Valencia Brøkharven. Even though I desired little else in that moment.

I was here to seduce Alistair and simultaneously save my brother. Valencia would simply be a distraction, no matter how lovely I thought her eyes were or how kind she'd been since I'd arrived.

"Sorry." Red warmed Valencia's cheeks as she lowered her arms and stepped away. "Remember how I spoke of the castle's unsettled nature when Alistair is gone? Well…" She laughed nervously, turning away from me to peer into the main part of the library. "Like I said—they don't usually come in here."

"And you don't know where they came from?" I hadn't expected ghosts to haunt Alistair's castle. There was much about the castle that I hadn't expected.

Valencia shook her head. "They were here when I arrived.

When I asked Alistair about them, he wouldn't give me a straight answer, as if he didn't know himself. They've never hurt me, but…" She shuddered, turning back towards me, "I loathe them. They creep me out."

"At least they don't seem to be aggressive." It would make navigating the home a lot more difficult, especially since Alistair seemed keen on leaving for long periods. His absence had me thinking about Cade, and my heart ached. I hoped he was okay. He'd been without medicine for days now if he was even still ali—

No. I refused to think of the alternative.

"It's getting late—I'll walk you back to your room," Valencia said.

I shook the darkness from my mind and nodded. I hadn't realized how exhausted I was.

——————

Valencia had gotten me back to my room with little trouble, and I had pounced into the bed, asleep just moments after my head hit the pillow. I was accustomed to waking with the sun rising, and today was no different, its rays peeking over the tree line as I stretched and rolled from the bed.

I washed my face in the basin in the corner. The water was cold, and I longed for a bath, but Valencia had spoken of going for breakfast together and taking a walk on the grounds afterwards. My fingers curled around the basin's edge, the water distorting my features as I stared down at myself. I tried to search my face for signs of my monstrosity. Could I mold myself into something capable of ripping Alistair's heart from his chest? The man had given me little reason to hate him, as annoying as he sometimes was, but I had to prepare for the possibility that the woman's words were the only way I would free myself from my curse.

Patting a towel to my face, a soft knock came to my door. "Lyra?"

Valencia's head peeked into my room, the blonde of her hair shifting down her shoulder as she leaned in. "Ready?"

"In a moment," I said, gesturing to my pajamas. It was the small nightgown of deep green that left little to the imagination, but I hadn't found anything else comfortable enough to sleep in. I wrapped my arms around myself, suddenly feeling self-conscious, and Valencia nodded before retreating.

When the door clicked shut behind her, I quickly changed. Much of Alistair's tastes bordered on silks, a standard fabric of Kahl's warm climate, in greens and golds, like his eyes.

I flushed at the thought of them and the power and heat radiating from them, only to chastise myself. If I lost myself in this, would I make it out alive?

"You need to remain focused," I told myself quietly, slipping a woven green shirt over my head. "For Cade."

My hair was a mess, a lost cause, really, so I barely paid it any mind further than running my hands through it as I pulled open the door and met Valencia out in the hall. She had propped herself against the wall next to the door, arms loosely crossed over her chest, and she offered a radiant smile when I appeared.

"I haven't said so yet, but having someone else here is incredibly nice. Alistair is gone constantly, and when he is around..." She frowned as we began our trek down the hall. I noticed it had not changed, except that some of the flower decor had started to look livelier in their frames on the wall. A few of the bugs fluttered their wings but did not move from where they were faceted, as if by magic, and I tore my gaze away from it to settle on Valencia. She had a strange look in her eye, one bred in loneliness, and my heart swelled for it. It had been only Cade and me for a while. I understood that loneliness.

"Yes, I'm here now, though I don't know if I'll prove to be better company than Alistair. My brother said I was somewhat of a grump myself."

Valencia laughed. "You sound like my sister, Dahlia. She always claims to be foul company, but hers is the only company I can stand on an infinite basis in my family. The rest?" Her nose crinkled in disgust. "Small, small doses."

"I can relate." Cade was the only person I had ever wished to be around. The ladies of the court were insufferable growing up. They'd never understood my desire to be a knight, never understood my fiery nature, or my disinterest in blushing and gossiping about potential suitors. "How many siblings do you have?"

Valencia glanced sideways at me. "Five. I'm the youngest, then it's Dahlia. The elder three are all brothers."

"And you all have dragons?" My curiosity was a hungry thing, insatiable, as I leaned close. I had always been fascinated with Bracaea's royal family and their dragons, but had never seen them in person.

It was the first time I'd seen Valencia's face light up, truly and radiantly. She was beautiful in that moment, her back straightening as pride etched itself in her gaze. "That's right. Many think we're given dragon eggs from the wild dragons in the mountains, but that's not true at all. We have to go and earn their respect. Only then do we get an egg and pass into woman or manhood to take our rightful place as part of the Family."

Another question formed, but I did not ask this one.

Valencia was here, and there was no dragon in sight. It didn't seem right, though, kind even, to ask her.

Still, she saw the look in my eye and understood me even though I did not ask.

"I tried twice. Both of them almost resulted in my death. Mother always said I must simply keep trying, and one day, when the time was right, I'd be gifted an egg from a godly clutch, but when I finally got mine, it never hatched."

I reached down, grabbed her hand, and squeezed. Her skin was impossibly warm. "I'm sorry." And I was, truly. Watching her family earn their dragons while the world did not give her hers had to have been difficult.

After a moment, her hand closed around mine, and the pain in her eyes disappeared. "Thanks, Lyra. I've had time to process and overcome it. Perhaps it will hatch when Alistair breaks my curse." She sighed wistfully. "If—"

I shook my head. "No, don't think like that. Did whoever cursed you tell you how to break it?"

Tugging her hand away, she slipped her hand on the railing of the foyer's staircase and descended towards the dining hall. "Only that someone dragon-touched will have my every desire. The only people I know that are dragon-touched are my family members, and...Alistair."

"Alistair is dragon-touched?"

"He will have to explain it. It's not my place."

Disappointed, I followed her into the dining room. There was so little I knew of our host besides being an arrogant mage running from the Council of Maega. I was hoping Valencia could give me insight into him without seeming suspicious.

Sidestepping a broom led by invisible hands as it brushed past us on the tiled floor, I took in the magnificence of the dining room as Valencia led us inside.

The Kahlian royal family was well-versed in their obsession with silks and other expensive tastes, but Alistair was not far off. Golden frames lined the walls, much like the rest of the house, their centers filled with delicate things. Some were filled with portraits of strange creatures, such as wolves with multiple sets of eyes and spindly limbs, while others bordered a plant that blossomed straight from the wall. The dark wood of the table was carved with intricate flowers and woodland creatures—fae of the Seelie Court, mostly, but I noticed some were creatures I'd only heard of in tales—goblins and redcaps and those of Neferíl's Unseelie Court.

"It's so strange," Valencia muttered. "The nature on the walls was all dead yesterday. I wonder what changed."

I ran my finger over a wooden rose carved into the back of the chair in front of me as Valencia took a seat to my left. Her nearness had me on edge, but she had already proved different from other ladies of the court. She didn't look at me with disdain, nor did she attempt to pull my hair or judge my clothes.

"Dead?" I asked, staring at the flowers blooming between extravagant frames.

Valencia nodded. "Everything about this place was dead or in some state of decay, but it's like something is bringing it back to life." She did lean closer then, and my pulse jumped eagerly. "I believe the house is tied to Alistair, somehow. Like his ghosts."

A flurry of movement gathered around us as I joined Valencia at the table; silver trays brimming with food rushed forward, suspended in the air, and sat neatly in the middle of the table. A small pixie, naked, with sharp teeth and untamed blonde hair, flew down to rest on Valencia's shoulder. She grabbed a fistful of Valencia's hair and began to braid it, and Valencia poured some sweetened milk into a small bowl and held it up to her. She cooed, a sharp sound that tinkled like a bell, and soon Valencia was swarmed with pixies as she laughed.

"Alright, everyone, but I have to eat too. Don't tell your host I was feeding you honey milk." She glanced sideways at me. "Makes them extra ornery. Alistair loathes it when I encourage them, but I can't help myself. I've grown fond of them. They're very different than what my family has told me of the fae."

"The wild fae are loyal to a fault, if you get on their good side," I agreed, watching the pixies take small handfuls of milk and bring it to their mouths.

We fell into a comfortable silence as I piled my plate full of fruit and various meats, struggling to ignore how ravenous I felt. It had been *so* long since I'd been able to have smoked meats and honeyed ham—meat of the north, which had been challenging to find since the war.

"What can you tell me about Alistair?" I asked, popping a blackberry into my mouth. "I don't know much about him, other than his inability to put up a fight and what Kraevians whisper of him in the streets."

"He really is a terrible fighter." Valencia laughed. "He makes up for it with his magical skill. I've truly never seen anyone better at wielding it, and the Bracaean family has constant contact with the mages of Ravenspire."

The mages of Ravenspire were renowned for their magical talents. It was where the Council of Maega resided, a group of mages that protected Bracaea. I didn't know much about them beyond my studies as a child, but the royal family of Kahl considered them enemies of the crown for their allegiance to Bracaea.

"He also saved my life," Valencia continued quietly, dragging me from my thoughts. "I don't know how he found me, but my curse—" she paused, a sheepish expression crossing her face. "I suppose you don't know, do you?" Setting her fork down, she laid her hands on her lap.

"I thought Alistair would have been here alone," I admitted.

"If I leave the safety of this castle, my form turns into that of the fae. And not just any fae — one of Neferíl's Court."

I blinked and turned to her. "What?" No wonder she couldn't return home. The faeries of northern Elvira and Bracaea had been feuding long before I was born.

Valencia's face was twisted in a mixture of pain, bitterness, and amusement. "I tried to return home after it happened, not realizing my form had changed. It wasn't until the guards tried to kill me that I realized what had happened."

"If this is overstepping, you don't have to answer, but how did it happen?"

Valencia was silent long enough for my question to feel intrusive, but she held up a hand when I opened my mouth to apologize. "No, it's alright. I went to a witch and asked her to free me from the prison of my home."

"Aren't witches notoriously unreliable?" I asked, shocked.

Valencia nodded. "I was desperate. My father was determined to marry me off to the right suitor, and I was far older than any of the other unmarried women in our Court. It was beginning to look undesirable."

I frowned and refrained from rolling my eyes. Court politics never quite made sense to me, but I knew the logistics of marriage, and it was often bred under the pretense of currency or power.

I reached out and laid a hesitant hand on top of Valencia's. "I'm sorry."

"The witch fulfilled my wish. It just wasn't... how I expected. I wasn't sure how she would free me from my obligations, but I *couldn't* marry Nasir. He's outright awful."

A chill ran down my spine. "You were to marry Nasir?" All the horrible things I'd witnessed beneath the scrutiny of Nasir's wrath pressed against my ribcage, and I pulled my hand away, horrified.

"Relations with Kahl were fragile. My father thought joining our houses would soothe old hurts. Seems I made it worse, trying to flee my fate. I wanted to be free, but not at the cost of innocent lives." Valencia sighed, pushing her chair from the table. "I also didn't mean to depress your morning. I'll leave you to it, but find me when you're done, and we'll go walk the grounds." She squeezed my shoulder and stood, leaving my mind with conflicting thoughts.

I couldn't kill Alistair. Not until he discovered how to break Valencia's curse. Doing so would doom the kingdoms. I stared down at my hands, at the curse that lay there with bated breath. I couldn't leave the safety of this castle until they were washed clean from the darkness that woman had laid upon them, and my tangled heart despaired: had I traded one prison for another?

My thoughts strayed back to the spirit that had chased us from the library. "Hey Val?" I caught her just before she left, her hand grazing the doorframe as she turned. "You said the spirits here are more restless when Alistair is gone. Does that mean when he *is* home, they're relatively quiet?"

Valencia nodded. "I barely notice them when Alistair is around. It's as if they fear him."

I nodded. "Thanks."

She gave me a soft smile, leaving me to ponder my thoughts. I needed to get back to that book, the one on fungi, but I would have to wait for Alistair to return before I braved venturing to the library again.

CHAPTER FIFTEEN
LYRA

*A*fter breakfast, I found Valencia, and she led me outside.

The grounds must have been beautiful once. Now, they were in a state of decay, with browned, crumpled flowers and dead leaves scattered over the fountain that rose high in the center. Valencia led me around the house, where a small garden was tucked away from the view of the front. The gardens were littered with stone benches, but many of them were also deteriorated, with a large crack through their centers.

"It's beautiful in its own sort of way," Valencia murmured, eyeing the gardens. "Thinking about how it must have been once."

I hummed in response. It was a shame because I *saw* the potential. There had to have been a plethora of flowerbeds once. "I wonder why Alistair stopped tending to it."

Valencia shrugged. "He's got other worries."

I might have scoffed and made a sarcastic remark had there not been a solemn look on Valencia's face. The words died on my tongue, murdered by my guilt. "Right. I suppose flowers are the last thing on the mind when there are curses about."

Valencia's smile did not quite reach her eyes. "Curses and mages and wars."

"Why isn't Alistair fighting in the war? I thought all the mages had to report to the king of Bracaea when the soldiers were called to war." A simple curiosity, and I knelt to pluck a leaf from the ground, marveling at the stark red color.

Valencia's shoulders tensed. "He saved me. After getting cursed, I foolishly tried to return home. No one recognized me, and faeries are not welcome in Vrona. Ravenspire was built to keep fae out, and I was stopped at the wall." Valencia went so still I swore she turned into a statue, and sympathy ran through me, cold as ice. I wanted to reach out and comfort her, but I had never been good at such gentle gestures, so I merely waited and listened, silent and patient, as she collected herself.

"I thought they were going to kill me." Her voice cracked, and she gave a soft shake of her head as she wrapped her arms around herself. "I hadn't seen myself yet, was too distraught to understand what the witch had done to me to know she'd given me what I wanted, but at the cost of turning into the very thing I loathed the most."

I frowned. "You didn't know. Witches are arguably more mischievous than the fair folk. You can never trust them to give you what you want without consequences."

Valencia sighed. "I know. I just wanted out of my obligations. I didn't *want* to marry the prince. I was not some prize to be won, not some cattle to be sold and bred for sons." Bitterness etched her tone, and I sank into her anger, letting it fuel my own. I was angry *for* her.

"You're so much more than that," I said. "We all are."

The smile that perked at Valencia's lips did not quite reach her eyes. "Funny enough, I dreamed of being queen when I was a little girl. I wanted it more than *anything*." She sighed wistfully, plopping down onto a stone bench with her hands in her lap. "My brothers used to tease me about it. 'You'll never be queen, you're the youngest.'"

"How awful," I said. I couldn't imagine Cade saying anything like that to me. He was the only one other than Alistair who knew I had always wanted to be a knight, and he'd supported that dream, as silly as it was.

"They weren't so awful all the time," Valencia said, waving a hand in dismissal. "Kept me from disappearing into the clouds. Yet...I've never given up on that dream. I *want* to be queen, but I don't want to have to marry to do it. Such a silly, foolish thing to want."

I shook my head. "I don't think it's foolish at all. Admirable, actually. It takes a lot of courage to rule." Never a dream of mine, but I admired anyone willing to stand up in defense of the people under their care. The royal families in charge now were doing a piss-poor job of it.

"It matters little. I'll never be queen. Perhaps in another lifetime, where women can rule without the aid of men, and I am the eldest child." Sad laughter passed her lips, and her words only enraged me, but she was right. Little could be done about the way things were, not in our lifetime.

"Say," Valencia said, changing the subject, "Were you able to find anything on breaking curses? We fled the library in such a rush..."

I nodded, falling on the bench next to her. "Just as I found something, the spirit interrupted. I haven't been courageous enough to go back." What other little research I'd attempted to do had yielded nothing but empty answers and frustrations, and my anxieties over Cade's safety had proven distracting the longer Alistair had been gone. My restless nature plagued me the most, eager to liberate Cade from wherever the city guards had taken him. Alistair still hadn't returned to share news of his fate, and my belly twisted mercilessly because of it. "Honestly, I haven't been able to think about it very much. Not when my brother—" My throat closed, cutting off my sentence, and my fingers trembled.

Valencia reached out to take my hands, but I pulled them away, too scared to touch her now that we were outside the castle. Her own hands fell back into her lap, and she smiled, genuinely this time. "If anyone can find him, it's Alistair."

I believed her. I had never met someone quite like Alistair.

"Is that a faerie ring?" I asked suddenly, gesturing to a circle of mushrooms growing some feet away. They weren't at all like the faerie rings in the city that the fae used to enter Kraeva, brown and dull in color, and Valencia shook her head.

"That's a deceptive one, but no. I remember Alistair telling me once that faerie rings were made with nemalyn caps."

"Those are the red and white ones, right?"

Valencia nodded, and a memory resurfaced: my father pleading with the king to let him harvest one for research. He believed it to hold something important, though I couldn't remember what. The king had refused because the caps were considered sacred, and taking one would destroy the portal between our realm and the fae world.

Suddenly, it clicked in my brain. The missing ingredient.

"It looks like Alistair has returned!" I looked up as Valencia gestured to Alistair, limping across the grounds. "It's best to leave him be until after he's had a bath. He's never well when he returns," Valencia said gently. She must have seen the look on my face, the desire to descend upon him and demand to know any news on my brother. I thought about ignoring her, but Alistair had already disappeared into the estate, and I still wasn't too familiar with the winding halls. No, but now that Alistair was home, I could return to the library.

"I have to go and check on something in the library. I'll see you later," I told Valencia, hurrying towards the estate.

CHAPTER SIXTEEN

LYRA

$\mathcal{I}$ wasn't sure how, but somehow, I'd found my way to the library by myself without getting lost or haunted by ghosts. I wandered the rows of books for a better part of twenty minutes before my frustration got the better of me, and I approached one of the fae strolling about the room. It was one of the short, rock-like creatures who seemed to pay me no mind even as I approached.

"Can you help me find a book on nemalyn caps?"

The rock faerie grumbled and chucked a small pebble in my direction, speaking to me in a language I didn't understand. It ambled off, and I frowned, rubbing the part of my arm the pebble had struck. I couldn't recall how Valencia had called about the wisp, so I sighed and continued my search. Perhaps the row of shelves I'd discovered that book on plants last time would have one on nemalyn caps.

I nearly gave up, my eyes sore from all the spines I'd read when I found it. The ancient, crumbling book with faded letters on its spine: Fungi and Their Multiple Properties, the same one I had seen just before the spirit had appeared. I tugged it from the shelf and sat right in the aisle, too eager to read its contents to return to the middle of the room. The inside was in a language I could understand, too, a relief as I turned the pages until the words' NEMALYN CAP' were spelled out at the top.

"Gotcha," I said, running my finger over the illustration of the nemalyn cap in the corner. Whoever wrote these tomes did so beautifully, illustrated on old paper that crinkled when I lifted the page to read.

Nemalyn caps are extremely rare, only found in the gardens of Eirwyn's court. They are used to create faerie rings with the aid of druidic magic. One should take care when handling these mushrooms—the circles on the caps release a toxin if provoked, which can cause fatal consequences unless the victim seeks out a healer immediately.

However, there have been studies conducted by a faerie scholar who wished to remain unnamed on the correlation between the stems of nemalyn caps and healing potions. Not much is known about the extent of their healing capabilities, but...

I quickly slammed the book closed and hurried to my feet. I didn't need to read anymore; I'd found what we needed. I wasn't sure how or when we'd obtain a Nemalyn cap, but perhaps this would be the answer I needed —a way to cure my hands without harming Alistair.

I murdered the hope in my chest before it could fester. Hope was dangerous, and I didn't know this would even work.

I needed to find Valencia and let her know what I saw. I shuddered at the thought of running into one of the spirits that haunted these halls, but the excitement over my discovery outweighed my fear, and I trudged out of the row of shelves and made my way towards the library door. A wisp stopped me before I could reach it, weaving through the air in front of me and preventing me from moving past it.

"What?" I asked it, feeling foolish, even though I was sure they could understand me.

The wisp gurgled and bounced before whizzing around my head and flying deeper into the library, back the way I came. Hugging the book to my chest, I hesitated. I did not want to delay the news to Valencia and Alastair, not when it could be the answer we were looking for, but it was apparent the wisp wanted to show me something.

Ultimately, curiosity prevailed.

The wisp trailed over to me again before zooming off, halting at a series of bookshelves. Despite its impatient nature, it moved gracefully, its tentacles drifting through the air slowly and methodically.

"Are you all so insistent?" I asked as the wisp floated back over to me and trailed around my head, disappearing around the corner of a shelf, only to reappear and bounce up and down. "Okay, okay. I'm coming."

Peering cautiously down the row the wisp led me to, I clung to the book in my hands like it was my lifeline. The bookshelves stretched for some time before coming up to a door, one I hadn't noticed before, and the wisp shot towards it until it burst through the door and faded away. Did it want me to seek whatever was behind the door? Something about the magical energy radiating from the wood had my heart pattering nervously as I approached. There was nothing to indicate where the door would lead or what lay tucked behind it, and I flattened a palm against the door for a moment as I hesitated.

I was startled as the wisp popped through the door, and I raised my hands to cover my face as if the wisp were going to lash out and strike me. My time in the fighting pits had kept me cautious, even as the wisp disappeared again. My instincts screamed at me to fight.

Ignoring them, I pried open the door and stepped through.

Inside was a small room. I was immediately struck with a waft of warm air; the room was stifling, and I stepped tentatively inside. There was nothing, no windows to shed light into the room, and there were a couple of steps down in the center where a pit of fire blazed beneath a stone.

No, I realized with horror. *Not a stone. An egg.*

I drew closer despite the thickness of the air, the heat, and the light of the flames bouncing off my face. The egg was gorgeous, a deep green tinged in gold. It was scaled, like the hide of a dragon, and I swallowed a lump that had formed in my throat. What was Alistair doing with a dragon egg tucked away in his castle? Dragon eggs were sacred, godly beings that were only gifted to the royal family in Bracaea. Last I recalled, mages weren't gifted dragons to ride.

"How did you find this room?" I flinched as Alistair materialized from the darkness, his eyes blazing green and gold. His anger was nearly as hot as this room, rolling off him in waves, and I straightened my back and slid my gaze over to the egg.

"What is actually going on here?"

His smile was chilling. "Answer my question, and I'll tell you."

"A wisp led me here."

"These wisps seem to be leading you around an awful lot."

I narrowed my eyes at them. "I can't tell them what to do— obviously, and this one was *insistent* that I follow it to this room. I answered your question, now it's your turn to answer mine."

I nearly shrank away from Alistair's imposing nature as he stalked towards me, his eyes a burning inferno. His anger was nearly palpable, a tangible thing I could taste in the air, but I held my ground, tilting my chin up to meet his gaze as he stepped closer.

"I will not be commanded in my own house. You are a guest here, and this room is off-limits."

My belly pooled with rage, only to be swiftly stifled as I remembered why I was here. If I wanted to break the curse on my hands, I would not do it by fighting Alistair Sylverhorn.

"I can't help you if I don't understand what's going on." *I need you to trust me.*

Alistair blinked, and for a moment, I thought he wouldn't answer me. Silence infected the room as he sighed and limped over to the top of the stairs that led into the small pit of flames that burned beneath the egg.

"Many assume it was gems and coin that I stole from the dragons to receive their wrath, but nay." His hand swept out, the fire dancing off his bitter features. "I sold my soul to a dying dragon in exchange for his magic. I was foolish to do so, but I wanted power. *Needed* it."

The echo of want in his tone was all too familiar; I had seen it many a time in the castle growing up, and that kind of greed sickened me. Not when I had seen the suffering of those in the lower districts. Not when I had seen what kind of corruption power wielded.

Noting the look of disgust in my eye, Alistair raised a hand to press to the nape of his neck. His anger had washed away, replaced with a haunted expression, and he laughed, though it lacked warmth. "I have earned your disgust, Lyra A'mar, but don't fret. I have recently grown disgusted with my actions as well."

"Why? Why do it?" I asked.

"Because…" he answered slowly. "I saw the corruption seeping into Ravenspire, saw the effects of Valencia's disappearance affecting Bracaea's royal family and, in turn, causing unrest in the mages. Greed is evil, and no others are greedier for power than those who wield magic." Alistair flexed the hand at his side, his shoulders tense. "Without it, I wouldn't have been able to escape and help Valencia seek her cure. I didn't expect the dragon sickness to plague me."

He didn't seem to be lying. I saw the truth cradle his eyes.

It was difficult to feel sorry for him despite the regretful tone of his voice, but I found myself stepping forward, my brow furrowed. "Dragon sickness? Valencia said you were cursed but…"

"She didn't go into detail," Alistair finished, nodding firmly. "I love that about Val. She's respectful when it comes to one's privacy." Stepping past me, he gestured for me to follow. "Come. Let us speak where it is more comfortable."

I spared one more glance at the egg before following.

CHAPTER SEVENTEEN

ALISTAIR

I led Lyra through the library, where the center sitting area was. A fire blazed in the fireplace, spilling warmth into the room and over the ancient tomes and towering shelves. I winced in pain as I lowered myself into one of the armchairs. Leaning my cane against the arm, I watched Lyra sit as well, only across from me. Her gaze bore a level of suspicion, but there was also a simple curiosity there, one I was finally ready to satisfy. Lyra had been here long enough and deserved the right to know who she was sharing a castle with. My bones ached, and I shifted in my chair, uncomfortable with the low-grade pain that radiated through my body. Rahfín was restless. Pressed up against my rib cage, he swelled, making it difficult to breathe. I longed for my bed, but it would be a long night before I arrived there.

"So…what is dragon sickness?" Lyra's impatience drew a smile from my lips, my pain momentarily ignored.

"The soul of a dragon possesses me." A half-truth. I *was* possessed by Rahfín, but I kept the grim darkness of the illness: that it would one day claim my life.

Lyra blinked at me in disbelief. "I've never heard of this."

I swept my hand out bitterly. "That's because it's never happened before. Not that I know of, at least."

Ungrateful pup. Rahfín's words washed through me. *I gave you the power of the gods, and you give me your bitterness as thanks?*

At what cost?

Rahfin shuffled in amusement and irritation, the heat of his essence brushing against the underside of my skin so quickly that I broke out in a sweat. *It's not my fault you failed to understand the burden of my weight. The cost for power is this, Alistair. Do not disappoint me.*

With that, his presence retreated, forming a sharp knot in the pit of my stomach as I grimaced. I would not have sought it out if I had known the cost to be this high.

"What does this even mean for you? Is this sickness curable? I suppose you wouldn't know if it's never happened before..." Lyra trailed off, dragging her teeth over her bottom lip. A dark thought that yearned to do just that fixed my gaze on her mouth. Something about her...I'd give anything to know what brought her pleasure.

"The only place I can think of that might have answers is the dragons in the Voiceless Mountains, and the only entrance is in Vrona. Until Valencia is cured..." I trailed off as Lyra's eyes lit up in understanding.

"You cannot return. She told me that you saved her."

The memory resurfaced, the fear in Valencia's eyes when the mages at Ravenspire had attempted to kill her. It had been foolish of them; one glance and I'd been able to see the princess beneath the mask of her curse, but perhaps Rahfín gifted me that power to see. Regardless, I had ferried her away, knowing her death would seal the fate of the two human kingdoms, and it had been a race to cure her ever since.

"And the egg?"

I sighed. "Nothing to do with me at all. That's Valencia's."

Silence fell between us as Lyra's eyes widened in realization. I didn't care to explain more, and she didn't ask even though I felt her brimming with questions. Getting Valencia's dragon egg for her had been one of the most challenging things I'd ever done, the thing that had gotten me exiled, but I didn't regret it. Not when Valencia was so sure it would hatch for her one day.

"Did you…" The fear in Lyra's voice caught in her throat, and I leaned forward, grimacing at my aching joints. Rahfín hadn't been merciful in using my body this time, and the lasting effect had been brutal. The bath I'd just taken had done little to soothe my pain.

"I found the place they took your brother," I said, knowing it was what Lyra was after. "I didn't get eyes on him, but I overheard them saying they're keeping him alive."

Lyra clung to the armchair like it was the only thing keeping her anchored, even as she pushed herself to her feet. "We have to go and get him right now."

I held up my hand. "Not so fast. We can't just go in there until we know what we're going up against. I have reason to believe that mages are involved. If there are mages in Kraeva, it can't mean anything good." I remained silent on Soria's involvement; Soria had always been eager to push magic to the limits, even to the detriment of human morality. Perhaps the king believed they were killing the sick as a mercy, a way to keep the city safe, but I knew Soria intimately. She had to be doing something to them, a way to foster her curiosity.

This meant the faster we got Lyra's brother out of there,

the better, but we couldn't go without knowing more. "Let me gather some more information about what is going on. They're keeping your brother alive for whatever reason, so he's not in any immediate danger."

Lyra didn't seem pleased by my suggestion, but she relented, her shoulders sagging as she sank back into the chair. "He's all I got," she said after a while, her eyes refusing to meet mine. Instead, her brow furrowed as she stared at some spot past my shoulder, her jaw clenched. "If anything happens to him…" The words hung heavy in the air, and I felt for her. I'd never had someone like that, a sibling or another person I cared for deeply. Not until Valencia, or, recently, how quickly Lyra was worming her way into my heart.

She could use that against you, Rahfín mused in my head. *Be careful, Alistair. You don't know the kind of woman she is or why Soria sent her.*

*Exactly. We **don't** know Soria sent her,* I argued.

Rahfín's scoff echoed through my mind, and my cheeks warmed in offense. *Her curse is written into Lyra's hands. Don't be a fool.*

Maybe I *was* a fool, but I pushed Rahfín's presence away anyway. I didn't need to hear it from him. I'd survived a long time without him; I'd continue to trust my gut.

"Have you found anything of use in the library?" I asked, eager to chase away the lingering suspicions of Lyra that Rahfín had infected in my mind.

Lyra brightened, holding a finger up and standing. "I'll grab it, but I've figured out what we need."

I grinned, pleased. "I knew you would."

Lyra flushed, a soft smile forming on her lips, and she shook her head. "I… don't thank me yet; it's not going to be easy to get." She disappeared down a row of bookshelves, only to return with a thick tome pressed to her chest. "We need a nemalyn cap."

My nose flared in horror. "What?"

Lyra nodded, offering me the tome. I took it from her, brushing my fingers over the spine of the worn volume. Lyra pressed close, the warm brown of her eyes catching in the firelight as her lips pursed. "The caps are poisonous, but the stalks…well, they can be used in some mixtures for healing purposes, if you know how to handle them."

"Unfortunately, I've never had the pleasure. If, and that's a big if, we can get our hands on one, I'd be willing to give it a shot. Especially if that's our only lead to a cure." I stared down at the illustration of the cap, frowning. Eirwyn's Court was the only place I knew them to grow, and getting into his castle and finding one would be a challenge. He wouldn't likely part with one, not without cause that would benefit his court. Though I was familiar with his castle, having visited my father several times after I was given to Ravenspire, I knew it wouldn't be easy to take one without Eirwyn's notice either.

"The only place I know they grow is in the Seelie King's castle, and the faerie king does not part with his things willingly," I said.

Lyra frowned. "Do you know him?"

I flashed a disarming smile her way. "Are you assuming because I'm fae that I know the southern king of the fae?"

Lyra flushed, and my gaze heated, spurred on by her embarrassment.

"I'm teasing." I sighed dramatically, falling back in my seat and staring up at her through dark lashes. "I know him, but…"

Lyra's face carved out her determination as she darted close, her fingers curling against the arms of my chair. "You *must* speak with him. It's our best chance."

Lyra's nearness had me on edge. I still couldn't place what

it was about her that warmed my blood or flooded me with desire. I had been fascinated with her since watching her fight in the pits, the untamed way in which she let go and brought down someone twice her size.

I stared up at her, and our eyes met. There was a silent determination in her stare, mingled with something I couldn't place…guilt, maybe? A quiet sadness that echoed throughout her gaze. I longed to comfort her, and I did not know why.

"Can I…?" Her words were hushed, and her nostrils flared as she lost courage. An electrifying tension hung in the air between us, and I slammed the book shut, setting it on a table beside the chair as she exhaled shakily. "Never mind."

But I wasn't going to let her go this time. I'd been denying myself the attraction I'd felt for Lyra since the moment I'd laid eyes on her. I couldn't deny it any longer. Suspicions be *damned.* I'd never denied myself what I wanted before, and I wasn't about to start now.

She'd returned to the chair across from me, and I stood, pinning her there with my gaze. "Can you what, Lyra? I never pegged you for someone who asked before taking what you wanted."

Her gaze heated, and she tilted her chin up, mouth drawn in a faint line. "We have other things to worry about than whatever *this* is." She gestured between us, but her tone was unconvinced as I sauntered towards her, ignoring the pain in my leg. "Plus, what about Valencia?"

"What about her?" My voice was low and rough as I drew closer to her, like a moth to a flame.

Lyra hesitated. "You two seem…close."

Commanding space, I trapped her legs between mine and grasped each arm of the chair, bending close. "We are. We are both on the same page about not denying ourselves what we want, even if that means other companionship."

Lyra exhaled again as my mouth drew down to the cusp of her ear. "We have all been under duress. Don't we owe ourselves a bit of a distraction?" I nipped at her lobe, relishing in the quiet noise that passed Lyra's lips as my mouth pressed against the skin between her ear and the start of her jaw. She smelled lovely, like the cross between cinnamon and vanilla, and she cocked her head to the side, granting me better access to her neck. I took full advantage, pressing small kisses to the line of her neck, tongue darting across the sensitive skin there and gasping when Lyra's hand found my cock through my pants.

"The two of you are having fun and didn't think to invite me? I'm offended." Valencia's voice behind me sent soft laughter, her breath brushing against Lyra's skin as she attempted to draw away, but she had nowhere to go. Her eyes were bright with desire as I pulled away, raising my head up to meet Valencia's gaze as she approached. An amused smile twitched at the corner of her lips. "Mind if I join?"

"*Gods,*" Lyra whimpered as Valencia stepped up to the back of Lyra's chair and began to run her hands down Lyra's shoulders and across her chest. "Let me—"

"Shhh, love. Let *us.*" Valencia silenced her as she managed to find the edge of Lyra's shirt, and Lyra leaned forward so that Valencia could tug it over Lyra's head, leaving Lyra bare from the waist up. I stepped back, taking a moment to drink in the sight of Lyra, her body writhing as Valencia's fingers darted gently over Lyra's nipples.

"Both of you are stunning," I breathed, my desire coiling deep in my belly. My erection was almost painful, aching with want, but I sank to my knees as the dragon inside me sent lust and the desire to worship through my veins.

Soft laughter broke the silence as hands intertwined, exploring curiosity and trust. Each gesture was careful, each touch a question and an answer, and the boundaries between us blurred. It was *intoxicating,* and soon, our whispers became the only sound in the library, a symphony of shared secrets and stolen moments.

Somewhere in the deep bowels of my belly, Rahfín's heat sprang to life.

CHAPTER EIGHTEEN

LYRA

Oh, gods.

At some point, Alistair had removed my pants, leaving me naked and doted upon by the two beautiful people who stood around my armchair. I would have been a fool to think I had never thought of it, never wondered what it would be like to touch either of them. With every searing kiss to my skin, I unwound, at the mercy of two otherworldly beings.

Valencia's mouth clamped down on my nipple at the exact moment Alistair's tongue plunged into me, and I cried out, overwhelmed with want. I had been with partners before, but never with anyone as intense as this. As Alistair's tongue worked its way around the sensitive spot at my center, Valencia showed no mercy to my nipples, her tongue darting delicately across one while her fingers worked around the other.

I could die here, in their arms, and it would be a mercy.

"Please," I begged, letting my head fall against the back of the chair, my fingers scrambling to cling to the chair's arms. My legs were draped over Alistair's shoulders, and my begging earned a low growl of approval from Alistair as he continued to send me closer to that edge. My stomach began to coil, deliciously so, and Valencia rose to press a hard kiss to my lips. I moaned Alistair's name into her mouth, one of my hands reaching up to keep her there, the other resting against the back of Alistair's head.

"Come for him, darling," Valencia murmured against my lips. "Come undone."

So I did. Letting go, I took a step off the edge and plummeted into oblivion.

I came down from the high of my orgasm slowly, breathing hard, feeling peace for the first time in a while. The violent ache had unraveled in my chest, and the warmth of Valencia and Alistair filled the air around me as Alistair ascended, his lips finding Valencia's before finding mine.

"Give me three days," he murmured against my mouth, suddenly drawing away. "Three days to scout the warehouse where they're holding your brother and ponder about the nemalyn caps." Before I could respond, he'd disappeared as if he were never there, and I glanced up at Valencia as laughter danced on her lips.

"He loves doing that," she said, answering my unspoken question. "Loves giving pleasure, but leaves before you can return the favor." She sobered as I rediscovered my pants and shirt and pulled them back on. "Not sure what that's about."

Still, his words had caused the edge of stress to return and cling to my rib cage. If anything were to happen to Cade...

No.

I scrambled to my feet, meeting Valencia's gaze. All this nervous energy had nowhere to go, and though Alistair had left to find out more about where they were keeping Cade, Valencia was still *here.*

"Since he isn't here for me to return the favor..." I stepped forward, backing Valencia against one of the bookshelves, relishing how her breath caught and the heat seared in her expression. "Tell me how you like to be pleasured, Your Highness."

She did, and the library was filled with soft sighs of pleasure as we locked ourselves away from the curses and other horrors of the world.

Alistair swept into the dining hall just as I finished my breakfast, three days after the incident in the library, just as he promised. My cheeks burned at the memory of his tongue, the desire in my belly begging for more. I tamed it; I needed Alistair to love me, not the other way around.

"I believe tonight is the night we go and get your brother."

A giddy excitement sang through me at the prospect, stilling any thoughts of intimacy. Many nights, I'd lain awake, terrified I would find out my brother had succumbed to his illness or the crown had killed him in an attempt to purge the plague in its city. Alistair had assured me they were keeping him alive, but what if he was wrong?

A small creature scuttled across the table. Its appearance resembled a mixture of a mouse and a bat, with leathery wings tucked against its furry body. I offered it a small crumb of my food as it pushed itself up on its two hind legs to look at me. A whiskered nose twitched as it snatched the food from me and immediately shoved it into its mouth, its canines long and pointed, its cheeks bulging.

Alistair smiled, and the gesture was so warm that my stomach flopped with silly desire. "Before we leave, though, I brought you a gift." He reached out a hand to run over the top of the creature's head as it scuttled over to him, and I watched the tender exchange.

Everyone told me you were a monster, I thought. *But I haven't seen that.* Alistair had been nothing but gentle with everything I'd seen him come into contact with. Nothing in his actions so far had given me any reason to believe he was capable of such monstrous things as the rumors had led me to believe.

"A gift?"

Alistair made his way over to me. He walked confidently today, his cane thumping against the floor as he approached. I noticed something shoved between his palm and his cane when he drew close enough.

I looked up and met the burning in his gaze as he leaned over my shoulder and set something next to my plate. Gloves. They were pretty, something the higher classes of ladies wore in the kingdoms. They were made of white silk and were dressed with flowers embroidered on lace at the wrist. I wasn't one for materialistic things, and I leaned to the side to stare up at Alistair before realizing just how close he was. I could sink into the warmth that radiated from him.

"What are these for?"

"They've been enchanted to keep your curse at bay. They'll still deteriorate, but keep your curse tucked away just long enough for us to save your brother."

I gripped the gloves so tightly in one hand that my fingers ached. I needed to spend as much time with Alistair as possible to get close to him, but my thoughts were flooded with panicked fear that something was wrong and that my brother wouldn't be okay when we finally reached him. It had taken too long, or something would happen when trying to get him out wherever they'd taken him. And the thought of leaving my newfound safety of the castle, even if it *was* haunted, left a sickened feeling in my stomach.

"I've seen the way you fight, Pit Viper." How he said my fighting name brushed up against the cusp of my ear and made me shudder. "But you're no killer. There may come a time when we must use your…ah, talents." He laughed. "These will help."

"Thank you." A quiet thrill zipped through me. "Do you think there will be a fight?" I tried to keep the hope from my tone, but Alistair saw right through it. He flashed me a toothy smile.

"I'm counting on it."

It had been too long since I had gotten to punch something. I never thought I'd miss the fighting pits so much, but my heart longed for it. If I had to, I'd go up against someone twice my size again.

I slipped the gloves onto my hands. They fit snugly but were soft and comfortable. I admired them silently for a moment before turning in my chair to look at Alistair, who had backed up to give me space. "What's the plan?"

"It will be all hands on deck, so Valencia is coming too. I hope some city guard has a soft spot for the fae." Despite its nefarious nature, I had yet to see Valencia's curse manifest, and a part of me was eager to see it. "We'll leave mid-afternoon to slip into Kraeva just before nightfall."

I nodded, ignoring the twist of guilt and fear in my belly. *I'm coming, Cade.*

"Don't worry, little flower. We're going to get your brother back."

Heart pounding, I scooted my chair back to stand. "I never actually expressed my gratitude for you agreeing to help me…" A good fighter knows when an opportunity presents itself to strike, and I saw one now, sitting in the curious expression on Alistair's face as I wove around the chair to face him. I didn't know if he'd be able to find a cure for my hands, so I had to shake loose his guard…just in case.

"Gratitude that will be repaid when you help me with our nemalyn cap problem." His voice was low, though, mouth parted as I reached forward to trail a hand down his chest. His heartbeat was slow and steady, like the pulse of magic in the forest after it rained, and I peered up at him from beneath my eyelashes, a satisfied thrill coursing through me when his gaze heated.

Perhaps I *could* make him love me. After the library…. well, it was all starting to seem possible. The consequence of such love… I wasn't sure at all what I wanted the outcome to be. Could I kill him? Or would I be swept away by his love as well?

"Or… if that's the kind of gratitude you prefer, I'll see myself out now." My tone turned coy, a breathy sigh escaping my lips just as my hand danced at the edge of his waistline, only to turn away.

His hand lashed out, clasping my wrist, and a satisfied thrill coursed through me as he tugged me back until I was pressed against him, my hand coming to rest against his chest once more. Our eyes met, and a fire burned at my core, begging me to reach down and slip my fingers into his pants. Instead, I buried my desire and leaned close, my lips dancing near his. I heard his breath catch. "Where did you come from?" He asked, and the corner of my lip twitched as I reached down and stroked his cock through his pants. It hadn't taken much to get him right where I wanted him, and he reached out to grasp my chin, his fingers long and slender as they curled delicately against my skin.

Just as I reached up to slip my hand into his pants, he straightened, his finger stroking the line of my jaw, and stepped back.

"Good day to you, Miss A'mar. I need to get some things in order and tell Valencia what we're doing with our evening, so if you'll excuse me."

Dazed and confused by his sudden rejection, I stood idly as he left. Still, I shook it away, knowing full well that I had gotten under Alistair Sylverhorn's skin. Once I knew Cade was safe and sound, I would double down on wrapping Alistair around my finger.

Shaking the lingering heat from low in my belly, I fled the dining hall back to my room. My blood sang with anticipation.

We're coming, Cade.

Valencia came and found me sometime in the evening. I'd been pacing my room anxiously, full of giddy energy. Between the tension of that morning with Alistair and the promise of finally getting Cade back, I'd nearly burst from the waiting.

"Are you ready?" Valencia asked as I opened the door after she knocked. She wore a dark cloak with a hood, her golden eyes blazing with the same energy I carried in mine —a nervous determination that weighed heavily on me.

"I brought this for you—It's supposed to be a cold one tonight," Valencia said, offering me a cloak that had hung over her arm. It was a lovely piece, black with intricate leaf designs woven into deep green threads. I took it from her and swept it over my shoulders, relishing in its warmth.

"Thanks," I said, pushing into the hall. "Where's Alistair?"

"Waiting for us at the front door. He was having Kalaea put some extra wards on the castle tonight, just in case someone tries to follow us."

I nodded. It was smart. Especially since Alistair mentioned

that mages were involved. I tucked my arms beneath the cloak and followed Valencia down the hall. I was thankful for her silence, too concerned about setting off for Cade to think of forcing idle chat.

Once we reached the foyer, my palms began to sweat beneath their gloves. Alistair knelt near the door in front of Kalaea, her fur gleaming blue in the dim light. Her three tails twitched, and then she was bounding away, disappearing down one of the halls as Alistair slowly straightened.

"We're going to have to do everything right, or things could turn to trouble fast," Alistair warned. He was dressed fancy for a rescue mission, fingers glittering with rings on nearly every finger and jeweled clips faceting his curls back. He wore no cloak, unlike Valencia and me, but his shirt was loose-fitting and a deep emerald threaded with silver, and his cane was gleaming in the torchlight.

"What can we expect?" Valencia asked, and I double-checked my gloves, taking care to ensure they hadn't deteriorated at all and that they were on snugly. It would be the first time I left the castle since I was cursed and had found myself here, and my anxiety flickered like a nervous bird in my belly.

"I've gone back several times, each at different times in the night, to try and scout out as much as possible. There aren't as many mages as I originally thought, likely to keep suspicions down since they're not exactly welcome in the south. It's good news for us, but one of them is Soria, Grand Mage of Ravenspire. She's strong and taught me everything I know. We shouldn't underestimate her."

Soria. That was the woman who cursed me. Thoughts of her caused the ache in my chest to fester and spread through my veins like wildfire. I'd love to take my glove off when I found her and see if the curse truly worked on humans.

I loathed those wretched thoughts, loathed the type of person she made me. Clenching my fists tightly, I strode forward until I was next to Alistair. "Is the plan to just stroll inside, find Cade, grab him, and leave?" It didn't sound like a perfect plan, one that was sure to end in trouble, and Alistair laughed and shook his head.

"No, no. I'll explain on the way." Cracking the door open, he slipped outside, and Valencia and I followed. The air was chilly, a nod towards the coming autumn, and I shivered beneath my cloak as I tugged it tighter around me. "The warehouse was warded after my first visit, so I haven't been able to get inside again, but I'm confident I can break them just long enough for us to slip through without arousing suspicion. Valencia, you and Lyra will sneak through the warehouse and subdue anyone you encounter, but refrain from killing anyone unless necessary. That's not why we're there."

"How large is the warehouse? We can't waste time trying to find my brother. The moment they know something is amiss, we'll lose our chance," I argued, my heart squeezing fearfully at the thought.

"It's not so large that we won't be able to find him fairly quickly," Alistair assured, tugging open the gate and stepping aside to let us through. "I'm going to distract the mages, so hopefully they won't even be looking for you. It's me they're after—Cade will be the last thing Soria is worried about."

I trusted Alistair, but there was an anxious twist in my belly, a fear that something would go wrong. Cade was innocent in all this, simply in the wrong place at the wrong time. If he died, his death would be a red stain on *my* hands.

"We'll get him," Valencia said, squeezing my shoulder. Her gaze burned with determination, and my fear turned to amazement as she stepped beyond Alistair's wards and her curse unfurled.

She was beautiful, her pale skin etched with a faint dusting of what looked like gold glitter. Her hair was long and flowing, a white-gold that cascaded over her shoulder behind long, pointed ears. When she shifted, I noted dragonfly-like wings trailing from her back, hanging low. They were semi-translucent, white, and etched with thin lines of yellow. She looked unrecognizable, and my stomach soured at the thought of Valencia trying to return home to a kingdom that vehemently *loathed* the fae. How traumatizing that must have been.

"Kaz!" Valencia called out quietly. A hawk descended from the trees and soared towards us. He was gorgeous, with light brown and white feathers and piercing orange eyes. He landed on Valencia's shoulder and stared at me.

"You have a bird?" I asked, still reeling from the sudden change in her appearance.

Valencia nodded, rubbing Kaz's head with her finger. "Kazimir is his name, or Kaz for short. He's my little scouting buddy. I nursed him back to health when I found him with a hurt wing. The pixies were bullying him near my home, and he hasn't been able to stay away, even when he got better."

I admired the sharp intelligence in his eyes.

"Here," Alistair said, pulling me away from my admiration for the hawk, "I have these for both of you. They'll help us when we need them to." Seemingly, something small dropped into his palm from the air, and two daggers with wicked curves to their blades. Their hilts were forged with syvler, meaning...

"Those are dragon-glass daggers," I said. Mainly wielded by Bracaeans, I had never seen dragon-glass up close but knew them to be sharper than most blades and usually imbued with some kind of magic.

"Indeed, they are," Valencia said breathlessly, her eyes widening at seeing them. "Those are beautiful, Alistair. Where did you get them?"

"For you. Never mind where I got them," he said, offering them to her. "If a mage has warded himself, these blades will slice through those wards as if they simply do not exist."

Valencia took them tentatively, eyeing them with awe and suspicion. "It's been a while since I've wielded a blade," she said. "I thought we weren't going to be killing anyone."

"Just a precaution." Alistair eyed her warily and then offered his hand to me, fist closed and palm down. When I reached out, he dropped a necklace into my waiting palm.

It wasn't anything fancy, just a nine-tailed fox charm in a side profile attached to a sylver chain. An emerald gleamed where the eye would be, and I admired how beautiful it was before slipping it over my head.

I immediately sensed magic as it washed over me, cold as ice. Goosebumps etched my skin, and I glared at him as he laughed, entirely too pleased with himself.

"What was that?"

"Protection," he said, sobering. "It'll protect you from the wards. When we find your brother, he may be tucked behind some. With that necklace, you can pass them and grab him."

This time, when I shuddered, it was from nervous anticipation. The forest seemed to swell around me, and off in the distance, two eyes blinked into sight from the shadows. It would have been terrifying if I had not had Alistair and Valencia with me.

All thoughts were now on saving my brother.

CHAPTER NINETEEN

LYRA

I thought it would be easy at first.

We reached the warehouse with little trouble, using Alistair's magic to illusion us past the guards at the gate. It was strange being back inside the city. The last time I was in Kraeva, my curse had flourished, and Soria and the city guards had taken Cade. A strangeness clung to the air, an unsettling nature that rested tensely on my shoulders. I cared not for it, pulling my cloak tighter around me as we stood near a cluster of trees by the docks.

"It will take me a moment to disrupt the outer wards," Alistair whispered, his fingers darting in intricate patterns to call upon his magic. "Once they're down, we'll only have a few moments to slip inside before the wards go back up, else we'll arouse suspicion."

"And those guards? What are we going to do about them?" I said, gesturing to the warehouse. Several guards patrolled the side of the warehouse, their movements stiff and precise. Each had a khopesh strapped to their waist, and Alistair cursed under his breath.

"They've upped the guards since I was here last."

"Do you suppose we could get into the warehouse through the water? Surely there's a water-breathing spell tucked up your sleeve..." I suggested, staring out into the bay. The water was dark and imposing, and surely there were creatures like merfolk and sharp-toothed fish that infested the shallows, but it was better to risk it than the certainty of being stopped by the guards.

Alistair made a face as if the prospect disgusted him, and he shook his head. "I'd rather not ruin my clothes unless the situation calls for it." His face sobered as he turned to Valencia. "The men of Kraeva love faerie company... Could you distract them until I can get the wards down?"

The moonlight gleamed off Valencia's skin, her eyes glowing vaguely in the dim sky. "Fine," she said finally, her finger reaching up to stroke the top of Kaz's head. "It shouldn't be too difficult." Tucking her daggers safely behind her cloak and away from prying eyes, she turned to murmur at Kaz, who took off and landed in the tree above us.

Rolling her shoulders, Valencia flashed us a toothy grin. "Watch and learn, loves."

Stepping out of the tree cover, Valencia straightened her back and sauntered towards the guards. They were too far to hear, but their initial reaction seemed defensive, with raised khopeshes and stern tones. After a few moments, one of them lowered his weapon as Valencia approached while his comrade remained poised and tense. Valencia's head lolled to the side, and the tense guard lashed out and grabbed her arm.

My eyes flickered over to Alistair as my stomach squeezed anxiously. This wasn't going to work, and I *needed* to get inside. We were so close to Cade.

Alistair's hand gripped his cane tightly, his knuckles white, but he appeared calmer than I did, distracted. "Wait," he whispered. "She's got it."

My skin crawled, my fingers aching, desperate for violence. One of the guards leaned close, seemingly entranced by Valencia, while the other snarled and tugged Valencia roughly towards the warehouse.

Alistair cursed quietly under his breath as the guards dragged Valencia away.

"I told you," I hissed as more guards rounded the corner. "We should have just gone into the water. Now we'll have to find Valencia too."

Gesturing towards the water, Alistair scowled, then sighed. "There are foul things that patrol those waters. We'll have to be careful if we go that way. I'll do my best to shield us."

Sucking in a breath, I dared not hesitate as I leaped into the water.

It took a moment to adjust, but I was quite the natural swimmer, having spent many summer months of my life sneaking away to some of Kraeva's local beaches and tucked-away bays to cool off from the desert's brazen heat. The merfolk problem had been a recent thing, recent enough that I hadn't the slightest idea how terrifying they were, as I had never come into contact with one before.

The water was warm, pleasantly so, despite the way it clung to my clothes and bogged me down. It might have been crystal clear had we come during the daytime, but night blanketed Feyrsia, and even as my eyes adjusted, I could not see further than a few feet in front of me. Fear of the unknown clenched at my stomach, but I willed it away and forced myself forward, cheeks bulging as I held my breath.

I had nearly reached the docks, lungs screaming for air, when I heard it. The soft lullaby that caressed the waters beckoned me to pause, to *listen*. I had heard tales of the merfolk and their wicked ways, stories of sailors stepping overboard to the sound of beautiful melodies, drowning themselves in their company. Some argued merfolk were fae, and as my head muddled with desire to seek out the source of the song, I was inclined to believe them.

I had strayed off course for several moments before the spell broke, and my mind became my own again. The desperate need for air had also stifled as Alistair brushed close enough for me to see him in the darkness of the water. I was thankful for the moon, for her light, however small, that pierced the ocean's surface. He gestured for me to follow, so I did, easily ignoring the merfolk's calls. Something grabbed my foot, and my panic roared as I glanced back to see the glowing visage of a merfolk, her eyes large and imploring. She looked vaguely human, mingled with the sea, her hair resembling seaweed and her skin shimmering with sparkling, fish-like scales. When she bared her teeth, several rows of them met me, all sharp and wicked. I mirrored it with a snarl of my own, twisting in the water and kicking her in the face as hard as I could with my free foot.

Her cry pierced the water as she let go, and I swam as hard as I could towards the warehouse, knowing that if she managed to get me again, I would be dragged to my death.

I shivered and gasped as I pulled myself up onto the dock inside the warehouse, coughing violently as water purged itself from my lungs. Alistair was above me, floating up into the air and landing gracefully on the dock beside me. He offered me a hand, but I continued to lie there, heaving until I could slip my glove back on.

"Through that door over there," he said once I'd risen. "I'll be right behind you."

The interior of the warehouse was almost cavernous, with wooden beams that stretched high above, like the ribs of an ancient beast. Lanterns swung from hooks on the wall, casting a warm, flickering glow that barely penetrated the shadowy recesses, and I stuck close to the wall, my fists aching for conflict. The air was thick with the scent of aged timber, mingled with subtle spices and rich leather. So far, no one was in sight.

Rows of sturdy shelves, cobbled together and made from the light wood of the local trees, lined the walls, cracking and groaning beneath the weight of crates, barrels, and bundles wrapped with burlap. Some packages were marked with strange, glowing sigils that I did not recognize, while others were sealed with wax bearing the insignia of Brûnheim. There were even dusty barrels marked with Bracaea's sigil, likely old furs or leather when they were still open to trading with Kahl for our spices and rum.

Alistair pressed up beside me, the silence of his steps jarring. "I have to find Valencia," he whispered. "The last time I was here, I overheard someone speaking about your brother as they were coming down that hall," he said, pointing at one of the hallways that led deeper into the warehouse. "I trust your skill, *Pit Viper*," he uttered, and I turned to catch his piercing gaze. "Be careful. If all goes well, meet me back in that cluster of trees outside."

I nodded, and Alistair hesitated, his gaze imploring mine before drifting down to my lips. An ache formed low in my belly, and I thought about kissing him. Not to deceive. Not with thoughts of breaking my curse. Just because I wanted to. Because *something* pulled me to him. It was frightening and alien, and Alistair stepped away before I could. A part of me was relieved.

"It's not me who needs to be careful. I've seen your fighting skills…or lack thereof," I teased, grinning foolishly when a playful scowl crossed Alistair's face, and he took off down a different hallway without saying anything.

I made my way through the shelves until I came upon the central part of the room, which was open and dominated by massive tables covered with tools and ledger books. Tangled ropes lay forgotten beneath the tables. Several small hallways branched off the main room, and soft moans emanated from the hallway Alistair had gestured to, accompanied by the cries of the sick. My skin crawled, remembering the conversation about the plague between my father and the king's adviser. Was this where they were rounding up the sick?

A faint glow at the end of the shelves caught my eye, and as I approached, I sucked in a horrified breath.

A ritual circle was carved in the center of the room, where a group of mages channeled at four spots opposite each other. A sick woman sat in a chair in the center, tied to it with a rope. Before her, on the ground, was what looked to be some sort of tooth or claw.

What are they doing? I thought as I slunk away, moving back towards the safety of the shelves and the shadows. The tooth was large, too large to be any common animal, and if mages were using it, it must've been something powerful. The fact that there were any mages in Kahl at all, being sworn enemies of the king, was concerning, but my thoughts quickly turned back to Cade as I slipped down the hallway Alistair had pointed out.

The hallway was narrow and dimly lit, its walls decorated with aged and splintering wood. Flickering lanterns hung at irregular intervals, casting unsettling shadows that preyed on my anxiety. I brushed my fingers against the wall and moved quickly, ears straining for any indication of anyone approaching.

Small side doors, some reinforced with rusted iron bands and others no more than warped wooden panels, lined the walls. Each was marked with an intricate rune and a number, likely nothing more than rooms to store different contents inside—spare tools, hidden caches, or perhaps even forgotten relics from a time when mages *were* allowed in the city. Soft voices sounded down the hall just as someone grabbed me from behind, covering my mouth before I could scream. They dragged me into an alcove housing a small grouping of moth-eaten tarps and nothing else, and I glanced up to see the sharp curve of Alistair's jawline.

"I haven't been able to find Val," he whispered. "I think they took her this way. Let me speak to whoever approaches, but remain hidden here and prepare to fight if they don't buy my lies." I nodded, and he let go, swinging past me and flicking his fingers at the torch above my head, snuffing it out with magic. He walked with silent steps, which explained how I didn't hear him approach.

"Who are you? I don't recognize your magic…" A voice called out from down the hall, and Alistair smiled, leaning against the wall to shield the alcove I was hiding in. I blinked, and he was a different man, tucked beneath an illusion with light skin and short, black hair.

"I just arrived at Ravenspire to offer my aid here. Soria said that I was to be expected. Has she not alerted you of my arrival?"

The other voice spluttered, flustered by the way his words failed to spill from his mouth. "W-w-well, no. If I may, we can go find her and—"

"Do you make a habit of bothering the Grand Mage when she's busy?" Alistair asked harshly.

"N-no—"

Alistair sighed, and I pressed a hand to my lips to keep

myself from laughing. "If I weren't a mage, I wouldn't have been able to pass through the wards outside. There was quite a ruckus when I arrived. A faerie girl had been trying to get in, and it made me curious about the security here."

"I can assure you, sire, that was taken care of. We took the faerie to a holding room for…interrogation."

Silence encompassed the hallway, and my stomach flopped painfully. Valencia came from a strong and capable family, but I still worried for her. My fingers curled into fists. If they hurt her…

"Take me to her, but show me where the healer's boy is first, so I can do what I was called here for."

"Healer's boy? He's strictly off limits. No one is to see him."

"Maybe *I'll* go and find Soria, since you seem to want to make my job more difficult."

Several tense moments passed, moments I was sure that the other mage was going to buckle and accuse Alistair of trespassing. I clung to the wall, preparing to throw myself around the corner at the mage, but something in the air shifted like it thickened with magic, and I heard the other mage sigh.

"No, no. That won't be necessary. Come along. I'll show you where the boy is, but you won't be allowed in the room until I hear verbal instruction from the Grand Mage that you are allowed inside. You must understand, I have my orders. I can take you to the faerie, however, afterwards. I'm sure Grahman would appreciate the help. She's extremely resilient to our tactics of getting her to talk."

"Wait a few moments and then follow. I'll silence your steps." Alistair's instructions were spoken so softly I nearly didn't understand them, and then he disappeared as he followed the mage down the hallway.

I waited several moments with bated breath and then took

off down the hallway, shifting uncomfortably as magic rolled over my skin. I would never grow accustomed to the feel of magic, but the silence in my steps *was* convenient.

"I'm surprised Soria wants you to see the boy." The other mage was a short, twitchy man, his hair so thin it might as well not have been there. His words gained confidence as he spoke more. "She has plans for him—plans that won't happen until we find Alistair Sylverhorn."

What did they want with Alistair?

"I'm surprised he hasn't been found yet," Alistair said, his voice even. I ducked behind a barrel, cradling the wall as the mage and Alistair halted next to one of the doors.

"I'm not," the mage replied sullenly. "Soria has spoken about how dangerous a mage he is, and how he harbors the soul of a dragon." The mage inhaled sharply, and as I peered over the rim of the barrel, his eyes gleamed with manic excitement. "It's why we're here. We all want a taste."

The mage's demeanor changed the longer he stood in Alistair's presence, and a chill slithered down my back as Alistair's back stiffened, but he ignored the mage's words, gesturing to the door.

"Is this the boy's room?"

"I—" The mage shook his head as if clearing his thoughts and then nodded. "Yes."

"Excellent. You said the faerie girl was at the end of the hall?"

"Yes. I'll take you to her now."

"That won't be necessary. I think it's time for you to take a nap."

"What?"

Alistair lashed out and pressed a thumb to the other mage's forehead, but nothing happened. The mage's face crumpled to anger and confusion as he flinched away from

Alistair's hand, and he took off down the hall, shouting in a strange tongue.

"I sense wards on the door, Lyra. Your necklace should keep you safe from them, but I mustn't let him get away. Meet me at those trees. I'm going to go and get our girl back." The rage in Alistair's voice was palpable, the same sort of rage that burned hot in the center of my chest as I rose from behind the barrel and stepped up to the door.

"Be careful," I called out to Alistair as he limped down the hall, but my attention was already turned to the door in front of me before I heard his reply. Reaching out a hand, I tugged it away as a sharp noise whistled through the air, like the snap of leather against leather. A large rune appeared inscribed on the door, and my heart thundered loudly in my ears as I grabbed the handle and tugged the door open. The necklace against my neck burned, and I hissed as I hurried through.

The room was small, decorated with nothing but a flimsy bed on an iron-wrought frame. Cade lay atop the bed, malnourished and dirty but *alive*. His chest rose and fell with unsteady breaths, and a sob rattled my lungs as I flung myself to him, the plague be damned. Now that I had found him, Cade would no longer be outside my reach ever again if I could help it. Not until he was better.

"Lyra?" His voice was weak, his eyes fluttering as fear marred his features. "N-no, no, no! You must leave."

"Shhh." I brushed his curls from his face, a hand drawing over to cup his cheek to soothe him. "You're safe now. I've come to save you."

"You don't understand. They *wanted* you to come here. But only…only after you…" His skin was ripe with fever, his hair plastered to a sweat-stained forehead. I quieted him, my stomach clenched in fear.

Cade slipped into an unconscious, fitful sleep, and I peered over my shoulder as I tried to decide what to do. I was going to have to carry him, but the entire warehouse might now know there were trespassers amongst their ranks.

Shouting outside stole my indecision, and I hefted Cade ungracefully onto my back.

If I had to fight my way out, so be it.

CHAPTER TWENTY

ALISTAIR

The mage was quick, too quick for me to catch up to him with my leg screaming in pain, but his words had sickened me. What was really going on here? And what, exactly, did they want with me?

Don't worry, Alistair, Rahfín mused. *I will rip them apart with tooth and claw if they try to take you from me.*

It won't come to that.

Let us hope not.

Lashing my hand out, I curled my fingers in an attempt to grab the mage by the leg and yank him back towards me. I must have missed, though, as he slipped through the door and his distant shouts filled the hallway.

Shit.

Several people stumbled out into the hallway, including the mage I had been chasing. One I did not recognize, but the other...the other was Kierda, a mage who had been kicked out of Ravenspire for dabbling in taboo magic.

"Gods...*Alistair?*"

Shit. Shit, shit, *shit.* How did he recognize me through my illusion? Perhaps it had slipped, a consequence of my pain, but I merely straightened and offered a grim smile. "In the flesh. I'd say it's nice to see you, Kierda, but my fae blood. It ah," I waved my hand in a flourished manner, offering dramatics, "well, I simply cannot lie."

Kierda glared down at me from pinched features, the thin trail of his hair quivering as he shook his head and turned to the other mage. "Seize him. Soria will be relieved to know our search has ended. Alistair has decided to come to us instead." Kierda's grin revealed the dark stain of his teeth. "Always so foolish."

I laughed as the dragon inside me woke, heat licking my skin. I didn't let Rahfín out, not when my bones were on fire, and the pain of his presence sank through me, but the temptation was there if only to watch him rip Kierda apart.

"I'm afraid I cannot let you do that." Flame burst to life in my palm, beckoned by magic, and I flung it at them as I stumbled backwards. I couldn't run, not with Rahfín's weight pressed against my leg, so I'd have to get creative to get past them and find Valencia.

They will not take you from me, Rahfín growled, his words echoing in my head. *Purge them with fire, Alistair.*

But I was no fighter. My tender heart had been foolish to think the power of a dragon would make me brave in the midst of danger. Perhaps that was what had drawn me to Lyra in the first place. The heat in her belly forged a strength I did not possess. My magic knew it, and the fire I flung at the mages before me was easily dodged as two of them brushed past Kierda, who sneered.

"Still the scared little boy, Alistair? Did you think your silly illusions and flashy magic could protect you forever?"

The illusion coating my features was useless now, so I allowed that magic to rest, shivering as the magic dissipated from my skin. His words had stopped hurting long ago when Soria had deemed me her star pupil, and my confidence had swelled.

Leaning against my cane, I stumbled backwards, raising my hands to call forth my magic. Kalaea had taught me some of the magic of her kind, and I tapped into Rahfín's power to manifest a small army of snakes that slithered across the floor of the hallway towards the approaching mages. Kalaea was the only one capable of making her illusions a reality in most senses of the word, but the snakes *looked* real as they hissed, their fangs protruding from parted maws.

One mage blanched immediately, a soft cry echoing from his lips as his eyes widened in fear.

"They're not real," his companion hissed. "You fool."

The words were ignored as the snakes pressed the mage up against the wall and kept him there. I smirked in satisfaction before a white-hot pain split across my back. I screamed out as the snakes immediately disappeared as I crumpled to the floor, and Kierda's feet stepped into my vision.

Rahfín roared, his rage echoing through my head as I writhed, unable to escape the pain that flourished through me. I had never felt anything like it; it was as if my very blood had betrayed me, as if my limbs no longer belonged to me. Two dark shoes stepped into my line of vision, and I glared up at Kierda as he stepped close, his breath rancid.

"It will be fun watching her tear you apart."

Spots appeared in my vision as Rahfín's presence pressed against my bones, begging for release. He wanted to tear this entire warehouse apart, to watch it burn beneath a maelstrom of fire. A part of me wanted to let him, but Lyra and Valencia were still somewhere inside, and I couldn't risk their safety.

Something wet and sticky struck my face, and I blinked as Kierda's eyes widened, his mouth coated in a thick layer of blood. He looked down at the same time I did, as a blade protruded wickedly from his chest, his shirt staining red with his blood. Surprise mingled with shock cradled his expression, and a surge of adoration coursed through me as Valencia appeared over his shoulder, her rage etched on her face and her golden eyes shining.

"I will kill you if you touch him."

Kierda slumped over and was dead before he hit the floor as Valencia pried her blade from his chest. She had already killed the other two mages, and I reached out to take her offered hand, groaning as she pulled me to my feet.

One day, they will not be around to protect you, Rahfín said.

Yes, well, one day, you will burn me away until there's nothing left but you, and I won't have to worry about needing any kind of protection.

The bitter bite of my words failed to amuse him as he huffed and curled against my bones, promptly choosing to ignore me, but Valencia demanded my attention in his stead as her fingers darted out to run over my cheeks.

"Are you okay? Where is Lyra?"

"I'm fine," I said, reaching up to curl my hands around her fingers and lower them. "Lyra found her brother, but we need to leave before we run into Soria."

"Is she here?"

I shrugged as I turned away from the fallen mages and peered down the hall back the way I had come. The torches created shadows that brushed the walls, and though it was silent, I knew it was only a matter of time before more mages came searching for them. Soria or not, we needed to leave. "I don't know. She was here when I visited this warehouse the last time, but I don't sense her now."

I don't believe she is here, Rahfín murmured. *I know her magical signature, and I don't sense it.*

"Rahfín says she's not, but it won't be long before she gets wind that I was here, and then we'll have to worry about her arrival." My eyes landed on Valencia's face, on the split of her lip and the swollen purple of her eye. Someone had beaten her.

"Who did this to you?" I whispered, brushing my finger against her cheek as a fresh wave of rage sang through me. "Tell me they don't still live."

Valencia's eyes darkened as she gave a slight shake of her head. "I took care of him."

Satisfied, I nodded. "Good." Cupping her cheek, I drew close, pressing a soft but possessive kiss on her forehead.

"Let's go find our girl."

Distant shouting echoed down the hall, and I pulled away from Valencia as a wave of magic infected the air. There were more coming. A lot more. "Change of plans," I said, meeting Valencia's gaze. "I'm going to provide a distraction. Find Lyra. Get her and her brother out. I'll meet you later."

Valencia hesitated, then nodded. "Be careful."

In my mind's eye, smoke curled from Rahfín's snout as he shook himself awake and urged his consciousness to touch Valencia's. *Don't worry, dragon child. I am going to keep him safe.*

Valencia's look was stern. "I don't expect anything less, Rahf."

As Valencia darted off, I turned back towards the approaching voices and gave myself over to Rahfín. It was the only way to keep them safe.

CHAPTER TWENTY-ONE
LYRA

The mage in front of me stank, his smile yellowed as he drew close, but he turned as Valencia burst into the room, granting me enough of a distraction to lash out, my fist crashing into his belly. He doubled over long enough for Valencia to pierce him with her blades.

The blade sank into the man's neck like butter, and the man spluttered up blood as he sank to the floor. Cade lay heavy against my back, and it was perhaps pure determination, will, and strength from fighting in the pits that allowed me to carry him out of the room towards the door that would lead us out of there.

"Hurry," Valencia whispered, wiping the dead mage's blood from her blade with his shirt before stalking back towards the door. She looked worse for wear, her face badly beaten, her wings crumpled against her back.

"Are you okay?" I whispered, readjusting Cade on my back. He was heavy but not overly so, and I followed Valencia towards the door as I stepped around the corpse of the mage. Alistair's wishes not to harm anyone had been ignored, but I was grateful. Fighting that mage with Cade on my back would have been a nightmare. "Where's Alistair?"

Valencia peered out into the hall, and I was relieved to hear the silence. "Offering a distraction," she said. "And I'll be fine once we're out of here. Come on. We're to meet Alistair outside."

Threat whispered in the air, thick with magic, and I readjusted Cade on my back before following Valencia into the hallway, where there were no other mages *yet*. My body ached for violence, an untamed and greedy thing, silenced only by my will to get my brother out and keep him safe. I would not let them take him from me, not again. It was just such a relief to feel the rise and fall of his chest, to hear the rattled, sickly breathing in my ear. He was sick, but he was alive, and that was all that mattered.

Unlike before, when we trailed inside, the warehouse had fallen into a chaotic flurry of panic. Wisps danced about the hallways, but instead of the soft, vibrant blue I was used to, these wisps were blood red and moving erratically.

We made it a few feet down the hallway when two mages appeared. The fire from the lanterns flickered across their faces, covered mainly by ceremonial hoods, and Valencia and I both halted as they blocked our way out.

"Look, Aishyn," one whispered, teeth gleaming against their smile. "Two little mice wandered in." They both radiated darkness, a chill that permeated the air and threatened to wrap around my lungs and squeeze. My breath curled in front of me. Valencia's daggers glowed in the dim hallway as she stepped in front of me instinctively, her shoulders tense with rage.

"Don't touch her." Her conviction sent a thrill through me, and the mages laughed as purple magic wove in the air in front of them, strung together by patterns made by slender fingers.

"We need her alive. You? We have no use for the fae here."

Valencia's wings fluttered against her back, and she glanced over her shoulder at me. "Keep him safe."

I bared my teeth in frustration. I could fight, but my arms were trapped beneath, keeping Cade on my back, and I was too afraid to jostle him or set him down in case more mages came and we needed to run. The opposite end of the hallway led deeper into the warehouse...no, we *had* to get past these mages, and I had to trust Valencia's skill with the blade.

One mage drew forward as a shard of purple magic shot through the air towards Valencia. She deflected it with one of her daggers, and the magic fizzled away, breaking against the enchantment on the blades. Alistair had thought of it all when he enchanted them.

Valencia's curse granted her the speed of the fae, and she put it to good use, her body a blur as she darted down the hallway. The mages did not anticipate it, and she managed to nick one of the mage's arms with her dagger before they realized she was next to them. They hissed in pain and flinched back, but Valencia showed no mercy, even when magic burned across her skin, and she yelped in pain.

I was trapped beneath the weight of guilt and frustration at not being able to aid, but Valencia brought them down with ease, chest heaving, and I drew forward in awe.

"When we are safe back in Alistair's castle, I would love to spar you," I said, earning an ornery smile from Valencia and a bark of laughter.

"It's a date, Miss A'mar. Until then, let's get your brother to safety." She nurtured her arm, spiderwebbed with what looked like the burn from electricity, and she hissed in pain as that arm fell to her side. "Something to worry about when we're safe," she said, noticing my worried stare. "They got my non-dominant arm, thankfully. Are you okay? Your brother?"

"He's heavy, but we're both fine. Thank you."

Valencia's smile was radiant as she pried her dagger from the dead mage's side. "Come on." A small songbird soared past us, fluttering around my and Valencia's heads before shooting forward, and I stared at it strangely as we followed it down the hallway back into the main room. Mages still chanted at the ritual circle, and when one of them saw us and attempted to stop, they imploded, their bones cracking and caving in on themself, followed quickly by the others, their cries a symphony of agony. We paid them little mind after that, bursting out the door, where the songbird shifted quietly and rapidly into Alistair.

"I saw a horse with a cart near one of the docks," he whispered, attempting to stifle a grimace as he clutched the leg he typically favored. Pain marred his gaze, and my arms screamed, finally beginning to buckle beneath my brother's weight.

"I hope it is close," I gasped, forcing myself to move. *Just a bit further. I can do this.*

Despite my fears, a strangled noise left me at my brother's resting form as Alistair led the cart out of town. We'd found the cart with ease, and Valencia had helped me load him into the cart as the horse whinnied anxiously. I wasn't certain why we weren't being followed, but I didn't question it too extensively as Alistair urged us away.

"Now that I've seen the plague that ails him, I believe there's something I can do to help," Alistair said, peering down at me from where he sat at the front of the cart. "It's very strange… if it's what I am thinking of… this plague isn't without its cure. I wonder why they have resorted to violence against those who are sick."

"There *is* a war going on," I said slowly, uncertain where Alistair's loyalties were. "And mages are known to be loyal to Bracaea. Perhaps…"

"They would not see to the health of Kahl's people." Valencia finished for me, staring at me in quiet horror from across the cart. "I'd like to believe my people aren't that horrible, but…" she trailed off, a look of disgust crossing her face. "I'm glad we got Cade out of there. It was horrible." She shuddered, and I couldn't help but agree. What they'd been doing to those people, what kind of experiments they were doing… it was awful, unlike anything I'd seen before.

I watched Cade as he thrashed about in his sleep, eyes darting beneath closed lids. He was thin, thinner than he usually was, his cheeks gaunt and dark circles etched beneath his eyes. The sickness had taken hold, small boils dotting his neck and cheeks, and my throat constricted. I didn't want to think what I would have done had I gotten there to Cade's corpse.

"Lyra," Valencia's soft voice tugged me out of my panicked spiral, and my gaze shot up to meet hers at the gentle swirl of gold beneath her hood. "He's not going to disappear."

The irrational part of me did not believe her, frightened he would slip away beneath my grasp. Cade was everything good about this world, soft and kind, despite the horrors that had faced Kraeva as of late. If the gods took him from me, I would come crashing down their door to seek my revenge.

"Get low and stay quiet," Alistair murmured as we neared the gate, "I'm going to get us past the guards." As Valencia and I lowered our heads into the back of the cart, I felt the wash of magic, and I suppressed the urge to shiver. It was like the slow crawl of bugs over my skin, and I never cared for it. Still, I remained as unmoving as I possibly could as the guards called Alistair to halt.

I waited with bated breath as the guards questioned Alistair.

"Just leaving with some leftover goods. I managed to sell most of my wares, but it's time for me to return home. My mother is in Nusa, and I come to Kraeva to sell her pottery. You're welcome to take a look in the back, if you'd like." I kept my eyes on Valencia as the guards murmured something, and then there was a shuffle of movement. I waited with bated breath—what if Alistair's magic didn't work?—as one of the guards peered into the back of the cart, his eyes lingering over me and then flickering to Cade and Valencia.

"Move along," the guard said gruffly, and Alistair pulled the cart forward. I exhaled a gasp, not able to properly breathe until we were well past the gates. Soon enough, Kraeva was but a small etching in the horizon, and I broke down in soft, wild laughter as I peered down at Cade again.

We'd done it. My brother was liberated from the city's clutches.

CHAPTER TWENTY-TWO

LYRA

We were met with no resistance and made it back to Alistair's castle without a hitch. At the edge of the forest, we'd ditched the cart and used the horse to carry Cade on its back. He still hadn't woken, though whimpering fits plagued him from time to time as the nightmares came to ail him. Once we reached the castle, Alistair whispered magic into his palm and then patted the horse fondly, watching it turn back into the forest. "It will find a safe way out of the forest," he explained as I hefted Cade onto my back. "I'll show you where we can put him close to my observatory, and I'll work on mixing something that can help him."

"Thank you." The exhaustion of that night was catching up to me, as my adrenaline was wearing off and paving the way for an emotional break. Tears pricked the corner of my eyes, but I willed them away. Tears could come later when I was safe from concerned eyes, and Cade was truly secure.

"I'm going to retire for the evening." The fae appearance was washed from Valencia the moment she walked through Kalaea's wards, and her eyes drooped with exhaustion. "Now that we've rescued Lyra's brother, it'll be time to ponder how we're going to get a nemalyn cap."

"Tomorrow," Alistair promised. "A discussion after we've all had some rest. There are things I need to do, fires I need to contain. We'll talk about it tomorrow."

Valencia reached out to lay a hand on his arm, noting the way his hands shook. "Alistair, you're running out of time—"

"I'm fine," he growled, tugging his arm away. "Lyra, come with me."

I shot Valencia an apologetic glance. Her eyes burned with unsaid anger, but she remained tight-lipped as I followed Alistair into the house, noting that Valencia was right: Alistair *did* look worse for wear, his limp more prominent, and his movements slowed. I didn't say anything, though, too concerned with getting Cade to a bed to anger Alistair further. Perhaps he was just led to exhaustion by the fighting we'd all just had to endure.

The room he led me to was next to his observatory, just down the hall from mine. The hallways had been shifting less and less, and Alistair pulled the door open so that I could get inside. An old, roll-top desk sat nestled against the wall across from the bed, framed by a fancy mahogany frame with posters that bore vine and flower carvings as they reached up towards the ceiling. Alistair, despite his pain, helped me lay Cade on the bed, and he woke with a fit, crying and screaming.

"Cade! Cade," I brushed his hair from his eyes as a violent cough overcame him, and he looked through fever-tinted eyes at me, his voice weak.

"Lyra?"

I shushed him. "You're safe now. Just rest. Alistair is going to help you feel better."

"Alistair? But—" Cade's eyes shuttered as he slipped back

into an unconscious state, and I glanced up at Alistair, my face drawn in pain and worry.

"Please help him." I could not stop the well of tears any longer, and they slipped over my eyes and down my cheeks. "He's all I've got, all I've ever had. I'll do whatever you ask of me. Just save him."

Alistair seemed to be working over something in his mind as he moved over to the bedside table and pulled a vial from within. "Lily's Milk," he explained. "I have it in every room... for the pain." He gestured to his own leg, and understanding flooded me as I nodded.

"It'll keep him sleeping until I can administer a cure. Seeing his symptoms...it's a nasty plague, but one that's easily treatable if handled properly. Nefarious things are going on, if they're using a plague to make people sick." Pulling the stop from the vial, he tilted it against Cade's lips. The furrow in Cade's brow instantly smoothed, and his eyes no longer darted beneath closed lids as he settled. The moment he did so, Alistair swept towards the door.

"I'll return momentarily. Stay with him, just in case he wakes, though I don't think he will. Lily's Milk is strong." I barely heard him as I wept, my head falling to rest on Cade's chest as I slipped onto the bed.

I wasn't sure when I fell asleep, only that I woke in someone's arms, warmth and the smell of a crackling fire and the sharpness of magic permeating the air as I glanced up to Alistair's face. He was no longer limping, his eyes blazing gold and green, and I was too exhausted to speak or wonder much of anything as sleep claimed me once more.

I stood before the edge of a cliff. Not a large one, but my stomach still clenched in fear at the thought of falling as I peered over the edge, only for a sob of horror to grip my lungs.

The corpse of a dragon lay broken and battered at the bottom, curled into a fetal position with shattered wings, the membrane between joints shredded. The sun glinted off its green and golden scales, and somehow, I knew it was Alistair.

I could not speak, even as a woman pried herself from the corpse of the dragon, her fingers stained red with Alistair's blood. In her hands was his heart, still beating. She glanced up at me, and I noted with horror that it was **me** *holding his heart,* **me** *with bloodstained lips as I bit into his heart and ripped away. It was* **me** *that killed him,* **me me me**...

I woke suddenly, the tendrils of my nightmare lingering like an unwanted fever. I pried the blanket off me as I rose to my feet, desperate to splash water on my face and cool my warm cheeks. My limbs were stiff like I walked through something thick, and I exhaled sharply as I drenched my hands in a basin in the corner of the room. The cold water was a relief, and I sighed happily as I pressed my head against the window pane and peered down at the front lawn of the estate. The grounds were beautiful, in an eerie sort of way, during the day. At night, however, they bred an air of unease, like a whispered promise against the nape of my neck or the subtle fear that someone was watching me. With what I'd seen in this house during my time here, I wouldn't be surprised if someone *was* watching me.

I shuddered at the thought.

I must have slept the entire day away because it was nighttime again. I wasn't sure how I'd gotten to my bed, having fallen asleep in Cade's room....

Wait.

Alistair had carried me in here.

My cheeks warmed at the thought, and I sighed, hoping Cade was okay. I'd hoped to remain at his side, but perhaps it was better this way. There was nothing I could do to aid in his recovery, and Alistair promised a cure. I had to put Cade's health in his hands. Remaining at his side would only stir my worry, and now that he was safe, I needed to turn towards the pressing matter at hand.

My curse. Valencia's curse. Alistair's sickness.

The nightmare washed over me again, the implications crawling through me like ice across a windowpane. I shuddered.

I didn't want to kill Alistair. In my attempts to seduce him, he'd wormed his way into my heart and made a home in its halls, curled against its hearth, and chased the cold away with his warmth. He and Valencia both. I loathed to think of the look on their faces if they knew what Soria had told me to do, what I'd kept from them in fear that it would resort to that.

Just as I made to turn away from the window, movement flickered from below. My fingers pressed against the sill as I leaned forward, my forehead laid against the glass. I peered down below. Was that Alistair? Where was he going?

Something compelled me to go after him. I longed to apologize for snapping at him earlier. My cruelty, as of late, had been bred out of fear, but that didn't make Alistair the monster. If anyone were to blame for my suffering, it was Soria.

Rushing over to the wardrobe, I opened it to find a fleeced-lined coat with dark buttons lining the front, and I tugged it on, not bothering with shoes. By the time I tugged my boots on, Alistair would be gone, and I wouldn't have the slightest idea where to find him.

I wrangled the door open, only to flinch backwards as a wisp met me at the door. Startled, it turned a violent shade of purple before sinking back into its vibrant blue, and the tendrils that hung from its body danced lightly as it darted from side to side.

"You must stop scaring me like that," I chastised as I poked my head out and peered down the hallway. The wisp made a soft noise, like a cross between a hum and a sigh, before darting down the hallway. When I didn't follow, it halted, bouncing up and down rapidly as it gurgled.

I held my hands up to appease it, too frightened of stirring up ghosts to speak. Already, they clung to me with bated breath, like if I made too much noise, they would come crawling out of the shadows to seek me out.

"Okay, okay, I'm coming."

"Where are you going?" I whispered as the wisp darted off, disappearing between trees as I followed it outside. I hesitated at the edge of the wards, hovering in doubt as I peered out into the darkness. "I can't see without you!"

The wisp was back at my side in an instant, curling up next to my shoulder and bathing the surrounding forest in a soft glow. My relief was immediate; I did not wish to accidentally run into fae.

A soft moan echoed, and I stepped forward, heading towards the clearing the wisp had been leading me towards. It wasn't far from the castle, and my gloves were snug in place, but I tucked my hands close just in case. Light filtered between the branches, and I saw what looked to be a large form as I approached, my heart in my throat. My anxiety would demand me to turn away, but my curiosity was insatiable. Was it Alistair? I dared not call out.

My breath caught as I danced at the edge of the clearing. A dragon rested in its center, breathing heavily as if he'd been injured. It was the first time I'd ever seen a dragon up close. The last time Bracaea's royal family had ridden to Kraeva atop theirs, I'd been too young to remember them clearly.

This dragon was lanky and four-legged, with dark green scales that looked as if they'd been dipped in gold. Horns curled at his head, and his breathing was slightly labored as he curled his wings against his body.

I can sense your anxiety, little human. Do not come any closer.

His voice was loud in my head, tinged with pain, and I flinched away by its sudden appearance, tentatively poking outwards with my mind until I brushed up against something significant and alien. *Who are you?*

One reptilian eye opened and stared at me. Its eye matched the color of Alistair's, and fear flourished through me and betrayed my courage as the dragon exhaled sharply. What was a dragon *doing* this close to the castle if it wasn't Alistair?

My name is Rahfín. Alistair and I share a body. As I said, do not come any closer, lest you wish to see how it feels to be eaten by a dragon.

I ignored Rahfín's demands as I stepped into the clearing. Heat rolled off the dragon and engulfed me and reminded me just how dangerous he was, but he wouldn't hurt me. Not if Alistair was somewhere in there.

My heart made a home in my throat. "Are you hurt? Let me help—"

Rahfín whipped his head around, rows of sharp teeth bared. Golden blood ran where his horns met scales, but otherwise, I couldn't tell where his injuries began. *You? Help me? My injuries go beyond comprehension, beyond physical nature. I will **unmake** him.*

"What does that mean?" Anger replaced fear and sank into me as I balled my fingers into fists. If he was talking about Alistair…

Rahfín's breath shuddered, heaving as he curled his lip back in disdain. *I owe no explanation. Not when he keeps the truth from you.* He snaked his head back, his head falling to rest on the ground, and I squared my shoulders and stiffened my spine, ignoring my impulse to flee.

"What truth? You're not making any sense—"

GO. The force of which his voice echoed through my head sent a current of magic blistering through the air, and I stumbled back, using the cover of the trees to shield me from the heat that rolled through the clearing. Somewhere nearby, a flock of birds shot off through the trees, squawking their displeasure. *Before I eat you. Let me lick my wounds in peace.*

I turned on my heel. *To the hells with you, you stupid fucking lizard.* I cast my thoughts out bitterly as I fled the clearing. I would speak to Alistair after he returned when Rahfín was tucked away, and I could talk to the man who saw sense.

The wisp had waited for me, and he led me back to the safety of the castle, where I remained in the foyer while I waited for Alistair. There was too much Rahfín had said to allow me any sleep without answers, and I tucked my feet underneath me as I found a chair to sit in where I could see the door. Alistair would not be able to sneak in and away from my questioning. I'd wait all night if I had to.

Somewhere off in the castle, a clock chimed three times. The castle bore an almost unnatural stillness as exhaustion tugged at my consciousness, tempting me to give in. A nervous energy sat in my chest, spurred on by Rahfín's words. *Not when I unmake him.* What did he mean by that? Was Alistair in danger? Was Rahfín doing something to him? I understood little about dragon sickness; there was no written record of it in the history tomes. I had never heard my father speak of it, but perhaps I would make time to research it in

Alistair's library. If there was any information on it, it would be there.

I yawned, digging my nails into my palm to keep myself awake, but I felt myself dozing anyway. I woke with a start to Alistair slipping a blanket over me, his fingers brushing against the hollow of my collarbone. I couldn't see his expression in the dimness of the foyer, but I straightened, forcing the sleep from my limbs.

"Alistair, we need to talk."

Alistair swept away from me less gracefully than I was used to him seeing. His limp was far worse, and he leaned heavily against his cane. "We can speak of things in the morning."

"No." I shoved the blanket from me and stumbled to my feet, my exhaustion forgotten as it was pushed away by my anger. "Since when could you *turn* into a dragon? What did Rahfín mean? What truth are you keeping from me?" I reached out and grabbed his arm, forcing him from climbing the stairs. "You will tell me the truth, here and now, Alistair Sylverhorn or I will leave and never return."

Alistair trembled beneath my fingers, and he turned suddenly, his eyes wild as he gripped my shoulders and shook me gently.

"I fear if I tell you the truth, you will leave anyway."

I narrowed my eyes at him. "You won't know what I'll do unless you tell me."

Alistair paused, his hold on me lessening as he sighed. "Mortal men were never meant to bear the weight of gods. My body is…not handling Rahfín's presence well. One day, he will consume me."

The news washed over me like a brush of cold water, and I stilled, pushing the blanket Alistair had draped over me away so I could stand. "Alistair," I breathed, horrified by his words.

"Why didn't you tell me?" I had been so concerned about Cade's safety that I didn't ever think to ask or wonder why his sickness seemed to fluctuate, what the cost was for carrying the soul of a dragon inside him.

"There are too many other concerns. I made my deal with Rahfín long ago. There's no changing it now." Alistair's face bore a bitter expression as he ran his hand through tousled curls, and I saw it now, the signs. The dark circles that covered the skin beneath his eyes. The burning in his gaze had nothing to do with desire or rage. The heavier limp in his walk.

"Tomorrow," I said. "Promise me you'll go and speak with Eirwyn tomorrow. We *need* that cap, Alistair. Curing Valencia could save you, could save us all."

Something warred in his expression, two conflicting emotions that I couldn't place. Anger and determination, perhaps? Fear and hope?

He sighed and then nodded, offering me a lopsided smile. "Who are you to command me, Lyra A'mar? Unless it is in the bedroom?" Noting the stubborn set of my gaze, he held up a hand: a peace offering. "Fine. But only if you promise to stop looking at me as if I am going to die, and go and *rest*. What are you doing up at this hour?"

I blinked, my smile sheepish. "Nightmare."

His face crumpled, washing away the playful, stubborn nature in his expression.

"I don't want to talk about it. I'm going back to bed," I said before he could ask. Guilt sang through me like shards of glass that caught in my lungs, and I turned away from him, unable to stare at the softness in his gaze. "Go and see Eirwyn," I demanded as if I could command someone like Alistair Sylverhorn. Only after his reluctant agreement did I ascend the stairs towards my room.

CHAPTER TWENTY-THREE

ALISTAIR

You cannot possibly be considering speaking with the King of the Wood.

No, I said, rubbing my eyes. *But I do intend to sneak inside his court to steal a Nemalyn cap. Your kind has to find a way to spare us both, and we cannot do that without Valencia's cure and returning her and her dragon home, even if it hasn't hatched yet.*

Rahfín seemed to contemplate my words. *You put too much faith in my kin. It is unlikely they will cure you, and even if they did, I do not know that I would go willingly. I quite like it here.*

Ire struck me fiercely, and I scowled. Yes, perhaps there was no longer any hope for me, but as I walked my grounds and stared up at my castle, I knew, in my heart of hearts, that I needed to save Valencia and Lyra.

It was the only way all of this would be worth it.

CHAPTER TWENTY-FOUR
LYRA

"How is he?" I looked up from Cade's bed to Alistair leaning in the door, a deep blue coat with poofy arms draped over his shoulders. His arms weren't through the sleeves but instead crossed over his chest, and he gave a faint smile. "He took the medicine rather well. I expect he'll make a full recovery."

I nodded, sighing in relief. "He's been awake a few times, and each time, he's more coherent than the last. He doesn't really remember his time in the warehouse, says he was too far plagued with nightmares and bouts of madness to recall, but he says he saw a *lot* of Soria." I stared at Alistair, attempting to gauge his reaction when I mentioned Soria, but there was none.

Instead, he pushed off the door frame and straightened. "I spoke with Eirwyn. We travel to his court today, and he promised to at least entertain our desire for a nemalyn cap, but we must move hastily. I fear we are running out of time."

I ran my gloved fingers over Cade's forehead and then stood. "Give me ten minutes, and I'll be ready."

Alistair turned away. "I'll meet you outside. Valencia has gone ahead to meet our escorts."

The air bore a chill of bated breath as I stepped outside, where Alistair waited for me. The trees rustled with the wind, creating a soft symphony of music only branches and leaves could sing as I stepped down the castle stairs.

"An entrance to the fae realm isn't far."

Following him, I halted just outside the castle's wards. "Wait," I said. "I just want to make sure—" I recalled when he spoke of these gloves and how their magic would one day fail to work, and I *needed* to know my curse was tucked away before I offended the Seelie King.

Alistair halted as I knelt, my knee digging into the soft ground. My hand was sweaty behind the silk glove as I inched it towards the ground, stopping just before I brushed my fingers over the blades of grass. I had never been one for fear. That had always been Cade's job. It festered within me now, though. Nature was a salve against the aching in my chest, soothing the violence that seemed to rattle my bones. Now that it had been ripped away from me, who was I?

I should have fought harder to become a knight.

You were not made for fighting, Ly, my father had told me. What did he know? My father had healing hands. What did he know what *I* was capable of? My blood sang tales of fire and rage, forged from the abuse I'd faced my entire life merely because I was a woman, merely because I was a woman without *power*.

I made my own power. I forged my own strength.

I hadn't bled and fought my way through the fighting rings beneath Kraeva to be called Pit Viper for nothing.

I was a woman, and I was strong.

I pressed my hand to the ground. If I could no longer nurture flowers, I'd nurture my rage.

But no. Alistair's magic held strong in the fabric of the gloves, even though I felt their wear in the pads of my fingers. There was no death, no decay or destruction upon the earth when I laid my hand against the soft soil, and relieved breath etched my cheeks as I stood.

The silence between us was profound as Alistair led me out into the wood. After nearly an hour of walking, I noticed a small road that wove through the trees, its grassy roots a little different than the rest of the forest. Had there not been small, magically lit lanterns dotting the path, I might not have noticed it at all.

"The King's Road," Alistair explained, noting my curious expression. "Most humans wouldn't even know of its existence because its only meant for the fae. Once you're on the path, you're safe from the forest's influence." A wry grin wormed its way onto his face. "Not for lack of trying on the forest's part, though. Best take hold of my arm now, *amori*. I'll keep you safe."

I was about to retort to his teasing tone when a low sound, a cross between some haunting cry and a humming noise, sounded throughout the trees. Alistair didn't seem shaken by it, but it curled against my limbs and beckoned me towards the trees.

I quickly took Alistair's arm, ignoring the soft laughter that fell from his lips.

"The forest seems...different." I'd braved safe parts of the forest from time to time to gather things for the flower shop, and despite the strangeness of faeries, I'd never felt like I was in any sort of danger. Not like I did now.

"The forest is sick. It's more apparent up north," Alistair said. "We are lucky to travel through these lands and not in the Unseelie Queen's domain. Neferíl's forest cries out—the wild fae there are dying."

That was troubling. I did not care for the fae, but that did not mean I wished for their ill will. "Does the queen know what caused it?"

"I am not too familiar with the going ons of the Courts, if I'm honest. I've spent more time in the human realm." He glanced down at me. "I know enough, though. Her throne has been taken from her, and King Eirwyn is preparing for war."

Even more troubling. The humans were already at war. What would it mean for Feyrsia if the fae were to declare war on each other as well?

"Do not fret about the troubles of faeries, though, Lyra. Your people have their own problems." He flashed me a serious expression. "*You* have your own problems."

"It doesn't mean I don't worry. Faeries are so ingrained into human life now—am I wrong not to be concerned? What if it bleeds into our world? What if more innocence dies, human and fae alike?"

The smile Alistair gave me was grim and did not bring me comfort. "True, but we can only worry about so much."

I didn't like his answer, but I didn't push him. We fell into silence after that, and I marveled at the world around me as we dove deeper into the forest. It was the deepest I'd ever gone, and the fae influence was ripe here, down to the moss-ridden logs and the soft laughter that echoed in the trees. I wondered if there were faeries out there hiding among the branches.

"If you're frightened, you're welcome to huddle closer," Alistair teased, drawing me from my silent observations. I realized how tightly I held onto his arm and forced my grasp to lessen, disgusted with how fearful these woods made me. "I don't bite," he said, flashing his golden canines in a gleaming smile. "Not unless you want me to."

I scoffed. "You wish."

"Maybe I do." His bluntness was startling, and I glanced up at him with a sharp expression as he threw his head back and laughed. "Did I make you blush, Lyra A'mar? Does it make you recall our shared time in the library? I haven't forgotten that moment, the way your legs curled around me when you cried out my name into Valencia's mouth…"

Heat clawed its way up my neck towards my cheeks, and I hid my face from him as his words made me remember that day, too. A welcomed distraction, one I'd crave again if I didn't fear his affections would distract me from what I really needed.

To make him fall without falling myself.

"We're nearly there," Alistair said, changing the subject. "Valencia should be on the other side of the stones."

I didn't know how much longer we walked before halting at another path that led up to a meadow of wildflowers and a circle of stones, all of them of various shapes and sizes. The circle itself was perfect, though, unnaturally so, and Alistair pulled away from me as Kazimir, Valencia's hawk, soared down from one of the trees and landed on one of the stones.

"Excellent," Alistair mused. "Kaz being here means Valencia is where she's supposed to be." He stepped up to the stone circle as it began emitting a low hum. I'd gone through plenty of faerie circles in my young lifetime to know I loathed it every time. I wasn't sure how the magic worked, only that it was ancient and wild, and I prepared myself for the aches and pains it would cause, knowing there was little point in trying to avoid them.

"Don't be afraid, Lyra," Alistair said, mistaking my hesitation for fear. "It is only uncomfortable for a moment."

"I'm well aware," I said, my voice clipped. "After you."

CHAPTER TWENTY-FIVE

LYRA

The moment we stepped through, tension thickened in the air. We stood in a meadow with a circle of stones matching the ones we'd just come from, nestled in tall grass that danced lightly in the breeze. Nothing seemed off, but Alistair's mood shifted immediately.

"We must move quickly," he said. Kazimir took off, disappearing through the trees as we moved towards the edge of the meadow ourselves, and my brow furrowed in confusion.

"Why?"

"I know where the king grows his nemalyn caps, but we have to act quickly."

I followed, but something inside me screamed that Alistair was behaving oddly. Shouldn't there be faerie guards to escort us to the palace? That's how it would have been done in Kraeva. The trees around me seemed to still as if they held their breath all at once, and I stared up at the canopy as sunlight peeked through the branches to hit my face. The forest was unlike any I'd ever seen, ancient and twisting. I thought I'd been in Elvira before, but I was so, *so* wrong. The faerie realm of Elvira was soaked in magic; it hummed in the air like a low vibration as if to remind us of its vibrant life.

A twig snapped, and Alistair stilled, his hand darting out to stop me.

"The king is expecting us, isn't he?" I asked. "Where is Valencia?"

When Alistair didn't respond, I quickly stepped in front of him and forced him to halt. "Is the king expecting us?" I asked again.

Instead of answering, Alistair pushed me back into the trunk of a tree, his body encompassing mine. At the start of my protest, he pressed a finger to my lips, hushing me.

"Shhh, they're coming," he whispered, bending his head close to mine. His breath tickled my face as his hands caged me between his arms, his body pressed close to mine. My fingers pushed roughly against the bark of the tree as I held my breath. Two faeries came into view, the gleam of their glaives shining in the dim light. Their boots padded against the soft grass, edging closer, and my heart pounded. How the hell were we going to avoid them? We were in plain sight, and all I could see was Alistair as he smirked down at me.

"Quiet, little flower. As long as you don't move..." he nudged closer, and I thought about shoving him away. Clearly, our arrival wasn't expected, and Alistair had lied to me about Valencia scouting ahead to speak with the king. The urge dissipated as his warmth enveloped me, and I realized I had nowhere to go and no one else to turn to.

Alistair was my only answer to salvation.

I stared up at him, studying his face. His eyes were a maelstrom of color, gold etched with green that tucked away the disease that riddled him. I had never seen or heard of dragon sickness before, and I wasn't sure what it was I saw in

Alistair's eyes now. The pain there, the fire—it was mesmerizing, and my mouth parted as I slipped further into the intensity of his eyes.

"Like what you see?"

"And if I said I did?" I whispered back, thrilled at the sharp inhale from Alistair. "Maybe next time, I'll be the one to get on my knees."

The intensity of Alistair's gaze pinned me to the tree as his hand reached up, his thumb coming to rest against my chin. I thought he was going to kiss me then, his mouth parted, but then he pulled away. His absence left a chill in the air despite Eirwyn's Court feeling like it was in the midst of summer.

"They're gone."

I shivered and then recalled why it was we had been so close in the first place. "You lied to me."

Alistair's grin was wolfish, the gleaming point of his canines granting him a wild look as he tapped his cane against the ground. "I did not lie. I simply withheld the truth. I was never going to be able to get us an audience with the king."

I narrowed my eyes at him, and the ache in my chest burned. "That's still a lie. The king doesn't know we're coming." The implications were breathtaking. If we'd come here without the king's knowledge, that meant... "You want us to steal a nemalyn cap from him." The realization horrified me, and I remained pressed against the tree trunk as I shook my head. "We can't. If we were to get caught, the consequences would be dire. Why not just ask him for one?"

Alistair sighed, leaning heavily against his cane as he waved his hand impatiently. "We are not exactly on speaking terms, he and I, not since he learned what Rahfín and I did. Dragon and fae magic don't mingle very well."

Kazimir flew down from the trees with a soft squawk of annoyance. Alistair glanced up as he landed on a nearby branch and ruffled his feathers. "Come," Alistair said. "We still need a nemalyn cap and have already come too far to turn around. I haven't the slightest idea on how to handle them, which is why—" he paused and then exhaled sharply. "I need you, Lyra."

His words sang pleasure through me, and a thought, unbidden, crossed my mind: how would that sound on his lips in another context?

"This isn't a good idea," I said, willing away my desire.

Alistair nodded. "I know, but what choice do we have?"

Kicking from the tree, I tucked my hair behind my ears. "Fine. But if we get caught by Eirwyn or his guard, you have to talk our way out of it."

Alistair grimaced. "Let's hope it doesn't come to that."

***

"This is Eirwyn's castle?" I stared up at the massive greenhouse, fabricated in the shape of a castle and embellished with sylver metal. Trees blanketed the glass walls and sailed high over the ceiling, preventing the sun from peeking through save for a few spots. We were still a ways off, but the castle sat on the edge of a cliff overlooking a ravine, and the distant sound of waterfalls echoed throughout the trees. It was breathtaking, and I couldn't imagine why the fae desired to leave this place. If I lived here, I would never tire of my surroundings.

"It is." Alistair's tone suggested he was not as impressed as I was; a grimace painted his face, and his finger flourished as magic sank into my bones. I had felt this magic before when I changed my face to be unrecognizable during my pit fights. Looking down, I noticed my arms were green. "We must blend in if we're going to get anywhere close," he said, and when I looked up, I blinked in surprise.

He'd transformed entirely. His skin color remained the same, but he was taller and broader in the shoulder. His curls had flattened, his hair long and drawn behind long, pointed ears. He looked elven, truly like one of Eirwyn's Court. The only thing that remained the same was his eyes, the swirl of green mingled with specks of gold.

"Where is Valencia?" I asked once I had collected myself.

"Kaz is leading us to her. My hope is that she found another way to the caps."

"Where are the caps?" I asked.

Alistair's gaze swept over me. "There's a meadow near his castle where the caps grow. We'll have to be careful, though. They're revered by faeries—as you know."

"I would have thought the forest to be crawling with fae," I said. Alistair moved quickly despite his limp, and I fought hard to keep up as his gaze trained on the canopy, where Kazimir soared through the branches.

"It's likely Eirwyn is having a ball or a tea party. It's rare that he isn't, so if the forest is empty of court fae, that's why. In fact..." he pondered. "If Valencia wasn't able to find us a way in, we may be able to sneak into the party and pose as a guest."

"What's he like?"

Alistair side-eyed me. "The king? Ah...kind and cruel. Merciless and forgiving. He's a walking contradiction, but his people adore him. He's been ruling for a very, very long time, way longer than the queen in the north, but I'm not too terribly familiar with him. My father is of his court, but my mother insisted I was raised in the human world, not here. She lives in Nusa now."

Nusa was a small village west of Kraeva, near the southern

tail of the Voiceless Mountains. It was renowned for its peaceful atmosphere, removed from city life. I could not imagine someone like Alistair growing up there.

"When did you go to Ravenspire?" I didn't mean to ask, but it slipped out of me anyway, my curiosity ever an insistent fly that demanded answers.

"When I was six," Alistair said without turning. We had arrived at a crossroads, a small clearing surrounded by trees that veered off in three different directions. I didn't have time to flinch from the implications of his answer. Ravenspire wasn't a requirement but often a solution to human parents who didn't want their magical children. The other option, however, was leaving them in the forest to its mercy. Both disgusted me.

"I'm sorry." I reached out to lay a hand on Alistair's arm, and he flinched, his eyes burning into mine. A strange expression crossed his face —a mix of sadness, disgust, and wonder —before it was replaced by one of indifference.

"I'm not. My mother did not want me after her failed attempt at suppressing my magic, and I learned a lot at Ravenspire." We took the path forward as I attempted to unpack the nature of his words, only to grow angry at a woman I didn't know. Why fraternize with the fae if you weren't prepared to raise a child with magic?

"Shit," Alistair muttered under his breath. The soft laughter of faeries wafted through the air, quickly growing louder. "If we just act naturally, they have no reason to suspect us."

"I have a better idea," I said. Before he could respond, my fingers had curled into his shirt, and I was tugging him off the path, where I pushed him up against a tree. "Go along with it," I said, peering up at him through my eyelashes before I danced my gloved fingers across his chest and used my free hand to slip over the nape of his neck, pulling his face down to meet mine.

He was warm, his hands coming down to wrap around my waist and urged me closer. I'd kissed many men in my life—women too—a welcome distraction when life at the keep had been insufferable, but something was different with Alistair. It was like kissing lightning, the raw edges of nature. It was as intoxicating now as it had been in the library, and my hand tightened around the nape of his neck, tethering him in place. The soft presence of someone behind me thickened and then passed, and I pulled away as soon as the voices disappeared in the distance, but then Alistair was curling his fingers into my shirt and pulling me close again, his lips crashing against mine again.

A noise echoed against my cheeks in surprise but quickly dissolved into soft moans as Alistair nipped at my bottom lip with his teeth, his tongue darting out to follow. Only after he seemed satisfied did he force himself away, nose flaring, eyes blown in desire. "You continue to surprise me, Miss A'mar," he whispered, straightening.

"I grew up in Kraeva's keep," I explained, my lips swollen from his kiss, my mind still a whirl. "You learn how to lose sight of guards when you have to."

"I'm surprised you didn't fight the guards, with all your physical prowess."

I glared at him, expecting his teasing nature, but there was no trace of it on his face, and I sighed.

"It's not proper for a lady to fight royal guards, Alistair."

He did laugh then as we shook the desire away and approached the castle grounds. Trees grew freely beyond the castle walls, dappling the grounds between beautiful gardens and fountains as far as the eye could see. Kraeva's Keep could not *compare* to the beauty of Eirwyn's castle. As we drew nearer, the sounds of conversing fae grew louder, and I picked at the lace stitched at my wrist. Being so close to the fae realm had me on edge, the swell of their magic pressing against me on all sides, but my anxiety loosened in my chest as I caught sight of Valencia as she hung close to a tall bush spiraling upwards in a trimmed, circular pattern. Kazimir clung to her shoulder, ever watchful as she caught sight of us and waved us over. Seeing her filled me with a sense of relief.

"The king is having a masquerade party, and I managed to snag us masks," she said, handing us each a mask. They were nothing fancy, simple gold masks that would only cover our eyes, and I slipped mine on as Valencia and Alistair did the same.

"Perfect," Alistair said, gesturing. "Just the distraction we need. Follow me and refrain from talking to anyone unless necessary. This will take everything we have to pull off."

CHAPTER TWENTY-SIX

LYRA

We walked through a great courtyard filled to the brim with flowers of various shades of gold and fluffy white petals. Giant cats—tigers and female lions—lounged about on soft grass on grey, stone benches, their eyes ever watchful as we approached. The entire ground was vibrant, almost unbearably so, and I struggled to refrain from shielding my eyes as we approached the king's castle, which was less a castle and more like a massive home shaped in the visage of a greenhouse. Crawling vines clawed their way up the side of the windows, and I couldn't help but stare at the two massive lion statues that stood tall and proud on either side of his sylver-clad door.

I picked at my gloves nervously as I walked beside Valencia and Alistair, a bead of sweat rolling down the side of my head as I glanced over at Alistair. "Are you sure about this? Walking through the front door?"

The corner of Alistair's lip twitched. "Eirwyn loves his parties. It would not surprise me if he didn't even know we were here."

The inside was much like that of the outside—trees stood tall, growing organically from the sun that spilled through the windowed walls. Blue butterflies flitted about, landing on massive flowers that grew on bushes around marbled pillars that decorated the walls, and the floor was naught but a continuation of the grass outside, bathed in wildflowers. It would have been beautiful had I not worried about my safety.

We followed the plethora of faerie bodies as they led us through the castle, and I noted with some surprise that humans were abundant in attendance. The world was changing. Just a few years ago, humans would have been too fearful of entering Eirwyn's Court, worried about getting trapped there. No longer, as I saw a human man making a faerie laugh, twig-like fingers pressed to his pale lips. Many others were draped over faerie arms, led to a tall door set with glittering gems, faint music trailing from beyond the opening.

"Try and stay out of sight of Eirwyn if you can," Alistair muttered. "He will be strong enough to see through my illusions."

Faeries mingled in beautiful dresses and suits made of grass clippings or spider-sewn silk, their swaying bodies otherworldly as the music played softly in the ballroom. I felt severely out of place despite my upbringing in the Kraevian court, and I glanced over at Alistair as he smiled at a passing fae.

"What are we doing here?" I whispered, annoyed. The last thing I wanted was to be swept up in a faerie ball; my knowledge of the fae and their politics was very little, but I knew the dangers of these balls. This was a sure way for a human to become trapped in the fae realm. I'd have to be careful.

"Blending in," Alistair uttered back, speaking so quickly his lips barely moved. "The caps are in a clearing off Eirwyn's gardens. Trust me—this is the easiest way in."

I didn't believe him, but what did I know of Eirwyn's court? I was out of my element, the fae-speech surrounding me like woven music that I couldn't understand. Almost immediately, a glass was pressed into my hands, filled to the brim with golden fae wine. A light, pretty music trailed about the room as faeries swayed or gossiped in groups in corners. It was so like human balls that I couldn't help but stare. There was no sight of the faerie king yet, but Eirwyn had to be here somewhere. It was his party, after all.

"I'm going to wander, see if I can't find the way that leads out to Eirwyn's gardens. Don't draw any attention to yourselves," Alistair said, already weaving through faerie bodies towards the other side of the room.

"Come, Lyra. Come and dance with me," Valencia said, tugging my arm before I could protest. Everything that came with court life appalled me, including dancing, but Valencia wasn't taking no for an answer despite my quiet grumbles. I passed off the faerie wine before it could tempt me, offering it to a faerie with pretty wings that fluttered when she moved. The music was intoxicating, as faerie music always was, and it threatened to drag me into a trance that would have me dancing forever, should I let it. Unlike Alistair, I didn't have an ounce of faerie blood in my family line to protect me, and the music didn't seem to affect Valencia the same. Perhaps her curse rid her of faerie temptations.

I recalled the several times I'd been forced through dancing lessons when I was younger, and it helped me here, though I made an effort not to touch Valencia, just in case my curse managed to manifest through my gloves. They'd held up for this long, but I sensed its desire beneath the fabric, its desperation to liberate itself from it.

"I am on edge too," Valencia whispered, noting how my gaze constantly darted around. "I grew up hating the fae courts. Alistair helped me see that it wasn't so black and white, but…" she trailed off, her gaze hardening. "The fae are very different up north."

"So I've heard. I'll feel better once we've gotten the cap and are back at the castle. I hope Alistair doesn't take long."

"He is notorious for taking longer than he should. He'd deny it, but I think secretly, deep down, he loves all of this," Valencia said. "Though he knows what kind of danger we're in, being here without the king knowing. That's sure to put haste in his step."

I hoped so. As the fae danced around me, I grew dizzy on their innate magic, swept up by the music that wrapped around me like the warmth of a blanket. Valencia and I danced until I was out of breath, and she tugged me towards one of the open doors that led out to a dim balcony overlooking the cliffside.

Pressing my arms against the sylver railing, I leaned over, my stomach plummeting as I realized just how far up we were. "The forest is beautiful, as strange as it is," Valencia said beside me, her cheeks pink from dancing. "Do you see the gardens? That's where we need to go."

I shook my head, gaze trailing towards the side of the castle. Down a ways, the cliffs jutted out from the castle, where I *thought* I saw the beginnings of a garden. I gestured. "Perhaps down there."

Valencia hummed, her gaze following where I pointed. Faerie lights dotted the trees nearby, bathing the canopy in an ethereal glow, and I turned and pressed my back to the railing, closing my eyes and relishing in the cool breeze that etched across my face.

"Lyra…" I opened my eyes to Valencia staring at me, her

mouth parted and her gaze heated. "Now that I have you alone, I wanted to revisit that moment in the library. We never got to speak of it. I—" she exhaled sharply, her eyes darting to my lips. "Can I kiss you?"

The question caught me off guard as Valencia swiveled around to stand in front of me, trapping me between her and the balcony railing. If I were being honest with myself, there was nowhere I'd rather be, and even though we stood amid one of the faerie courts, I nodded.

Valencia flung herself at me, her lips crashing to mine. Kissing her was like waking a flame in my belly, and it roared to life as her fingers curled into the fabric of my shirt at my waist, pinning me in place. Her tongue darted out to trace my bottom lip, and I sighed against her mouth, my fingers curled against the railing. Perhaps it was the influence of the fae, or maybe it was just the exhilaration of kissing Valencia, but my head swam.

When I pulled away, Valencia's eyes shone, and she exhaled sharply. "I could kiss you forever," she admitted, fingers coming up to trail the curve of my jaw. "I thank the gods every day that Kalaea brought you to us."

Guilt wormed its way into my gut at her words, Soria's curse echoing in my head. *The only way you can cure it before it claims your life is to find Alistair. Pry his heart from his rib cage. Feast on it. Make sure he loves you when you do. Only then will you be free of this terrible darkness, Lyra A'mar.* I felt it even now, how the curse lingered inside me, how it cradled my bones and twisted my lungs.

I smiled, swallowing my guilt. "Me, too."

Valencia studied my expression, hers turning to confusion, but before she could question me, my eyes trailed over her shoulder, and my entire body went cold.

"Shit," I hissed, scrambling forward and dragging Valencia out of sight.

"What?" She asked, glancing back towards the ballroom.

"I think I saw Soria." I couldn't have been certain, but I'd remember the woman who cursed me anywhere. She haunted my dreams and plagued my waking thoughts.

Valencia paled. "Are you certain?"

I shook my head. "I reacted too quickly, so I can't be sure, but it *looked* like her."

Alistair appeared before Valencia could respond. "I found where to go."

My eyes flickered to Valencia before returning to Alistair. "I think Soria is here."

Alistair's lips pressed into a thin line, though he did not look as concerned about the news as Valencia and I did. "Her being here would be strange, but not completely out of the realm of possibilities. We need to hurry, then."

CHAPTER TWENTY-SEVEN

LYRA

listair led us away from the party and through a deserted hallway that led deeper into the castle. Miraculously, we did not encounter any servants or guards, but perhaps it was a miracle that the ball was taking place. Most of the castle would be there.

"You're not worried about Soria?" I asked, now uncertain it was even her at all. It was but a quick glance as she passed across the open door, and the more time that passed, the less certain I had seen her.

"Do not mistake my dismissal of it for anything but the desire to get this nemalyn cap and get out of here," Alistair said, leaning heavily against his cane. "I cannot afford to worry." His gaze slid to mine. "Not when we're about to enter the king's sacred grove."

I shivered at Alistair's words. This heist kept getting worse and worse.

We walked until we reached the gardens. They were extraordinary, with small, cobbled paths carved through an abundance of flower beds and rose bushes, and trees with vibrant lights dotting their trunks stood tall in various places.

"This way," Alistair whispered, ignoring the few faeries that trailed through, flutes of wine in their hands. "Towards that cluster of trees, just there. The meadow is beyond there. It took some time, but I managed to find a crack in the wards that keep everyone out. We'll need to hurry."

We all moved through the gardens with bated breath. An eager nature settled low in my belly at the prospect of being so close to a cure. Once we reached the cluster of trees, Alistair gestured to a small break in the trunks.

"This…this is incredible," I breathed, stepping tentatively through the tree line into the clearing. In the middle stood a triangular stone that jutted sharply from the ground, wreathed in moss and white lilies, and a shimmering magic echoed through the air above it as if something was tucked away, just out of sight. The sun bathed the meadow in an ethereal light, and nemalyn caps grew in abundance here, their red and white caps gleaming and beckoning.

Come and pick us.

"We must hurry," Valencia said in hushed tones as we all stepped into the field of wildflowers and mushrooms.

"We have to treat this delicately," I said, recalling what I'd read about them. "Mishandling any of these caps could prove disastrous beyond measure."

"And we're only taking one," Alistair said, his voice sharp. "One will go unnoticed. Any more than that, Eirwyn would not rest until the thief was found."

"Just one," I agreed. I feared the wrath of the elven king, and something whispered in the etches of my mind, encouraging me to leave the nemalyn caps be.

"Do either of you have anything sharp? I'm going to need

something. Especially sylver-made. The nemalyn cap will be less resistant to faerie metal."

Valencia shrugged as Alistair scowled. "I'm afraid I didn't think of that," he said.

A scowl of my own spilled across my lips as I knelt, prying a knife I'd plucked from Alistair's dining room table out of my boot. "Must I do everything myself?"

"Who were you planning to stab with that?" Alistair asked, his tone tinged with amusement. I ignored him as he leaned heavily against his cane, ever watchful as I padded around the meadow, taking care not to touch any of the nemalyn caps.

"Are these still being used to make portals?" I looked up, first to Valencia, then to Alistair, who shook his head.

"No. Only druids can make portals, and for whatever reason they've retreated to their groves. Perhaps it is the sickness that ails these lands."

I remembered Alistair telling me on the way to Eirwyn's castle about the forest's disease, but Valencia seemed troubled by the news.

"What sickness?" she asked.

"It's more apparent in the northern part of the forest," Alistair said, studying the caps. "An unnatural rot that's hurting even the fae."

A part of me wondered if it was mages hurting the fae. Bracaea's hatred towards the forest would only make sense. Another dark thought festered inside me: what if Soria being here had something to do with the sickness Alistair spoke of?

"Lyra," Alistair murmured, dragging me out of my speculations. "Can you safely harvest one of these caps?"

I rolled my shoulders and knelt, where a nemalyn cap glowed softly against the tall grass. "I think so, but I hope you have a bag capable of holding this."

The air thickened, and the sharp taste of magic dashed

across my tongue. I sensed Alistair approach me from behind as I glanced up and sought out his gaze. "I need you to be ready to catch it with the bag. When I cut it, the cap must not touch the ground."

Alistair's lips cracked into a smile as he glanced over at Valencia. "If you wouldn't mind…" Gesturing to his leg, his smile faded. "I'll spare you both the embarrassment of seeing me attempt to kneel." He winked as Valencia approached. "Thank you, *amori*. I only get on my knees when I intend to fuck something."

I rolled my eyes at his vulgarity as Valencia took the bag from his outstretched hand and bent down next to me, holding it out for me. Her nearness set me on edge; she smelled lovely, like the stench of flowers after it had rained.

"Ready?" I whispered, hovering the knife inches from the stalk.

"No," Valencia answered truthfully, and I laughed, taking care to steady my hand before I quickly flicked it through the mushroom.

I cursed as the cap teetered dangerously close to my fingers as it fell. "Catch it!"

I grinned with satisfaction as Valencia caught it with the bag, closing the top and tying it shut with the strings woven in place.

"Thank the gods that's over," I said, exhaling slowly and raising to my feet. I still gripped the knife tightly in my left hand as I turned towards Alistair, and that sick, aching in my chest blossomed again, fed by my curse.

Kill him.

Eat his heart.

Liberate yourself.

Wait. WAIT.

Not yet.

But the curse fed my innate desire for violence, and my eyes skimmed over Alistair's body, trailing over the curve of his neck and the soft points between his ribs where his heart would be. The hilt of the knife was slick in my sweaty palm, and it shook slightly as I met Alistair's gaze...

"Halt!"

A voice called out across the meadow, sparing me from my murderous thoughts, and I quickly slipped the knife back into my boot as several faeries materialized from the trees. They were all clad in sylver armor and gleaming helms, their glaives held high as they surrounded the three of us. Valencia shuffled closer to me on instinct, and I felt the shadow of Alistair envelope us both, but there was nothing to be done. The faeries had us surrounded in minutes, but before they reached us, the bag disappeared from Valencia's hands, echoing behind the swirl of magic that cradled Alistair's palm. I glanced up at him as one of the faerie guards spoke in the Kahlian language.

"King Eirwyn would like a word."

CHAPTER TWENTY-EIGHT

LYRA

We walked back through the gardens, and I took better care this time to admire how it was filled to the brim with flowers of various types and colors. A few of the giant cats lounged about on the grass, ever watchful as we walked by.

I picked at my gloves nervously as I walked alongside Valencia and Alistair, and a bead of sweat rolled down the side of my head.

"Please," I said. "The treaty holds strong between our people. I am close to the royal family in Kraeva. It would be unwise…" I trailed off once I realized the faerie guards were not listening. Or perhaps they simply didn't understand me. Regardless, I followed willingly, knowing if I were to resist, it would only end with us in chains. I had never seen Eirwyn's guards before today, and they bled an intimidating nature that humans were incapable of possessing.

A sharp pain flourished through my side, and I hissed through gritted teeth as I stared at the faerie that had poked me with a blunt wooden stick. It didn't *appear* to be a weapon, but it still hurt. A darkness shadowed the edge of my thoughts: what did a faerie's blood look like?

I quelled that darkness inside me as Alistair stepped between us, his lips drawn back over his teeth. He spoke quietly in a lilting, pretty language, and though I couldn't understand him, tension thickened in the air as Valencia grabbed my arm and tugged me close to her side. I was glad for her comforting presence in that moment, the aching violence rattling around my chest.

The faerie guard relented and led us not back towards the ballroom, where I'd spotted the king last, but rather back to the front of the castle and up a half-circle of stairs, slightly decrepit in nature but still beautiful; each crack was filled with what looked like starlight. A massive wooden door sat at the top; if this were anything like a human keep, that would lead to the throne room.

I inhaled slowly. The king housed treaties with humans. We were not in danger.

So why didn't I believe it?

Perhaps it was due to the nemalyn cap nestled in the bag Alistair had tucked away with his magic. Or maybe it was simply the way the guards had treated us when they found us.

Somehow, I knew we would not see the king's mercy.

They led us into the throne room after a quiet conversation among the faerie guards stationed at the door. Their dialect was familiar; I'd heard it spoken in the shadows of taverns or among the grassy parks of my city, where faeries would frequent with brave humans and wine. It was a slow dialect, beautiful in its own right, like the whispering of wind or the bustling of creeks.

The throne room was massive, with gleaming round tables made of sylver and more nature than should rightly grow inside. My own greenhouse paled in comparison to the flora that thrived within the halls of the king's castle. The roof was nonexistent here, just a canopy of trees, and birds and butterflies alike flew about, creating a facade of calm.

I was anything but calm as we approached the king.

His mask clung delicately to his fingers as he sat casually on his throne. His crown was beautiful, a wreath of gold and red leaves among sunbursts of sylver upon his long strands of blond hair and long, pointed ears. He stood, and it was as if the very room shivered beneath his presence. I lifted my chin and gritted my teeth; I had stood in front of powerful men before and did not falter then. I wouldn't now, either.

King Eirwyn said something in faerie as he descended the stairs, and the guards beside me responded before leaving the room. It was just the four of us now, with Valencia's hands wrapped around my arm.

Eirwyn's smile was unnerving as he approached, a swirling glass of golden wine in his hand. Just the sight of it made my head spin; my hand drew back up to my lips, remembering my kiss with Valencia.

After taking a sip, Eirwyn offered the glass to me.

I thought about refusing him. I knew how dangerous faerie wine was. A lot of people in my kingdom indulged, only to wake up trapped in faerie deals or having no recollection of what they'd given freely to the fae folk they'd been sharing the wine with. And that was faerie wine deluded with human wine and outside the forest, where its magic could not seep in and change you. I'd only sampled it one other time when Cade dared me to when I was younger, and each time, I was reminded how much I loathed it.

"Come now, little fawn," the king said softly. He spoke in

Kraevian, his accent making it sound far too pretty a language than it was. "I do loathe your language and need you to understand me." His free hand lashed out to cup my chin delicately as if the act itself wasn't offensive. Tilting my head up, he slipped the lip of the glass against my mouth, and I shuddered as magic rolled over me. Everything grew vibrant. I almost felt the warmth radiating from the trees, almost felt their willful contentment. Birds chattered overhead, and if I focused, I understood what they were saying. My eyes shot upwards, marveling at their quiet exclamations.

"Excellent," the king murmured, releasing his hold on my chin. As he pulled his hand away, I noticed his fingers were littered with rings—giant gemstones set in sylver or lion heads mounted upon skin. I sensed Alistair's anger beside me, though I wasn't sure why. He and Eirwyn had to know each other, surely. Perhaps it was the fact the king seemed to be ignoring him?

"Now that we can discuss important matters, you can tell me why the three of you were trespassing in my sacred grove?"

I stared down at my hands, covered beneath the soft silk of my gloves. I hated these gloves. They made my hands look too proper and dainty, too calm despite the wrath they longed to inflict.

"Your Majesty, if you'd just—"

"I did not bid you permission to speak, Alistair. Had you grown up in my court, you might have learned a thing or two about *manners*."

Alistair exhaled sharply from my peripherals.

"Say something, I *dare you*." King Eirwyn spoke with a deceptive calm, and I swallowed the lump of fear in my throat. He was exceptionally more terrifying than King Mahlar was, but perhaps it was due to my upbringing in his castle that soothed my wariness of him.

"Good boy," Eirwyn purred, turning his attention back to me. "What use do you have for a nemalyn cap? Unless you wished to use my Speaking Stone for something? Speak quickly, for I grow impatient." He paused as he swept away from us, possessing a grace only known by the fae. It was infuriating. I lowered my hands to my side, clenching my fingers in an attempt to curb their tremble. Beside me, Valencia's hand trailed down to curl around my wrist. A warning. I did not have the means to piss off the elven king of the fae.

The king bent, running his fingers over the head of a slumbering white tiger at the stairs that led up to his throne. The thump of the cat's tail hitting the grassy floor was nearly silent, heard only by my otherworldly state caused by the wine.

"We believe it can cure a plague."

"Lyra." Alistair's whisper was drenched in a warning tone, but I ignored it, prying my arm away from Valencia's soothing grasp and stepping forward just as Eirwyn returned to sit on his throne.

"Can't you simply grow more? There are plenty in that meadow. We only need one," I said.

Eirwyn laughed as a bird flew to settle on the arm of his throne, its tiny head cocked to the side as if it were listening. "Foolish girl. I do not give mortals godly gifts with nothing to get in return. And *no*, I cannot grow more. They're created by druids, I'm afraid, and they've all scurried off to their groves. The wood sings a sad tune, and they fear its sickness." He paused, his finger tracing the arm of his chair. "A plague you say? You are not the first one suffering strange illnesses that have crossed my borders as of late." His eyes narrowed. "I was too lax on their hospitality, and my people have suffered for it. What reason do you have to remain free of my dungeons?"

I twisted my hands together. *Shit.* "My father is the royal healer of the Kahlian royal family. The last—"

"Nothing but failed excuses. Guards!" The king snapped his fingers as guards materialized. Alistair tapped his cane sharply against the ground and strode forward.

"My king, I ask for but one favor. Let us strike a faerie deal."

King Eirwyn laughed again as guards stepped up behind Valencia and me. "Alistair Sylverhorn wants to make a *deal*? How will you slip out of this one, I wonder? No, I don't think I would like to strike a deal with a dying man." I blinked, and all of a sudden, Eirwyn stood before Alistair, his fingers wrapped around Alistair's throat. Alistair did not struggle, and the king tilted Alistair's head to the side as he leaned close. I might have thought the movement to be intimate had I known better. I was too far away to hear what the king whispered to Alistair, and one of the guards hissed at me.

"*Move,*" they whispered, striking at my leg with the bottom of their glaive. "Or we will make you."

I'd like to see you try, I said sullenly as the guards turned Valencia and me towards Alistair, who appeared just as angry as I felt when the king let him go. There was a fear that struck Alistair's eyes, one that infected my own as it sank, a heavy weight, in my belly.

He didn't argue anymore after that and refused to look at me when I passed him.

"I tire of their presence." The king sighed, waving his hand in dismissal. "Take them away."

CHAPTER TWENTY-NINE

LYRA

They led us deep below, where the earthy smell of the forest was thick, and darkness was chased away only by the dimly lit torchlight that lined the walls between cells. The cells were mainly unoccupied, save for one when we first entered. The goblin was dark green with glittering black eyes and sneered as we passed, his long, bony fingers curled tightly around the sylver metal bars.

The guards urged all of us into the same cell, one at the end of the thin hallway, and the door was barely shut and locked before Alistair was urging me back, his presence swelling like a great and terrible beast in the shadow. My back hit the cold wall behind me, and one of Alistair's hands pressed against the wall, trapping me beneath his gaze.

"What the *fuck* were you thinking?" He whispered, his breath tickling my face. I sensed Valencia moving to intervene, but Alistair held up a hand to stop her. "Have you little sense? You told me you grew up in the Kraevian castle—have you never spoken to a king before?"

"Of course I have." Offense trailed through me like poison, feeding my anger, and Alistair scoffed, lips pulled back over his teeth.

"Eirwyn is not like your mortal kings, Lyra. If he has any sense, he'll go and aid Kraeva in eradicating the Blooming Dahlia to prevent it from spreading to his people."

My anger howled at the implications; it sang. It filled my ears with a dull roar as panic formed in my throat, making the world spin. I ducked beneath Alistair's arm and shot towards the bars of the cell. I needed to get out. The walls were closing in, and my breathing was coming too quickly. Panic prickled against my skin and pinched the air from my lungs. I needed to get out. I needed—

"Lyra." Valencia's voice was gentle, her face swimming into my vision as she took my face in her hands. Look at me. *Breathe*." I stared at her, trying to focus on the freckles of her nose or the intensity of the gold in her eyes. She was strange, alien as a faerie, her fingers longer than they were when the curse didn't ail her. I saw her, though, saw her within the concerned swirl of her expression.

I inhaled with her, held my breath, and exhaled.

We did that until my anxiety became an unwoven thing that was liberated from my lungs, and I slumped. "I—I spoke out of line," I admitted. "I should not have been honest with the king."

"Faerie wine," Alistair said quietly, trailing his hands through his hair. He looked just as rattled as I felt, but the anger had also left his face. "If you're not used to it… it isn't your fault, Lyra. Not really. I apologize for directing my anger at you."

Overcome with dizziness, I nodded. "Tell me the nemalyn cap is still safe."

Alistair nodded. "Tucked away from prying eyes. I dare not retrieve it until we're safe from this place."

"Thank you," I whispered to Valencia, who offered a faint smile and pressed a gentle kiss to my forehead. The wings on her back shifted as she dropped her hands to her sides and stepped back, granting me some room. Anxiety still clung to me like a second skin, but the cell didn't feel quite so imposing.

"Do either of you have any ideas on how to get out of here?" I asked.

Valencia and Alistair glanced at each other, and Valencia shook her head.

"I have never been in the faerie realm before, let alone Eirwyn's domain," Valencia said.

"There is no way out until the king decides to be merciful. Could be tomorrow. Could be a hundred years from now," Alistair said, limping over to the corner. The jeweled eye of his cane gleamed, and I stared at it a moment before realization came crashing down upon my shoulders.

"A hundred *years*?"

Alistair's laugh was bitter. "Welcome to Elvira, Lyra."

Exasperated and tired, I turned back to the bars of the cell, my fingers curling against the metal. They were cool to the touch, the chill seeping through the silk of my gloves, and I noted with some horror and disdain that my gloves had begun to fray and wither as if the spell placed upon them to keep my curse at bay was starting to fail. I was running out of time.

Faerie-forged metal looked weak, but in all reality, it was one of the strongest metals in all the land. The only stronger, perhaps, was the dragon glass found in the Voiceless Mountains.

Alistair was right.

We wouldn't leave here unless the king willed it.

We were locked away in our cell for an unknown time before someone came to visit us.

"Hello, Alistair."

Her voice called at familiarity, and I looked up only for a chill to run the course of my spine.

Soria stood in the safety of the hallway, her furs gathered around her shoulders, as she stared into the cell with an amused and calculating expression. Her visage had changed from when I'd seen her in the ballrooms. She no longer looked Kraevian; her skin was porcelain pale, and her hair was spun silver with braids lining one side of her head. Her eyes were the same, though, and I would recognize her voice from anywhere.

"I've been looking everywhere for you," she said. Tension rolled through the cell as Alistair pushed off the wall he'd been leaning against to stand straight. "Kierda told me you paid the sick a visit at the warehouse in Kraeva. You shouldn't take things that aren't yours but..." her gaze flickered about the cell, "I suppose that's why you're here, isn't it?"

"I'd say it's lovely to see you again, Sor, but I can't lie," Alistair said. "What are you doing meddling with fae? It's no secret you loathe the Courts."

Soria's eyes narrowed, her finger running along the bars of the cell. "Information you're no longer privy to, Alistair. Not since your exile. Where are you hiding the missing princess's egg? If you would just return it, perhaps I could speak with the royal family and we could cure that sickness of yours."

I glanced over at Valencia, her anger a tangible thing in the air. We all stayed a fair distance from the front of the cell, but Valencia moved to step beside Alistair, slipping her hand into his. "Don't listen to her. You know intimately how she lies."

Soria's eyes fixed upon Valencia. "Is this faerie your new plaything, Alistair? My, how the mighty have fallen." She clucked, her tongue clicking against the roof of her mouth in disapproval, and she turned away.

"I'll see you soon, Alistair. Until then, you're at the mercy of the king."

The tension Soria caused remained long after she left, and Valencia turned to Alistair the moment Soria disappeared, her hands cupping Alistair's cheeks. "Her words are poisonous, Alistair. Do not let them hurt you."

"I'm fine," Alistair uttered, tearing away from Valencia's comfort. "Let's just focus on how we're going to escape."

As if by some miracle, a quiet squawk echoed from the shadows of the hallway, and Kaz's small head appeared as he landed on the ground before the cell with something small in his mouth.

"Kaz," Valencia whispered excitedly. "How did you get in here?"

The hawk cocked his head to the side and dropped something on the floor, his wings flapping with urgency. Valencia reached through the bars and held it up to the torchlight.

A small piece of metal. Disappointment ran through me at the same time Valencia grinned with relief. "I can work with this," she told us, her fingers closing tightly around the metal. "Something one of my brothers taught me when I wanted to know something tucked behind locked doors."

Valencia snaked her hand around and stuck the metal piece into the lock. After several moments, the lock clicked, and the door of the cell swung open. My heart leapt to my throat in anxiety and excitement as Alistair strode forward.

"Incredible, Val," he whispered.

"They never suspect ordinary lockpicks," Valencia said with a smug grin. "They always prepare for the magical attempts, but never the simple ones."

"Oi," a voice called out from the darkness, and the goblin materialized at the front of his cell. "Do ol' Grünt a favor and lemme out."

"Can't trust a goblin. One of the tricky fae," Alistair said.

I eyed him warily. "Can't trust any of them."

Valencia laughed. "She got you there, Alistair."

"Make it worth ya while," the goblin hissed, snapping his fingers. Trails of pollen slipped from his hands and collected at his feet, and I chewed on my lower lip as I glanced back at the others.

"He could be a distraction. We're not getting out of here without one."

"She's right," Valencia said, darting her finger across Kaz's head as he landed on her shoulder. "It's possible Eirwyn already knows we've escaped our cell."

Alistair's fingers flourished with purple magic, his eyes smoldering in the dimness of the dungeon. "I'm capable of giving our distraction. Leave him. He was locked up here for a reason."

Still, I hesitated until the muffled sound of the guards was heard from above.

"We have to go," Alistair hissed, just as something shifted in the shadows behind the goblin. It took form, pulling all the heat from the dungeon and making me shiver, but I couldn't discern what it was. It looked like naught but limbs and claws, a shadow figure with disjointed legs that bolted out from the back of the cell and snatched the goblin.

It was gone before the goblin even had time to scream, and I stood before where the goblin had been, stunned, as Valencia grabbed my arm and tugged me close.

"Stay still," she whispered, her breath tickling the cusp of my ear. "They're coming."

I didn't have time to wrap my head around what had happened to the goblin as Alistair stepped up next to us, and his magic fell like a blanket over my skin just as the guards appeared, their expressions wild.

They raced past us, sputtering in nervous tones, and I realized I couldn't understand them anymore. The effects of the faerie wine must have worn off, and I stared up at Alistair from behind Valencia. Her body was sandwiched between us, my back pressed up against the cell of the goblin that had disappeared, and the hair on my neck prickled like I was being watched. I was desperate to turn around and look, but doing so would shatter Alistair's magic.

"Did you see where the goblin went?" I whispered.

"No, but I don't want to stick around for it to snatch us as well. Probably another one of Eirwyn's, so we must move quickly," Valencia replied, her breath tickling my ear.

I trembled. My instincts screamed at me to get away, but I held my ground as the faerie guards checked our cell, argued with each other, and then disappeared back up the stairs. Alistair waited an uncomfortable amount of time before he waved his hand, and the magic dissipated. As he did so, something brushed against my back, like the tips of some sharp fingers, and I shuddered away, my gaze darting fearfully behind me. But there was nothing there. Nothing but the void of darkness that made up the cell. Whatever had happened to the goblin, he was gone now, and I loathed to think where he might have been ferried off to.

"Is it safe to go up?" I whispered. The air was thick with

trepidation like the darkness had eyes and teeth, and I was eager to liberate myself from the anxiety of this place. The goblin's sudden absence made the dungeons thick with the threat of danger. "What do we do now that we're free? Especially now that the guards know we're not in our cell."

"Follow me," Alistair said, brushing past towards the stairs. "I have a plan."

CHAPTER THIRTY

ALISTAIR

My mood soured as I hobbled past Valencia and Lyra towards the stairs. Seeing Soria *here*, of all places, sent warning bells off in my head, and my anxiety made Rahfín anxious, which in turn caused the pain in my joints to scream.

"What is your plan?" Valencia asked, following behind me as I nurtured the wounds inflicted by Soria's appearance. She brought out demons in me that I had tried to smother long ago.

"I used to travel here sometimes during my mage studies," I said, pushing away thoughts of the past before they could fester. "There are secrets tucked away if you know where to look. We must hope that they still exist." I loathed this place. Memories of my childhood were bleak, and being back in Eirwyn's castle pried them to the surface.

As we neared the top of the winding, dark stairs that led out of the dungeons, I paused at the door and cocked my head to listen. They had led us through the gardens to a small house that led down into the dungeons, a layout designed to discourage a successful escape, should someone manage to get out of their cell.

"Once we're free of Eirwyn's walls, we just need to make it back to the human world. Kalaea will be able to ferry us home from there without being tracked," I said, fingers pressed against the wood of the door. "We must hurry. Eirwyn will not be as merciful if he catches us." I also did not know where Soria might be, but her being here had me on edge. If she were to capture me…

I couldn't think about it.

"Let's just get *on* with it, Alistair. I do not wish to linger," Lyra hissed as she danced close to Valencia. She was rigid, her gaze darting behind her shoulder several times.

"Afraid of the dark, Miss A'mar?" I teased, earning a slight slap to the arm from Valencia.

"Not the time," Val whispered.

I chuckled bitterly, even though I found no amusement. It was oddly quiet on the other side of the door. Rahfín's possession gave me a keen sense of smell and hearing, and I heard nothing save for the peaceful symphony of faerie heartbeats littering the castle. It was not like Eirwyn to fill his home with anything but the constant celebration, so the silence was jarring. It reminded me of my own castle and the shards of myself that haunted its halls.

"Stay right behind me," I said. After receiving confirmation from both women, I steeled myself and pushed the door open. I half expected guards, but there was nothing, no one in the gardens. A gentle breeze sifted through the air, tousling my curls, and I shook them from my eyes as I peered about. It didn't make sense. Eirwyn's gardens were massive, with varying flowers as far as the eye could see. Nighttime filled the gardens with monsters, shadows lying in wait as we passed them, but there should have been guards. No one came to haunt us or recapture us.

"Something's not—" The burst of magic manifesting stole the sentence from my lungs as I turned and snapped my fingers, washing a protective spell over Lyra and Valencia just before whatever imposing threat reached us.

"Get down," I cried out to them, just as the gardens filled with mages. My eyes locked with Soria as she led at least half a dozen mages into the gardens, their eyes fixated upon me. The sharp stench of magic filled the air, sending my senses buzzing to life, and Rahfín shifted angrily in his fleshy prison, searching for a way to force me to lose control.

"At long last," Soria said, her words accompanied by a simpering grin. I didn't recognize the mages that had come with her, but it had been some years since I had fled the Order at Ravenspire. "I couldn't get you while you were behind the safety of faerie magic, but now I think it's finally time you come with me."

I blinked and said nothing at first. Seeing Soria after all this time was a painful reminder of how quickly the mages turned on me when I was plagued by dragon sickness; their faith in seeing the dragons as gods blinded them to the point where they failed to aid me when I needed them the most.

"I'm afraid I can't do that," I said finally. I sensed Valencia and Lyra behind me, knelt behind a bush of roses where I had shielded them from the magical impact the mage's presence caused. "How did Eirwyn let you past his walls? You are no friend of the fae." Eirwyn did not maintain relations with the North and had minimal contact with the mages of Ravenspire. It had been even less so since the human kingdoms went to war due to his continued support of Kahl.

"Eirwyn is a fool." Soria sneered, fingers trailing over

flowers as she walked closer. "And he is…preoccupied with other things tonight."

I narrowed my eyes. "What did you do?" My mind was racing; I needed to figure out a way to get out of here with Valencia and Lyra safely. The hole in the garden wall was too far to get to now that there were mages in the way.

"Now, now, Alistair. It doesn't matter. You're going to come with us back to Ravenspire, and the women will be left here for Eirwyn to come collect. Unless you want to make this difficult…" Tension thickened in the air as magic brushed up against me, urging Rahfín awake.

Let me out. I'll show these pups what true magic feels like, Rahfín growled, making my bones ache. *Release yourself to me, Alistair.*

How much of me will you take this time?

Rahfín blinked a scaled lid at me in the cusp of my mind. *You know the cost.*

I shook my head. *Then no. I will resort to my magic for this fight.*

He relented, sinking back into the marrow of my bones, and I shuddered as magic washed over me. "I'm afraid I can't do that," I said, meeting Soria's gaze.

Soria clicked her tongue against the roof of her mouth in disapproval, snapping her fingers. The mages surrounding her began to move forward as she exhaled her disappointment. "Such a shame. You were my best student, Alistair. It saddens me to see what you have become."

Her words preyed on my self-loathing as I ducked beneath a bolt of purple magic that shot towards me. It hit the wall behind me, webbing across the grey stone, and I pried my own magic from my fingers and flung it at a mage at random.

"Alistair!" Lyra's panicked voice caused my head to turn, but she had thrown herself in front of me, shielding me as a mage lashed out with a dragon-glass dagger. He hadn't expected her, and Lyra managed to wrangle his wrist and twist his arm until the dagger dropped to the ground. I was too stunned by Lyra's protection to react with gratitude, and Valencia scrambled from her hiding spot to snatch the dagger away from the mage who dropped it.

"Leave him alone. He's not coming with you." Lyra urged herself in front of me, her anger a tangible thing as it infected the air around her. She held her arm out in front of me as if that would protect me from the wrath of the Grand Mage, and Soria tossed her head back and laughed.

"Foolish, stupid *child*. Who are you to stop me? Tell me, how's your curse? I see Alistair has denied its right to play with those silly gloves, which just won't *do*." On her last word, Lyra hissed in pain and gripped her wrist, flinching away.

The gardens fell prey to chaos as magic flung about, unbidden and untamed. The three of us defended ourselves as I flung up an invisible, magical shield, or Lyra stabbed a mage that got too close. It was only just barely enough as Soria and the other mages walked forward, trapping us against Eirwyn's castle. If we stalled for too much longer, Eirwyn's guards would alert him to our escape, and we would truly be trapped.

Once more, Rahfín's presence washed over me. *I can get us out of here.*

My leg screamed at me, threatening to buckle as magic lashed out and sank into my ankle. I cried out, managing to stand afoot by some sort of miracle, and I looked up as a faerie guard stood at the door, their mouth agape as they took in the sight before them. They bolted, and I knew it would only be moments before Eirwyn was upon us, too.

"Let me *go*. You will not touch him." Lyra's voice carried out from the garden, and my gaze snapped to her, thrashing in

Soria's arms. The Grand Mage held her close, intimately so, and whispered something in her ear.

Lyra's nostrils flared as disgust and horror stitched itself in her expression, and Soria laughed and pushed her forward, holding a hand up for the other mages to halt. The air thickened with the stench of magic, and Rahfín brushed up against the underside of my skin, begging for release.

So, I gave it to him. I braced myself as Rahfín took over, ripping my skin asunder and forging deep green and gold scales. I lost control of myself, my mind shutting down to cope with the pain, and everything darkened.

CHAPTER THIRTY-ONE

LYRA

I stumbled towards Valencia and Alistair, whose eyes were wide with panic and rage.

"Get back," Valencia breathed, grabbing hold of my arm and tugging me away as Alistair twitched and shifted, his limbs cracking, snapping, and reforming until a massive dragon stood before us. It was the first time I'd seen Alistair shift into Rahfín, and my heart leapt out for him. It didn't look like a painless thing.

Now that I've been let out, we can stop toying with those beneath us. Rahfín's voice washed through my head, a demanding presence that sent a shiver down my spine. I wanted to bow to that voice, to worship the ground at its feet. I wanted to *kill* in its name, the desire sinking through me so heavily that I gasped. *We must go. He is coming, and I won't be chained to his cells ever again.*

Eirwyn had arrived, his eyes blazing with rage. Several faerie guards accompanied him, and behind us, Soria and her mages had disappeared as if they'd never been here at all.

"Stop." Eirwyn's command felt solid as it slammed into me,

beckoning my legs to obey. At first, I could not move, and I reached out to Valencia, only to realize something was wrong with my hands.

The tips of my fingers poked through, a contrast against the dirt-stained white of the glove. They were deteriorating as if the magic had suddenly failed. I recalled Alistair telling me they would not hold forever. I cursed them. *Why now?* I thought, burdened with panic. Maybe Soria had done something to them.

"Time to go, little flower," Valencia said, not realizing as Eirwyn strode forward.

I had always admired my courage. I had used it to forge strength within myself when the world wanted to keep me down. The thought of hurting Valencia or Alistair or the idea of being left behind, however, filled me with such intense fear that I didn't know how to move.

"I can't." I whimpered, hating the terror in my voice.

"We have to—" Valencia glanced back and visibly paled, noticing the decaying gloves on my hand. "*Fuck.*" She made it to Alistair, shouting something I could not hear over the roar of my own anxiety. Alistair—or rather, Rahfín—lowered his head in acknowledgment before pressing low to the ground, granting Valencia access to his back. My heart pounded; they were going to leave me.

A strange acceptance washed over me as I clenched my fingers into fists. The faerie guards were shouting, but I had long since been past the point of understanding them. I made peace with the idea that I would have to fight them. I didn't know what my curse would do to them. I had never had the chance to see it. Could I kill them? Could I watch the life drain from their eyes? The prospect of death was not unknown to me, but I knew it was different than the fighting I had done in the pits of Kraeva's belly. I had never killed anyone before. I didn't know if the violent aching in my chest craved such murderous intentions.

Rahfín roared and shot up into the air, buffeting with his wings as he danced closer and grabbed me with one of his feet, his claws curling around me protectively. I didn't have time to comprehend it before he shot up over the treeline. The motion was so sudden it took my breath away, my hair whipping around my face as Eirwyn's castle drew further and further away.

My scream was ripped away from my lungs as my stomach plummeted, and Rahfín climbed higher until he soared through the clouds. I squeezed my eyes shut, forcing my arms out so that I would not touch Rahfín by accident, but my mind begged me to cling to his toe, desperate for security. *Oh gods. Please don't drop me.*

I won't, Rahfín mused. *Open your eyes, Lyra. You'll only get one chance to see a sight like this.*

After my stomach settled, I found the courage to open my eyes.

Rahfín had dipped back below the clouds and soared over the trees, and the vast size of the forest was breathtaking. A sea of green, Elvira was as beautiful as it was haunting, an indescribable thing that filled me with simultaneous joy and sadness.

I understood it now. Why the Bracaean family treasured their dragons above all else.

I was free.

The feeling was intoxicating.

Something flew past us quicker than I could get my eyes to understand what it was, and Rahfín veered sharply.

Mages, he seethed, and my fear made a home in my chest once more as the sky began to light up with magic. It was frustrating not being able to see nor hold onto anything as Rahfín climbed once more towards the clouds.

There's a storm ahead, he said. *I'm going to try and lose them in it.*

That didn't sound pleasant at all, my stomach clenching mercilessly as Rahfín dipped and dove to avoid the wrath of the incoming mages. Rain crashed down upon me as Rahfín shot into storm clouds, and the corners of my eyes darkened as I nearly passed out.

Don't worry. I see a cave. If we can just make it there...

Rahfín roared as he jerked to the side as if struck. A monstrous creature, something similar to a bat, only nearly Rahfín's size, shot past me, and I closed my eyes again. If I was going to die, let it be swift. I loathed the helpless situation I was in and only opened my eyes as I felt Rahfín slow.

Are you okay? I asked.

I'll be fine, he said, wings buffeting as he straightened and lowered me to the mouth of a cave. *Hurry. The cave is not big enough for me, so you and Valencia will have to hide inside while I lead them off.*

No, I thought with panic. *Give us Alistair.*

I hit the ground harder than I would have liked as Rahfín released me, the howling of wind ripping at my clothes and hair. He straightened as Valencia slid off his back and down his leg, landing way more gracefully than I had. My shoulder screamed in protest as Rahfín took off, and Valencia gestured for me to follow.

"Come, Lyra! He means to lead our trail away before returning to us!"

I stared out into the storm-soaked horizon and hesitated. Would he be safe? Why did I worry so much for his safety when it was my task to kill him?

After a moment, though, I followed Valencia into the cave.

There was nothing I could do. Alistair was at Rahfín's mercy. I could only be glad that there was no sight of those massive bats about.

The inside of the cave was pretty shallow, but it was dry, and I wrapped my arms around myself to will away the chilling bite the storm had brought. Valencia moved quickly to ensure there was nothing else in the cave with us, and I sank against the wall, teeth chattering.

"Don't come near me," I said, my voice curt as Valencia moved towards me. "I don't…I'm not sure if I will hurt you." I pressed my hands beneath me, between my back and the stone wall. It was cool to the touch, but numb fingers were better than accidentally brushing against Valencia.

"You'd never, Lyra. I know you wouldn't. I trust you." She kept her distance, though, jumping as thunder crashed through the sky. It was a miracle there was light in the cave at all, with the yowling storm brewing outside, a call to my own anxiety as I pressed my hands harder against the wall. *I* didn't trust myself.

"Alistair," Valencia breathed, her gaze flickering from me towards the mouth of the cave. Lightning cracked across the sky, momentarily filling the cave with light, and my head whipped around as Alistair stumbled in, once more a human. He pitched to the side, his face wrought with pain as his fingers splayed out against the cave wall. After a shuddered breath, he waved his hand, and a purple light flickered across the mouth of the cave, trapping us inside. Then, he sent out a cluster of light that darted about the cave, bathing us all in a soft glow.

"We're safe," he whispered, his breathing ragged. Eyes bright, he moved further inside and forced his back to straighten as I scrambled to my feet. "We're safe."

CHAPTER THIRTY-TWO

LYRA

I shivered violently from the cold as Alistair remained near the mouth of the cave, peering out into the growing storm. It seemed Alistair had shaken the mages from their pursuit, but anxiety rolled off Alistair in waves, and I stayed pressed against the back wall as my teeth clattered together. My clothes clung to my skin as I sunk down, and it was a long time before Alistair turned, purple magic still trailing from his fingers as he wove it over the cave's opening again, and again, and again. Despite his earlier weakness, he seemed to have recovered, and Valencia knelt beside me, her skin glowing in the dimness of the cave.

"They won't find us here. I've made sure of it," Alistair said, and I was grateful. The grand-mage Soria's words had rattled me. *I see now. You've gone and fallen in love with him. Don't forget to heed my words, child, or your monstrous, foolish little heart will kill you.*

"Lyra?"

I peered up at him as he said my name, his eyes glowing vaguely in the dimness of the cave. Dragon sickness was a quiet plague, never outright baring its teeth, but only in the eyes. It was always so apparent in the eyes.

Magic soaked the air as the gold in Alistair's eyes glowed brighter, his mouth drawn in a pursed line. "Are you alright? Rahfín didn't hurt you, did he?" His voice lowered, his eyelashes thick from the rain. My heart thundered against the halls of my chest, my stomach flopping between fear and desire as my gaze darted from him to Valencia, her faerie form glowing lightly in the dark cave.

I shook my head, my head still warring with everything I'd just seen. Watching the dragon rip itself from Alistair's skin filled me with nothing but worry for him, and I stood, desperate to reach out and comfort him. When I started to do so, however, I remembered: my gloves were gone. My curse was free.

"Don't come near me," I whispered, my voice lacking strength. "My gloves. They—they're gone."

Alistair's eyes flickered to my bare hands, mouth pressed in a faint line. "It's alright, Lyra. We've got the cap now. The moment we're back at my castle, I'll use it to make the cure."

I nodded, though my heart thundered with adrenaline. I was a well of untapped energy and nothing to do with it, the exhilaration of everything that had just transpired toppling me over the edge.

"Can I kiss you?" His question caught me off guard, and I froze as my eyes snapped back to him, and I studied the pathways of his face, the curve of his jaw, and the patience that warred with impatience in his eyes. "Because gods, Lyra, I can't stop thinking about you. I thought Soria was going to kill you, kill the both of you." He shuddered, his gaze smoldering as he took a step closer, his hand reaching out. "Now that we're safe, I don't want to hold back."

I stepped away, my back hitting the wall. My fear was

monstrous, clawing at my insides like a beast trapped inside a cage. My desire willed it away, and a battle ensued, twisting together in my belly.

"But—"

"We're not going anywhere in this storm," he whispered, but he'd halted, waiting for my permission. My gaze flickered back to Val, the hungered heat in her eyes making my mouth dry. I wanted this. Did that make me selfish? To want both of them? We were trapped in this cave with nothing to do but wait for the storm to pass, and my desire made a home in my belly, a hungering beast.

"My hands," I whispered, turning back to Alistair. My small, murderous hands. Would they hurt him? Gods, what I would give to touch him. "We're not in the safety of your castle."

"Do you trust me?"

After a fearful moment, I nodded.

His fingers curled around one of my wrists, and I flinched, terrified of the sight I would surely see unravel before me. Would he pucker and decay like all nature had done before? Would he wither and slip away, destroyed to naught but ash before me? I shivered, unable to bear the idea...

But no.

He was fine. The skin of his fingers remained unharmed, his eyes chasing mine as if to assess my feelings. "It is only your hands that are a danger to us, Lyra." His other hand reached down to snake around my free wrist, and he clasped them together, drawing forward to raise them up and pin them against the wall over my head. "Keep your hands above your head," He commanded.

I obeyed, even as he pulled his hands away, even as I squirmed, desperate to move.

His fingers reached out, cupping my chin. He tilted my

face upwards, and I didn't deny him as desire pooled like betrayal in my belly. Everywhere his fingers touched left a trail of pleasure, like the smallest of lightning that snaked across my skin, and I suppressed the urge to shudder myself. He took care to keep away from my hands, his eyes blazing as they met mine.

"Can I kiss you?" He asked again, his voice low, hoarse.

"Yes," I said before I lost my courage. He was made of lightning and did not hesitate, rushing forward to push me harder against the wall as his face fell to meet mine.

He kissed me roughly. He was all muscle, tucked away by the deception of his lean body, and I pressed my hands so tightly against the wall of the cave they ached. I was lost in him, his tongue darting out to demand my lips part so that he could gain entrance. I gave in too quickly, a soft moan etching my cheeks, and his hands left my face to rest on either side of my head. I forgot the cold and wet clothes as my desire thrummed, a heartbeat all its own at my center.

A crack of thunder shook the cave, and we both stilled, his gaze boring into the side of my head as I turned to look at the cave's entrance. The storm raged on outside, a blanket of rain shielding us from any wandering eyes.

"Perhaps we should—ah." I exhaled sharply as Alistair distracted me, his mouth at my neck. I met Valencia's gaze, her mouth parted in desire as she stood some feet away, and my eyes fluttered as Alistair sought a sensitive part of my neck.

"Hmmm?"

"I would tame this storm if it granted me the ability to get back to the castle," I managed to breathe out, my voice soft and full of want. "I can touch you there," I said with a little more force. "I can touch *her*." Valencia smiled, teeth sharp. Lightning cast the cave in a sharp light once more, followed by thunder, and Alistair chuckled against my skin.

"We're going nowhere in this storm, little flower."

"I want you. I want you both." The confession slipped from my mouth unbidden, a source of my desperation. Storm be damned. I wanted to pave pathways across the slope of Alistair's face, wanted to run my fingers through his hair. I wanted to feel the thrum of Valencia's heartbeat beneath my fingers. All of these that I had hungered for but never acted on after that day in the library, despite wanting it. I had never wanted two people so desperately before, but I hungered for them now, like I was starving and tempted with food I could not eat.

Fool.

Alistair pulled away so quickly that I shivered, the cold returning to me all at once. I hadn't realized how much *warmth* rolled off his body until it was gone. The lightning lit up Alistair's form as he stood tall. "The dragon that slumbers inside my bones hungers for beautiful things, Lyra. It hungers for you: your stubborn nature, your drive, your kindness. I want to devour you, and I don't think I can wait any longer."

A thrill sang through me. A small voice in the back of my head cautioned me to his words: *What if he wants to eat my heart?* But my lust sank heavily in my groin, spurred on by the heat of his stare. I buckled.

"What are you waiting for?"

My words were the only encouragement he needed to move forward. He grabbed me so quickly that I scarcely had time to react. He was gentle as he laid me on my back, where the cool stone of the cave seeped into my back. "Stay still, little flower," he commanded as he shrugged his shirt off, revealing the hard lines and slopes of his muscles. I drank in the sight of him as he ripped a strip of fabric from his shirt.

"What are you doing?" I asked as he leaned down towards me.

His smirk held traces of amusement. "Tying your hands. Unless I can trust you to keep them to yourself?"

After a moment of silence and contemplation, I shook my head. "Go ahead."

He looped the fabric around my wrists and tied them together. Not so tightly that it hurt, but tight enough that my hands wouldn't slip through as he raised my hands above my head once more. This time, when my wrists met stone, I felt the shiver of magic slip over my skin and found I could not pull my hands away.

"You're so beautiful, Lyra. Like a glittering gem of starlight in a sky of darkness," Valencia whispered, her voice rough as she sank to the ground, her fingers slipping between her legs as she watched the two of us.

"Do you trust me?" Alistair asked again, his face hovering above mine. The heat of his skin sank into my damp clothes as I tore my gaze from Valencia and stared up at him, searching his expression for deceit.

Yes.

No.

"Yes."

He hovered close before he lowered himself to kiss me again. This time, his kiss was slow, and my lips were swollen by the time he pulled away, his fingers dancing at my waist.

Go lower, my desire begged, but they did the opposite, chasing my shirt up until he began lifting it over my head. Before it passed my eyes, however, he stopped, and I was blind, the cold pebbling my nipples as I heard him shift above me.

"Alistair?" I asked, but no response was given, and my body tensed in anticipation. I could sense his presence, but I could no longer see; my ears strained to listen above the sound of the storm outside. "Alist—*oh.*" A gasp replaced Alistair's name on my lips as his tongue flicked across my left nipple, the sensation sending a current of desire shooting down my belly to settle between my legs. His breath was heavy against my breast as I moaned, his other hand drawing up to cup my right breast.

"I want to kiss every inch of you." His voice sank into me. "I want to worship you in every way you deserve. Gods, Lyra, you have unmade me." His mouth clamped down on my nipple, and I arched my back into him, craving to be closer as sensation washed over me. It was almost too much as I clenched my thighs together, craving some inch of friction. I wanted him to touch me. I wanted him to consume me.

I nearly whined when his mouth left me, when the air between us felt too far. I was bathed in darkness, lost in a sea of black as I squirmed against the cold, stone floor. "Alistair, *please*."

His laughter filled the space between us, his fingers ghosting my waist as he tugged my pants off. The air was chilly against my bare skin, but the heat that permeated from Alistair kept the cold at bay.

"Gods, Lyra. Nature could not hold a torch to your beauty."

I wanted to respond, but I moaned instead, his fingers ghosting my skin as his breath pressed against my inner thigh. He was close to my center, the hot air he exhaled teasing me as I opened myself up to him.

If he were going to kill me, what an end it would be.

"Try and stay still for me, little flower," he whispered. "I'm going to worship you now." And then his tongue darted out, and the soft echoes of my moans sank into the walls of the cave.

My shirt over my eyes elevated my other senses, and it was like his fingers were made of lightning; he wrapped his hands around my upper thighs as I began to squirm, rolling my hips up into his mouth, craving the friction of his tongue. Being unable to move was exhilarating. Being unable to see was even more so.

"Gods, Alistair. Please—" He showed no mercy as he forced me down, and his tongue plunged inside me. I had never been quite so overcome by desire like this before, and my moans mingled with the thunder as Alistair's tongue carried me higher and higher until I peaked and then…

"Oh, *gods*, Alistair—I'm going to—"

"Yes, come for me, *amori*."

And so I did. I spiraled, my legs curling delicately around his head as he carried me straight into oblivion. Every ounce of me relaxed, and I let him pull away as I exhaled sharply. My mind flooded with peace. For the first time in a very long time, there was no aching rage in my chest.

Alistair nipped at my thigh as he moved away, and I twitched, still coming down from my orgasm. The cold stone beneath me was cool against my heated skin, and I sighed softly as Alistair pulled my shirt back down and stared deeply into my eyes as if he were searching for something there.

"I'm going to fuck you now, while she watches," he whispered, and I shivered, my shirt bunched up at my wrists as Valencia's quiet moans etched into the stone. "It's her favorite thing to do. And then when I'm done fucking you," his words paved promises into my skin, his lips etching the curve of my jaw just below my ear, "I'm going to fuck *her*. And after that—" His teeth nipped at my neck, and I moaned. "She's welcome to have you however she likes."

He pulled away long enough to dance magic into the air, to weave his finger slowly over his body and strip his clothes away. He was lean, full of hard muscle, and I drank in the sight of him now that I could see.

"Are you just going to sit there or are you going to fuck

me?" I asked, my voice hoarse and laced with my teasing nature.

Alistair's eyes darkened, and he leaned forward, his hands grabbing my hips to drag me towards him as he positioned his cock at my center. I writhed in anticipation as my bound wrists went taunt, and he slid into me slowly, a low moan echoing out from his lips at the exact moment my breath hitched. Once he filled me up, he paused and then began to thrust slowly, one hand coming down to rest next to my head, the other to cup my cheek as he kissed me.

"*Fuck*, Lyra. You feel so good," he murmured against my lips, and as he pulled away, he straightened, his hands grasping my hips as he continued to fuck me. Magic poured through his fingers, sank into my skin, and ran along my veins. It filled me with electrifying want, and I gasped, desperate to pry my hands from their prison and claw at Alistair's back.

"Alistair, please," I begged. "Fuck me just like that."

"You like that?" He mused, voice rough, his thrusts quick and sharp. "You're so fucking beautiful, Lyra." His compliments fueled the flames of my desire, and I rolled my hips in time with his thrusts, pressing my head back against the stone of the cave. At one point, I glanced over to Valencia, brow furrowed, her moans mingling with mine as she touched herself a few feet away, and as I locked eyes with her, Alistair's magic-imbued fingers drew pleasurable circles over my clit. At that moment, the three of us were one, all gasping breaths and writhing bodies, and it made my desire soar and crest, hovering once more at the edge of that cliff.

"I'm going to come, *amori*," Alistair said, fingers digging into my hips as I rolled them, urging him to his orgasm. He'd already taken me to mine; it was his turn. "Oh, *gods*." He thrust sharply as he came, body shuddering forward to press against mine as his hands came to rest on either side of my head. He pressed his forehead to my shoulder, breathing heavily, and I turned to press my lips into the curl of his hair.

"I do hope you're ready for round two. It's my turn," Valencia said, earning a tired laugh from Alistair as he kissed the hollow of my neck and pulled away, rolling onto his back on the ground next to me and wincing in pain as his hand went down to massage his knee.

"Give me a moment."

But Valencia was relentless. "Just lie there, then. Enjoy the feeling of my tongue wrapped around your cock." Valencia winked at me as she dropped to her knees between Alistair's legs, and soon, the cave was once more filled with the mingled moans of pleasure.

CHAPTER THIRTY-THREE

LYRA

The storm cleared up the following morning. Though I desired to tangle myself against Alistair and Valencia as they fell prey to sleep, I couldn't risk my cursed hands touching either of them in the middle of the night, so after our intimacy, after Valencia curled against Alistair and the soft sounds of their sleep encompassed the air, I found my clothes. I burrowed further inside the cave, finding solace in sleep despite the dull roar of the rain outside.

Alistair woke me sometime the next day when the rain had cleared and paved the way to a sunny day, warming the cave and hinting at promise. We had successfully stolen a nemalyn cap. With it, Alistair could add it to his cure, and Valencia could go home to end the war. With any luck, it would also cure my hands. My heart ached, burdened with agony now at the thought of having to kill Alistair. I couldn't. I wouldn't. I'd let the curse take me before I peeled back Alistair's rib cage and stole his heart.

"How are we going to get back to your castle?" I asked, peering out of the cave. We sat nestled in some mountainside surrounded by the forest, with no way down as far as I could tell. "Are you able to shift into a dragon at will?" I turned back to look at Alistair.

He nodded slowly as Valencia rubbed sleep from her eyes. "Yes, but it enacts a price each time I do. I don't know how many more times I can do it safely." He seemed to ponder something silently for a moment before sighing. "There's no other choice, though. I brought us here to keep us safe, but there's no way down, and it will be faster to get to the faerie circle this way. Once we're back at the castle, I need to find Kalaea to up the wards, and then I'm going to see if I can do something with the nemalyn cap."

"The tome I read on them told me to handle them carefully. Don't let it touch anything, and I'd wear gloves, just to be safe." I stared down at my bare hands, my stomach plummeting at the implications. "You're going to have to carry me like you did last time. My hands…"

"If the cap doesn't work, Lyra, we'll find another way," Alistair murmured, hand reaching out to curl in my hair. "I've finally found you. I think I've been looking for you two for a very long time." His gaze darted between Valencia and me. "Now that I have you, I'm not so keen on letting go. You're *mine*. Your curses cannot have either of you."

The possessive nature of his words sent a flurry of excitement through me, but it sauntered away when Alistair turned and stepped onto the lip of the cave. "Be right back," he said, winking as he stepped off the ledge.

I couldn't stop the gasp from freeing itself from my lips as Valencia sighed. "So dramatic," she muttered, just as a massive dragon shot up past the mouth of the cave.

So he is. A deep voice rumbled in my head, filled with amusement. *Come, Valencia. Feel honored that you are given the chance to ride upon my back once more*. As the dragon landed just outside the cave, Valencia trailed past me, pressing a gentle kiss to my temple as she passed.

You, Lyra. Rahfín snaked his head around to stare at me, golden-green eyes blazing. Looking at him made me want to drop to my knees in worship, my innate self tugging apart at the seams. It was easy to believe why the Bracaeans thought they were gods. *Lie on your stomach. It will be easier for me to pick you up.*

How embarrassing. I couldn't help the feeling as it coursed through me, but I did as he asked, lowering myself to the ground and pushing my arms out so that he didn't accidentally touch my hands. The faster we got back to the castle, the better.

Rahfín got us back to the faerie circle quickly, with no mages or faeries in sight. I decided after he lowered me to the ground that if I could avoid flying that way again, I'd gladly do so. In my attempts to avoid touching anything, my hands still brushed the grass, where it curdled and died. Panic hammered against my chest as I quickly rolled over and drew my hands to my chest, immediately forgotten when Rahfín shifted back into Alistair. He cried out in pain and crumpled, his face still bearing some of Rahfín's characteristics. Scales lined the side of his face, his eyes snake-like as his wings slinked into his back, the soft cracking of bone echoing throughout the meadow.

"Alistair," Valencia said, pressing a hand to his back. "No more. You cannot shift anymore, or he will consume you."

"I know," Alistair growled, his voice half-sounding like Rahfín's. "What choice did we have? Give me a minute and I'll be fine."

"But you need to—"

"What I need—" Alistair seethed, his jaw locked in anger and pain, "is to get back to the castle. Once I make your cure, I can take some Lily's Milk for the pain. Just *give me a minute.*"

Valencia's lips pursed, but she pulled her hand away from Alistair and darted over to me, her eyes falling on the dead spot in the grass. "Are you alright?" She asked, her voice lacking the exasperation it had with Alistair.

I nodded, even as tears pricked the corners of my eyes, and I gripped my wrist as if I could protect the world from its wrath. "I only hope this cap is the answer to our problems."

Valencia nodded, her smile lacking warmth or hope. "So do I."

Kalaea greeted us on the other side of the faerie ring, her tails darting in different directions as she sat in the grass before the circle. The moment I came through, I stumbled away, pressing my hands to my knees as I threw up. My stomach then protested loudly, reminding me I had had little to eat since arriving in Eirwyn's woods, and I wiped the back of my mouth as Alistair limped towards Kalaea and began speaking to her in low tones in a language I did not understand. It had taken him time to collect himself, but somehow, he had pulled it together, though his limp had gotten significantly worse, and the sickness clung to his face.

"Kalaea's going to accompany us back to the castle," Alistair announced just as Kaz swooped down to perch on Valencia's shoulder. "She says there has been a strangeness in the woods, different from what it has been as of late."

My stomach twisted at the thought. If Kalaea was worried, then it was something to treat seriously, and my eyes scanned out across the trees, noting that Elvira did not feel any different than it usually did. Still, I kept close to Alistair and Valencia as we followed Kalaea home.

I nearly wept when the tall spires of the castle came into view, a relief so profound it stole the breath from my lungs. Kalaea wove through the trees, an ethereal beauty, her feet causing flowers to bloom wherever she walked. She bounded away the moment the castle came into sight, and I nearly bolted through the gate, grateful for Kalaea's wards to keep my hands from killing anything.

"How long?" Valencia asked Alistair.

"Give me a few days, but it shouldn't take that long. I'm sure the two of you will find a way to occupy the time." Though his words hinted at his teasing nature, exhaustion riddled his tone, and he climbed the stairs slowly. Once more, I cursed myself for not paying more attention to my father's practice. Perhaps I could have helped more.

"Let's start with some breakfast," Valencia said, sliding her arm through mine. "Trust me. He won't rest until he sees it done," she said, noting my hesitation. "And I've tried to offer aid. He won't accept it. Best to just stay out of his way and let him work."

I didn't like it, but I relented, allowing her to lead me towards the dining hall as Alistair limped up the stairs.

CHAPTER THIRTY-FOUR

LYRA

"I believe I've done it!" Alistair's excited exclamation came days after our heist at Eirwyn's castle. I had nearly gone mad with waiting, but Alistair had locked himself in his observatory and doomed Valencia and me to wait, wondering when he would turn up. We had settled into one of the sitting rooms, telling each other tales of our times growing up in the opposite kingdoms. When he finally appeared in the doorway, his eyes lit up with eager anticipation. In his hand were two vials of a swirling green liquid. The sight of them made my stomach clench in anticipation.

"They're certainly the right color," I said as Valencia hurried to her feet. I did the same, and Alistair's cane tapped against the floor as he moved towards us, offering us both a vial each.

As it dropped into my palm, I couldn't help but stare. It had felt like so long ago when Soria cursed me. It scarcely seemed possible to be here, holding a cure that might break the curse my hands were under. I was almost afraid to drink it. What if it didn't work?

Valencia didn't carry such hesitations as she tore the stopper off the top and immediately drew the vial to her lips. The liquid disappeared as she drank, and she shuddered, her face growing pale. "Oh, that makes me feel *awful*," she said. "But I don't care, as long as it works."

"Come," Alistair said, looking at us both. "Let's go and test it."

I gripped the vial in my hand as we rushed outside and stood at the edge of the wards. Valencia exhaled slowly, shaking her hands as she hesitated at the edge of the gates, her eyes trailing back to look at Alistair and me. "Even if it doesn't work," she said, "we can all say we tried."

After that, she stepped outside the wards.

Nothing happened.

A strangled noise, a cross between a sob and a shout, passed Valencia's lips when she remained herself. The cure worked. She no longer bore the resemblance to the fae. It was incredible, and she immediately threw herself against Alistair, her fingers cupping his cheeks as she kissed him. "Thank you, Alistair. *Thank you*."

Alistair laughed and slung an arm across her shoulder, turning to me. "Your turn, Lyra."

But anxiety made a home in me. Seeing Valencia get her happy ending was all I ever wanted, but what if it didn't work? I stared down at the vial in my palm, heart pounding, and feared the alternative. My fear angered me, and I fed that flame, using it to curb the anxious *what-ifs* as I raised the vial to my lips and drank.

Valencia was right. It tasted awful. It went down quickly, and immediately, I broke out into a sweat as if I'd just poisoned myself. A noise of disgust cradled my throat as I pressed a hand to my stomach and then tentatively took a step outside the wards.

The forest slanted as I grew dizzy, and I knelt, hovering my hand above the grass, just as I did before we left for Eirwyn's woods. *Come on, Ly. What are you waiting for?* I thought to myself, pushing my hand onto the ground.

The moment my hand came in contact with the grass, it began to die. I ripped my hand away as the implications crashed down on me, and my disappointment and rage roared in my ears. I couldn't hear, couldn't tear my eyes away from the dead spot amid green.

I stood suddenly, stumbling back into the safety of the wards. It'd worked on Valencia. Why didn't it work on me?

"Lyra, I—" Alistair started, but I ignored him as I made my way back towards the house. Neither followed, and for that, I was grateful. Tears blinded my gaze, and I don't know how I managed to find my way to Cade's room, but I did, and I flung myself inside and sank against the side of his bed. Alistair had been keeping him in a magically induced coma. At the same time, his body and the medicine fought the Blooming Dahlia, so I still hadn't had the chance to speak with him since rescuing him from the warehouse, but I was desperate for his advice as I wept.

"I know what I have to do, Cade, and I don't think I can," I said anyway, reaching out to him. He looked better than I'd seen him last, less sickly, and he no longer thrashed about as if nightmares plagued him. I took comfort in knowing that no matter what, he would be okay. I imagine he'd tell me that it would be okay, as anxious as he was all the time.

"You always know what to do, Ly," he used to say. "Follow your heart."

My heart wanted to spare Alistair, but I'd doom myself in the process. Was I ready to die?

I stilled when I heard a soft knock at the door, and then

Alistair appeared. He did not comment on my state or the fact that the cure had failed. He merely gestured for me to follow him silently and then turned without looking to see if I would come.

After a moment, I wiped the tears from my eyes and stood, padding out of the room after him.

He led me down a winding staircase off the foyer, and my anxiety conjured up all kinds of nasty *what-ifs* until we paused at the door. It was anything but simple, painted a deep green, embellished with golden flowers that somehow grew straight from the wood itself. The doorknob was also gold and round, carved with intricate swirls.

"Your flower shop may be out of reach, but I thought you might like this in its stead, at least until we can break your curse." Alistair's hand pressed against the doorknob as he spoke, turning to glance at me. My heart thundered as I stared at him, my curse taunting me in my ear. *Kill him. He loves me. I can see it in his eyes. I know now. It's the only way.*

"What's beyond the door?" I asked.

His smile brightened, sending a wave of guilt through me and murdering the impulses my curse urged through me as he pushed open the door. I followed him through.

We were somehow outside, somewhere that I'd never seen before. The house was situated in an open plain, filled to the brim with flowers as far as the eye could see. Rolling hills dotted the horizon, and before me sat a sparkling lake and a waterfall that disappeared over the edge of a cliff. There were no trees, not that I could see, and I felt a tear prick the corner of my eye at how indescribably *beautiful* it all was.

"Alistair, I—" The words lodged in my throat as I tentatively followed him down the front steps, relishing in the warmth of the sun and the soft breeze that caressed my cheeks. My fingers itched to trail through the long flowers that grew here, but I refrained, fearful of seeing the destruction they wrought.

"Kalaea warded this island. It's a haven from your curse," Alistair murmured.

"I will not test it," I said, my brow furrowed sadly. "I couldn't bear it if you're wrong."

If I offended Alistair, he did not show it. "This place is my gift to you, so do whatever you want. I'm sorry, Lyra. I don't know why the potion did not break your curse."

Ignoring his apology, I looked out at the open field. "This place is for me?" I swallowed the lump of emotion that threatened to overwhelm my throat. "I haven't done anything to deserve it." He started towards the lake, and so I followed, tentatively, drinking in my surroundings. The flowers were beautiful, and I didn't quite understand how some of them were able to grow so well in the conditions they were in, but I marveled at them all the same.

Alistair laughed. "Do I need a reason?"

My confusion remained. I was not accustomed to receiving gifts without strings; it was always to give my mother my forgiveness for her absence or my father's gratitude for attending some royal party I had begged him not to make me attend. Gifts were often pretty things to mask the nature of their deceit.

"Yes," I said finally. "You do."

Alistair sighed, and I steeled myself against his ire. I would not cower at his aversion to my stubborn nature. I would stand taller and push back should he judge me.

But he did no such thing. Quite the contrary.

"Because you *do* deserve it, Lyra. You've been wonderful. This is my way of saying thanks for aiding me, for showing me what strength is." He paused and pulled away, turning so that he made sure to meet my gaze. "You would have made a wonderful knight. The world is cruel for not seeing that merely because you're a woman."

I searched his eyes for that deceit, the same deceit that had been there when my mother promised to stop leaving on trade ships or my father promised not to force me to attend more parties. I waited for the line that would sour this gift, waited for Alistair to turn this beautiful place into a poisonous one.

"Lyra," Alistair said, shaking me from my anxiety. "Are you alright?"

I forced a small smile, my stomach twisting. "Yes, sorry. It's beautiful, Alistair. Truly. I—is this place magic?"

Alistair stared at me for a long moment before responding. "I just use a little magic here and there to keep the flowers healthy, but this island *is* one of the islands of Amëa. You might have heard of them—they're north of Feyrsia and thought to house the home of the gods."

"The gods?" I had heard of the Isles of Amëa, but as a distant thing in a history lesson that I barely paid attention to when I was younger. Still, as I looked around, I could see it. *If the gods were to dwell anywhere in our realm, it would probably be here.*

"It's why Kalaea's magic works so easily here," Alistair said, stepping up to the edge of the lake. "I come here to think sometimes. I think it'll be good for you now, which is why I'm giving it to you. It'll be yours to have, whenever you need to get away."

My fingers darted out towards his shoulder, intending to get him to face me from where he stared out at the lake, but he turned before I could do so, and I lost my courage, my fingers falling to my side. The grass rose up to caress my legs, and I lowered my gaze as I forced my desires somewhere deep and dark where I could ignore them.

Why? I found myself thinking. *You have been freer here than anywhere else. Why are you fighting to return to a life you were miserable in?*

It was Cade. I knew it in my heart. I had protected my little brother my entire life, drawing our bullies' gazes from him to me so that he would be safe. Perhaps he was the only reason I longed to return. Would he survive the cruelties of the world without me to stand in front of him? Once Cade recovers from the plague, he will go back home. Did I truly deserve to wish to stay here, where it was kind and lovely, when I'd be sending him back to Kraeva and its war-torn state? How could I, when the curse was doomed to claim my life, should I keep Alistair safe?

If Valencia can prove her survival, it might not be war-torn for long. The thought was a desperate one, but I realized I did not wish to leave this place. I wanted to stay here with Valencia and Alistair, where I was shown kindness and genuine care for the first time by people who did not owe it to me. But I couldn't do it, couldn't seek all of this paradise, with the darkness of what I had to do harbored inside me. That secret would haunt me and fester inside me until I was sick with guilt.

I had to tell Alistair. If I didn't now, I never would, and it would tarnish whatever *this* was.

"Alistair? I have to tell you something. Something about my curse."

He held a hand up, his head turning away to listen. "Lyra, something is wrong."

I furrowed my brows. "What do you mean? Alistair, this is important. Soria told me to ki—" but my words were silenced, a prickle at the back of my neck causing them to die in my throat. Alistair's gaze swept over something behind me, his mouth drawn in a severe frown as a whisper of wind trailed through the air, promising trepidation.

"I think we should go back," Alistair said suddenly, turning to face me fully. He was distracted, no longer staring at me, and his anxiety rolled from him, thick as smoke.

"Okay," I said, my courage dying as it withered inside me. *Soon*, I promised myself. I wouldn't go any longer without telling him what Soria had told me would break my curse.

Alistair's face crumpled as he noted my defeated expression, his hand darting out to curl around my chin and tilt it up so that my gaze would meet his. "Let's go back inside the castle. Once I make sure everything is alright there, we'll talk. Valencia is preparing to return to Vrona and end the war. We'll see her off."

Sadness gripped my heart and threatened to crack it. "Is she coming back?"

Alistair looked as sad as I felt, but he tucked it away better than I did as he shrugged a shoulder. "I do not know, nor does she. She wants to, though."

I nodded, knowing that the moment he knew the truth, he might never look at me again as he did now: full of adoration. I would lose him, lose them both.

It was for the best. It was the right thing to do.

Following him back towards the door, I took care to study the flower-rich fields one last time. The vibrancy of the petals was otherworldly, much like what I would find in the faerie side of Elvira, and I inhaled deeply as I followed Alistair back through the door.

The screaming began the moment we entered. The door slammed shut behind us, and Alistair limped quickly through the house with me hot on his heels. Shadows enveloped the place, an unnatural darkness in the corners that seemed to stretch out and grab us as we passed. Alistair pried open the door once we reached the top of the stairs, only for us to find ourselves in a room I did not recognize.

"Shit," Alistair muttered, just as the screaming became warped, loud and quiet, all at once. "Stay here, Lyra."

"Like *fuck* I am," I protested, following behind him. "You don't know how to fight, and I think that's Valencia screaming. You'll have to knock me out if you want me to stay behind."

The anger that burned in his eyes when he turned to face me was met with a challenge as I faced him head-on, my lips pursed. Fear settled heavily in my chest, but the longer I listened, the more convinced I was that Valencia was in danger, her howling cries full of its own anger mingled with fear.

Alistair's shoulders sagged, his hand reaching up to grasp the nape of his neck. "Yes, yes, how foolish of me. Stay close, though. Kalaea is trying to protect the house from something, which is why it's shifting."

I nodded, my fingers curling into the back of Alistair's shirt. "If something's hurt her…"

"I have no doubt you'll make them pay for their crimes," Alistair agreed, prying open the door and spilling us into the hall near the front foyer. Another shout sounded, followed by the soft laughter of a woman, and Alistair hesitated, an immovable force that I barreled into.

"Alistair, what the fuck?"

"Soria," he breathed, earning a strangled exhale of realization from me. Soria was here? How? She'd told me she didn't know where Alistair was, and that's why she'd cursed me to find him. We clung to the shadows of the hallway, but another cry from Valencia had me slinking around Alistair and shooting off towards the stairs.

"Hi, Lyra. Alistair."

As Soria came into view in the foyer below me, a sight unfolded. Valencia tugged hard against the restraint of someone who held her, arms twisted behind her back. Her face was bloody, with thin cuts lining her face, and Soria's fingers tapped against her arm, expressing her impatience.

"Let her go," I said, my fingers curling around the wood of the banister.

"Not one more step, love. We're not here for you, *or* for her. Though it's curious: why does Alistair have the missing princess of Bracaea? Perhaps he wishes to harbor her to keep the kingdoms warring?"

Her accusations sickened me as Alistair swept around the corner and halted at the top of the stairs.

"Let her go." His words echoed mine, and my fear made me dizzy as Valencia cried out, another weeping wound etched along the curve of her cheek. "Harming a member of the royal family is treason, Soria."

Soria threw back her head and laughed, lowering her finger before mocking a bow. "Come with me, Alistair, and I'll leave the girls alone. We've already found her dragon egg." She gestured to a mage beside her, and I noticed he cradled the egg I'd found in the library; its scales gleamed in the torchlight of the foyer. The sight of it in his hands, of him *touching* it when it wasn't his, felt so inherently wrong that I wanted to rip his skin off, but I couldn't move from where I stood.

A tense silence filled the air before Alistair's cane tapped against the wood of the stairs, and he began his descent. "Fine, fine. You have me. If I find you have harmed either of them after such an agreement, you know what I'll do."

Soria sighed, all the amusement draining from her face. "Sure, sure. There's no need to involve Rahfín in this. Now come along."

"Alistair, no. She'll kill you." I reached out to grasp his shoulder, a desperate move that had him turning and slowly removing it. A soft, sad smile had graced his lips, and he pressed a gentle kiss to my knuckles.

"The two of you have made a man out of me, Lyra. I would go with her ten times over to keep you both safe. Never before has anyone ever made me feel this way, and I want to protect it, nurture it. I'll gladly serve my fate if it means both of you remain here, where it is safe." Lowering his voice, his tone took a serious note. "Get Valencia home. End this silly, stupid war."

"I grow impatient. Come quickly, or I'll cut her throat."

Soria's warning had Alistair turn from me as a flood of tears threatened my eyes, and I hovered in place, knowing Soria was not one for empty threats. I met Valencia's gaze, and I willed her to understand that the moment she was free, I would do whatever it took to keep Alistair from going with Soria.

"Good boy," Soria purred, drawing her hand to sling an arm across Alistair's shoulders as if a mother had finally found her long-lost child. "In all honesty, I grew tired of waiting for her to kill you, so I took matters into my own hands."

A look of betrayal crossed Alistair's face as he glanced up at me, where I had stilled, my own horror crossing my face.

"I meant to tell you. I tried—in the fields back there." My shoulders shook as the tears finally spilled over, my thumb jutting back from where we'd just come. "I tried to tell you what she told me to do to break my curse."

Alistair's lips parted, but no words came out, silenced by the hurt in his eyes. It was the last thing I saw as Soria snapped her fingers, and the three of them disappeared, Valencia dropping to the ground as I rushed down the stairs to her.

The castle became dark and silent.

Silent and still, just like my rage.

CHAPTER THIRTY-FIVE

ALISTAIR

The moment we walked past Kalaea's wards, I prepared to relinquish myself to Rahfín, knowing that doing so would seal my fate. He was so strong now that I sensed him ripping me apart from the inside out. One or two more shifts, and I wouldn't shift back at all. Alistair Sylverhorn would cease to exist, doomed to have nursed Rahfín back to health at the cost of my own life.

I had made my bed. It was time for me to sleep in it.

Even though Lyra's cut deep. My heart shattered when Soria spoke the truth, but I had to keep them safe, just as I needed to keep the castle safe. Some would call me a fool, but I wasn't going to go willingly into whatever evil thing Soria had planned.

"Not so fast, Alistair," Soria said, sensing my resistance. "Can't have you going back on your word and shifting on us. Not *yet*." She struck the back of my head, and when I went unconscious, it wasn't due to Rahfín taking over my body but rather the thick sense of magic drawing me to sleep.

When I woke, I was naked and chained in an empty room, my arms pulled apart as the chains attached to opposite walls. It wasn't a large room by any means and was empty, save for the runic circle drawn in blood beneath me. I sat on my knees in one circle, my leg screaming out in pain, and there was another circle situated across from me, where Soria sat, still as stone, fully clothed, an eerie smile painted on her lips.

"What is this?" My throat was dry as if I hadn't been given water for some time, and the tips of my fingers tingled. I was weak and tried as I might to sit up straight; I could not, my shoulders screaming in protest as I fell forward. "Soria, if you wanted me naked, all you had to do was ask."

"Shhh," she cooed, ignoring my vulgarities. Her head tilted to the side as I stared at her through my hair. "Keep your strength. You'll need it when the ritual starts." A soft sigh cradled her mouth as she produced a wicked dagger from her side, and she spun the tip of the blade against her finger. "When you took that dying dragon into your heart, it made the Circle of Maega *very* curious. Why you? What gave you the right to harbor a god in your skin?"

"It's killing me, Soria." Frustration sang through my weakened bones, and while I sensed Rahfín, he was disconnected, like a far-off dream. I tried to reach out to him to communicate, but our connection had been severed. "What did you do to me?" I never thought I'd miss Rahfín, but kneeling here, naked before the implications of a ritual, made me afraid.

I didn't want to die alone.

"That's because you're not strong, because you don't know what I know." Soria laughed, the tone touching the edge of madness. "The Circle of Maega wanted to kill you, but I thought it was such a waste. Why kill you when I could learn how to chain your dragon inside *me*? What power could I wrought if I could control him?"

Horror sank through me at her words, at the implications. I fought against my chains, but I was way too weak, and the movement caused the room to slant. I stilled, fearful of blacking out, and then my rage came undone, rattling around the prison of my chest. "That's not how power works, Soria. There's always a cost."

I sensed Soria standing, and then she was in front of me, her fingers drawing over my cheek, like a lover might or a mother comforting her child. "The cost is you, Alistair. I loved you, loved you more than your whore of a human mother ever could. Why? Why did you have to go and search for that power?" Her fingers hardened against my cheek, and I groaned as she scratched down my cheek and turned away.

"No matter. I am prepared to lose you if it means I can have *him*. Make peace with yourself, Alistair. The ritual begins when the full moon rises."

CHAPTER THIRTY-SIX

LYRA

*H*urt and anger cradled Valencia's face the moment Alistair and the other mages walked through the door, and we were alone. "What did Soria mean? Did you come here to kill Alistair all along?"

Fear blossomed in my chest, my heart cracking at the hatred that burned in Valencia's gaze. "Val, please—I don't expect you to trust me...I don't want you to, because I don't deserve it. I just need you to let me save him."

"You're right. I *don't* trust you." Valencia's anger did not diminish, her fingers padding gently against the wounds on her face as she straightened. "How could you? I-I cared for you, thought I might even love you..." Her voice cracked, and she stumbled away towards the stairs. "I suggest you leave, Lyra."

"I never intended to kill him. Soria spoke those words to me, yes, and I did lie to Alistair when he asked me if I knew what would break my curse. I didn't want him to send me away, not when Cade, not—" A sob shook me to my core, and I curled my fingers into a fist, pressing it tightly against my leg. "I was never going to hurt him. I'm not a monster." When Valencia did not speak, I stilled. "I'm going to go and save him. If it kills me, so be it, but the monster here is Soria, Valencia. Not me."

I turned, and as my hand pressed against the doorknob, I felt Valencia's grasp on my shoulder. "I'm coming with you," she said grimly. "You should have told us, but you're right. Soria's a monster, and Alistair is in danger. Plus," I met her gaze, at the burning rage in her eyes, "they have my dragon."

"What's our plan?" It had taken us all morning and well into the afternoon to return to the warehouse. Once we'd left the castle, Kaz had flung down from somewhere in the trees and somehow communicated with Valencia that he knew where Alistair was. It didn't surprise me that Soria had brought him back to the warehouse, but seeing where they'd been holding Cade filled me with sickness and rage.

"The plan," Valencia hissed through clenched teeth, the daggers Alistair had gifted her strapped to her waist. "Is that we're not going to hold back this time." She glanced over at me and then at my hands. "You don't have gloves anymore," she said, eyes sliding up to meet mine. "We're *not* holding back this time."

I nodded. The thought of killing someone should have frightened me like it had before, but I was blinded by my determination to get Alistair back. He might never forgive me; I'm not sure I would in his position, but in my heart, I knew I loved him.

"Let's go. Whatever they're doing, they're not going to wait around for us to save him," I said, pushing up from where we'd hunkered down behind two large barrels on the docks.

Moving as quickly and as silently as we could, we darted towards the door we'd used to get in last time. When Valencia reached out to push open the door, I hissed and flinched back as the swell of magic cracked and popped into the air. "Wards," she muttered, nurturing her arm. "I don't know how we break them down without Alistair."

"Wait, could you use your daggers? Alistair said something about them cutting through wards on mages, but perhaps it could be used..."

"Lyra, you're a genius." For a moment, it was as if nothing had happened, as if Valencia and Alistair hadn't discovered what it would take to free my hands. She looked at me with such fondness that I wanted to claw my adoration for her from my lungs, to pry it from my chest, especially when her gaze hardened and shifted away. She cleared her throat and unsheathed one of her daggers.

"I'd step back—sometimes wards have magical backlash when they're tampered with," she warned, and I stepped a few feet away, anxiously looking over my shoulder. The air was thick with the threat of danger, but there was no one outside, no mages or guards watching for intruders.

Valencia drew her blade forward slowly, with a calm preciseness I could never achieve with a blade. I was too chaotic, too eager to strike out at my enemies to wield the patience of a dagger, though I envied it. The air cracked like miniature thunder, my hair frizzing up like it did before it rained, but then there was nothing, and Valencia pressed her palm to the wood of the door and pushed.

We both burst into the warehouse, this time not caring to remain quiet, but there were no mages, no ritual going on in the main room. "It's not so large that we cannot find him if we hurry," I said. "But we should split up, cover more ground."

Valencia nodded, veering off towards one of the hallways.

"If it starts to be too long, meet back here, and we'll figure out what to do from there. And Lyra," Valencia hesitated, and my heart stuttered, a flurry of hope that, for whatever reason, she might say she still cared.

But then her face hardened again, and she shook her head, disappearing down towards the hallway across the room. There were blood marks where the ritual had been held the last time, but I no longer heard the symphony of the sick, nor did I see any ritual circle. I knew better than to hope the evil going on here was over, and I took off down the hallway they'd been keeping Cade, moving further past the room where I'd found him.

The hallway ended, splitting off left or right, and I halted quickly, throwing myself back behind the wall as two people walked down the hall away from me.

"It's going to start soon. Soria says we're all required to be there, to witness the birth of a god." The mage's voice was tinged with untamed excitement, fading away as they disappeared down the hall, and I immediately followed them.

They *had* to be talking about Alistair and Rahfín.

The two mages led me unknowingly to a small room where voices could be heard speaking in hushed tongues. I waited several moments and then dared to peek inside.

The room was full of mages, maybe a dozen or so. They all surrounded Alistair, who was naked and chained in the middle of the room, his arms splayed out like he was welcoming someone for a hug. They hadn't had him very long, less than a day, but he looked extremely malnourished and sicker than when I'd seen him last. A rune had been carved into his chest above where his heart was, and dried blood coated his skin.

My rage yowled; it *screamed*.

I cried out and launched myself at the first mage inside the room. I caught them by surprise, my fist lashing out to crash into their jaw, and the curse worked instantaneously, peeling back their skin and sending decay rampant through their face. They died screaming, clawing at their neck, but I'd already moved on to the next person.

"It's her, it's the one Soria cursed!"

"I've heard of her, it's the Pit Viper."

"Someone grab her!"

But no one seemed eager to do so, not after watching the mage I'd struck die so horrifically. I didn't give them the choice, though, bringing down two more before one had the sense to try and contain me with magic.

The mage in front of me held a hand up, and I slammed against an invisible force and was then held in place. No matter how much I thrashed, I could not break free, and my cries of frustration only earned the laughter of the mages surrounding me.

"Frisky little thing, she is," another one purred, courageous enough to grab a strand of my hair and lean close. "Ready to watch the dragon mage die?"

"Let him go," I growled, throwing my head forward and headbutting the mage in the face. He hissed and stumbled back, blood flooding out his nose, and then the room went silent and still, unnaturally so.

"I expected you, Lyra, but not so soon. I also would have figured Valencia to abandon you both to return home." Soria's voice trailed from the door, and I glanced up to see Soria with Valencia writhing in her arms. She no longer had her daggers, and the moment her eyes locked on Alistair, she cried out and attempted to free herself from the shackles Soria had imprisoned her in.

"Now that everyone is here," Soria said, ignoring Valencia's attempts, "We may begin."

CHAPTER THIRTY-SEVEN

LYRA

Soria bound Valencia and me to the wall, much like Alistair had when he bound my wrists in the cave after escaping Eirwyn's. Try as we both might, we were unable to free ourselves as Soria went up to Alistair and cupped his chin, gently tilting it upwards as she whispered words too low for me to hear.

Alistair's eyes flung open, and he darted about the room, his chest heaving as he gasped for air. When his gaze fell on Valencia and me, fear struck them and then flickered back to Soria. "You promised," he said. "You promised to leave them out of this."

Soria shook her finger at him as she moved back until she stood in a small circle across from him. Only then did I notice a ritual circle on the floor. Soria had ignored all the mages I killed, and the ones that lived remained still and silent like they were waiting for someone.

"I promised not to kill them, but now they get to watch me kill you."

"Bitch," I hissed. "Why curse me? Why force me to find him for you if you could do it yourself all along?"

Soria smiled but did not look my way. "Because, Lyra, you got in my way, and I don't very much like people that *get in my way.*"

Her words were like a bucket of cold water had been dumped on my head, the realization that she'd just cursed me because I was in the wrong place at the wrong time, painful like she'd struck me. I was sick and angry all at once, and I flinched away from her words like I could erase them if I just stopped poking her.

"Do all the mages of Ravenspire behave as you do? My father—" Valencia began, only for Soria to interrupt her.

"Your *father* is weak," Soria snarled, eyes darting over to Valencia. "Stuck in the past, unwilling to look to the future. It's disgusting." Soria snapped her fingers at one of the mages. "Force their mouths shut. I tire of listening to them." The mage nodded and raised his hand, and try as I might, when I opened my mouth to speak again, I couldn't.

Don't panic, Ly. But I was—it swelled in my chest and made me dizzy. I recalled Valencia calming me in Eirwyn's cells, and I attempted such practice now. I needed to keep a clear head if I was going to figure out how to save Alistair.

The necklace he'd given me was supposed to protect me from mages. Perhaps...I stilled my panicked heart, exhaled slowly, and began to push against my bounds. With a dizzying sense of satisfaction, I moved an inch. An inch was something. I could work with an inch.

Soria raised her hand and began to chant in tongues, the magic casting shadows about the room. Alistair fought weakly against his chains, but it was of no use. His eyes sought mine, and beyond the hurt and betrayal, there was something else: fear and adoration.

Soria lashed out, sliding her dagger across her palm, and her blood fell against the floor as she moved towards Alistair, her eyes glowing brightly in the dim room. "I'm sorry, Alistair. I wish there were another way." She said, and I beat against the magic that held me in place, trying to cry out, frustrated when I couldn't.

Pure, unadulterated fear struck Alistair's face just before it fell to peace as Soria brushed her bloody hand against his shoulder, holding him upright, and then plunged her dagger into his heart.

The silence was deafening. My scream rattled in the halls of my lungs, trapped behind the magic that sealed my lips. Tears fell down my cheeks as Alistair slumped, and Soria carved his chest open and pried out his heart. Curled around it was a silvery light in the shape of a dragon, and she plucked at it with two fingers, dropping his heart, forgotten, to the floor. The silvery tendril of magic hung limply in the air, and Soria's laugh was unhinged, filling the room as the mages continued to stand still and silent.

"Finally, *power*," she whispered, tilting her head back and swallowing whatever it was that had been curled around Alistair's heart. Beside me, Valencia was struggling just as hard as I was, her tears cascading down her face, her cheeks red with emotional distress.

I don't know how I slipped out of my bindings, but suddenly, I was stumbling forward, my hand reaching out to curl around the throat of the mage that had silenced Valencia and me. His screams of terror were quiet behind the dull roar in my ears, and I shoved him aside, doomed him to his painful death by my curse as I shot towards Soria.

I never reached her.

A painful grunt passed her lips, followed quickly by a

violent cough that produced blood. She grasped her stomach before Alistair's bleeding corpse and groaned in pain, and our eyes locked. She snarled, opened her mouth to scream, and exploded. Blood and gore shot out in all directions, bathing me in what was left of her, and I blinked, stunned, as I stood before the shimmery visage of a dragon.

Lyra. Rahfín's voice washed through me, and the sound of him filling my head was a relief so immense I nearly collapsed. A mage reached out and grabbed my shoulder, but then he was taken away as the ghostly visage of the dragon shot around the room and began to murder every mage that dared to stay behind.

I stumbled towards Alistair, unable to touch him for fear of causing further harm with my curse, and I howled, collapsing to the floor just as Valencia reached my side. She was sobbing too, only she reached out to cup Alistair's cheek, and I threw my head back and wept, ignoring the taste of copper and iron on my tongue as my tears washed some of Soria's blood into my mouth.

Please, I cried out, brushing up against Rahfín's consciousness and finding Valencia's as well. *Please do something. Bring him back. You did this to him. Bring him back.* I was never one for begging, but I did so gladly, pressing my hand to the floor next to Alistair's heart.

Are you both prepared to pay the price? Rahfín's ghostly form landed in front of me, a shadow of his size. After freeing himself from Soria's body, he'd taken shape, looking more like a dragon now and less like just a worm, and I stared at him through tears.

What is the price?

It has to be worth the same as his life, something of your heart.

Something of my heart… What about my flower shop? I loved

the little shop well enough; it had been a way to break free of the pressures my father had tried to place upon me.

Rahfín's stare pierced through me for a moment before shaking his head. *Your love for your flower shop is not strong enough, not if you want me to pluck Alistair's soul from Death's domain. How much do you love your family, Lyra?*

My heart thundered painfully in my chest. *My family?*

Rahfín's head dipped. *Would you give them up to save him?*

My gut screamed at me, my terror clawing at my throat. *What do you mean? I cannot let you kill them...*

No, no. Nothing so large. Your family will not remember you, and you'll never be able to return home. The realization was painful. Could I trade my brother's memories of me for Alistair's life? *Will I be able to say goodbye?*

No, but I can ensure that he will be healed from the Blooming Dahlia and that the flower shop the two of you share will flourish. He will not suffer, Lyra. I can promise that much.

A single tear fell down my cheek as I stared down at Alistair, at the lifelessness in his eyes. My heart warred with itself, with my newfound love for Alistair and my sibling's love for Cade. I didn't want to lose either of them, but I knew a sacrifice was required. I couldn't have both.

I demand to say goodbye. I'll do it, but not without telling my brother I love him, I said finally, tears soaking my cheeks. I didn't fight this hard to save Cade to lose him before we spoke.

Rahfín blinked, contemplating, then nodded. *Very well.* Snaking his head forward, his snout brushed my brow, and then I stood in the bedroom of Alistair's estate, where Cade lay awake in the bed. His eyes widened as they landed on me, and I rushed to his side.

"Lyra, is that—is this real? Why do you look so weird, like you're here but not here?"

I shushed him, uncertain how much time Rahfín would give me. I felt strange and weightless, and I sensed my body still back at the warehouse. It was as if the dragon had cast my soul to Cade to speak. I could not take his hand in mine, my fingers passing through his, and my heart ached as I met Cade's gaze.

"I don't have much time, but Cade—I don't know what to do." I exhaled shakily and then explained everything to him. I left nothing out, beginning at the flower shop when Soria had cursed me. The closer I came to explaining the cost of bringing Alistair back, the tighter my emotions wound in my chest, and I was close to tears by the time I had choked out the words.

"I don't want to lose you, but I love him. I don't know what to do, Cade."

"Lyra…" Cade pushed himself up against the headboard, sitting with a soft smile. "If you truly love him as you say, then you should go and be with him. I'll be okay." His gaze hardened fondly when he met my hesitation, and tears of his own shone in his eyes. "Really—I'm a grown man now. You don't need to protect me anymore. I have the flower shop, and I have Father. I'll be fine." His gaze searched my face, his curls bouncing as he cocked his head and laughed. "'Sides, do you really expect magic to keep me from remembering you?" He closed his eyes, and a single tear rolled down his cheek. "The very forces of this world could not make me forget my sister."

His words did little to soothe the maelstrom of anxiety that plagued my belly. "But Cade…"

"No, Lyra. You've sacrificed much in your life to take care of me, to soothe Father's ambitions for us. You gave up the one thing you wanted more in this world to work at the flower shop with me. If this is the place where you truly belong, I won't be the reason you give it up. Go—go tell that dragon you've said your goodbyes and save Alistair."

The tears spilled over my cheeks then. "I love you, Cade."

"I love you, too. Now, hurry back, before it's too late."

I blinked my tears away, taking one last look at Cade's face. I memorized the gentle curls that fell against his forehead, brown peppered with grey, and the gentle way he looked at me. I memorized all the freckles that prominently showed on his nose during the summer months and how healthy his skin looked as if he hadn't suffered the plague at all. I memorized it all until I blinked and was back at the warehouse again, with Alistair's corpse before me and Rahfín staring at me expectantly.

Take them, I said. *Before I change my mind.* I wept again, hanging my head over Alistair's corpse as tears fell against his bare skin. I took comfort in knowing that I was able to say goodbye.

And you, Valencia— Rahfín turned, staring at Valencia. *Your dragon. I need a body, and he is not yet born. He may never hatch for you. Give him to me; let me once again roam as I once did, a free dragon of the Voiceless Mountains, and I can bring Alistair back to you.*

But... Valencia's gaze flickered to Rahfín, only for her shoulders to sag, and she nodded. *Very well.*

"Rahfín..." I spoke aloud, uncertain, as I stared down at my bloodstained hands through swollen, tear-stained eyes. "My curse..."

Rahfín paused. *Your hands. If you are not attached to them...*

My heart fluttered in fear. *Would one work?*

Rahfín snaked through the air surrounding us. *Perhaps. It's not as certain.*

Anguish and hesitation burrowed within me. I could

handle losing one hand. I don't think I could bear to part with both. *I'll take my chances.*

Rahfín didn't answer. Instead, a soft light filled the room, etched into its walls until it was nearly blinding. I squeezed my eyes shut and hissed in pain as my right hand, my dominant hand, was severed at the wrist. I dared not open my eyes until the light faded, and the first thing I noticed was that the wound on my wrist had already healed. It was strange; as I held up my arm, it was still as if I could feel my fingers even though there was no longer anything there.

A groan emitted from Alistair as the chains slipped away, and he slumped to the floor. A red and angry scar ran over his chest above his heart, and Valencia and I both shot forward, straight into Alistair's arms. For a panic-stricken moment, I feared my curse had not been lifted despite losing my hand, but as my left fingers darted across Alistair's cheek, nothing happened, and I sobbed with relief.

"Why does my chest feel heavy and light, all at once?" Alistair rasped. "And where is Rahfín? I don't...I don't sense him anymore. Is he alright?"

Valencia laughed and hiccuped, her hand cupping Alistair's cheek. "You silly, silly man. We just saved your life, and all you ask about is the dragon that nearly killed you?"

Alistair smiled, no longer sickly in the face, and when our eyes met, I noticed the gold in his green eyes was gone. He sobered, and for a moment, I wondered if he still wasn't going to forgive me.

But then he reached out, past Valencia, whom he'd tugged close to rest her face against the side of his head, to pull me close too, his lips finding mine. "My heart belongs to both of you, for as long as you'll put up with me," he whispered, taking turns to pepper kisses between us. "Now—I need you to tell me what the *fuck* happened here. Whose blood are we soaked in? Why am I naked?"

I laughed, nearly hysterical, and a low crack shot through the air, silencing the three of us. Had more mages come?

Another crack, and my gaze sought out the source: Valencia's dragon egg had finally begun to hatch.

CHAPTER THIRTY-EIGHT

LYRA

A FEW MONTHS LATER.

"You said Valencia is coming—when is she to arrive?" I lay with my head in Alistair's lap as he wove wildflowers in my hair, humming a quiet tune I did not recognize. The soft sound of water cascading over rocks sounded in the distance, and I peered up at Alistair as he smiled fondly down at me, finger reaching down to trail gently over my nose and cheeks.

"Any moment now. She's coming the quicker way."

"Oh?" I said, but my question was answered before Alistair had time to open his mouth as a shadow passed over us and a dragon sailed overhead, banking to the side before landing gracefully nearby.

Prepare yourselves. She's been daydreaming about coming to see you both for nearly a fortnight, Rahfín grumbled, and I laughed as Alistair helped me sit up and then pulled me to my feet. I still wasn't quite used to having only one hand, but staring up at Alistair and watching Valencia slide down the back of Rahfín to greet us? Having them both here and healthy was well worth the cost Valencia and I both paid to save Alistair and cure my hands. Even if my heart ached, grieving a brother who would never recognize me. Alistair had illusioned us once, some weeks ago, so that I could check on Cade. Since the war had ended, Kraeva had returned to a vibrant city free from sickness and rage, and I'd never seen Cade happier. The flower shop had been overflowing with customers, and he'd barely had time to say two words to me, his face blank with recognition, before he'd moved on.

My heart still panged whenever I recalled the way he'd looked at me, like he might have looked at a stranger on the street. Kind and casual, with no notes of familial love in his eyes. I had told Alistair I never wanted to go back there after that. Cade was happy, and Alistair was alive and well. Everyone had gotten a happy ending, even though Valencia and I had made sacrifices to get here.

I'm still surprised you let her ride upon your back, I teased, earning Rahfín's disgruntlement.

Only the two of you, and only when I'm in a good mood.

"It's so good to see both of you," Valencia said, drawing close. She'd reclaimed her royal nature so easily, wearing the regal black and gold of her people. Her hair was pulled back into an intricate braid to keep it out of her face while riding, and a small, syvler circlet was donned on the top of her head. She kissed Alistair first and then me, reaching down to grasp my left hand and squeeze.

"How is everything? I remember you being anxious to return home."

Valencia nodded, though a small smile graced her lips. "Yes. I wasn't sure they would receive me. My family believes our dragons choose us because we are worthy, and I gave up any hope of having a dragon egg hatch for me." She peered up at Rahfín. "Rahfín could have returned to the mountains, but his decision to remain close gained them their favor. I also went and visited Cade."

My heart leapt, and my question lodged in my throat. *How is he?* I wanted to ask, but I was too afraid of her answer.

She seemed to know what I wanted to ask, though, and her eyes sparkled as she reached out and squeezed my hand. "He's doing wonderfully. The flower shop was *packed* when I visited, and he even mentioned you."

"What?" I asked, astonished. My gaze flickered over to Alistair, fearful that her words would tear him away, that somehow my sacrifice would be deemed unacceptable, but no. He was alive and breathing, as he had been since we brought him back.

"I asked about his family, and he mentioned a sister who was traveling. He looked like he couldn't think about it too hard and changed the subject, but it was something. The bond the two of you share…it doesn't surprise me that the magic of your sacrifice is struggling to hold," Valencia said gently.

"Thank you," I whispered, grateful for her words. I didn't know what the news meant or if I'd ever be able to see Cade again, but it was enough to know that he was thriving and that he had some memory of a sister.

Valencia smiled and nodded. "Now that the war has ended, the two kingdoms are thriving again. It's going to take some time to get back to normal, but—" She reached out and grasped the nape of Alistair's neck and then mine, tugging us both towards her so that the three of us pressed our foreheads together. "I've been granted the freedom to leave court life. Will you both still have me as I am?"

I pulled away suddenly, uncertain I'd heard her right. I glanced up at Rahfín as he kneaded the ground with his claws, his head snaking around us as if to listen in. Heat permeated from him just like it had when he possessed Alistair, and I stared at Valencia, gauging if she was serious or not.

"Of course we do, Val," Alistair said, pulling her into a hug. "Things have been dreadfully boring without you."

I nodded in agreement. "*Dreadfully.*"

A low noise echoed out from Rahfín as he lay down, his head the last thing to hit the soft earth. *I think I'll stay for a while, too.*

Alistair laughed, his consciousness brushing up against mine and Rahfín's. *But Rahfín, I thought you were going to rejoin the other dragons in the Voiceless Mountains after ensuring Valencia was welcomed back home?*

Rahfín snorted loudly. *I won't be questioned by a human. This place is lovely enough.*

Alistair reached out and splayed his hand over Rahfín's side, and as he and Valencia spoke excitedly about the day ahead, I couldn't help but smile.

I had finally found home.

ACKNOWLEDGMENTS

I want to take a moment to thank my great aunt, who introduced me to Studio Ghibli's Howl's Moving Castle when I was a child. This book is a love letter to that movie and my admiration of Sophie's strength and the love she and Howl share. That movie (and the other SB films) altered my brain chemistry, and I love implementing their influences into my works.

I'd also like to give a shout-out to my husband and his endless support. This book tested me in many ways, and he was always there to help me through a frustrating spell when the characters weren't cooperating, or when I hit a stumbling block and needed to bounce some ideas off a fellow creative. Shout-out to my sister for being the same kind of rock. Both of you are amazing and I am endlessly grateful for you both in my life!

Thank you to Katie, who is always down to read the messiest of my drafts and offer insight on the stories I create. Forever grateful. <3 Thank you to Sam at scrollworkedits for the developmental edits and for offering suggestions to strengthen this story. It wouldn't be where it is today without you.

And as always, thank you to the readers. Whether this is your first Dugdale book or your fifth, I am endlessly grateful for the support and those who allow me to nurture my dream. May magic always find you <3

Continue past the acknowledgments to read the first chapter of each Romancing the Realms novel: five steamy standalone romantasy books!

ABOUT THE AUTHOR

Jordan Dugdale lives with her family in the small town of Liberty, Missouri. Growing up, Jordan found herself fascinated with fantasy. She would often hunt for dragons with her little brother, or shoot at aliens in video games with her father, or write fantasy stories with her sister. Her upbringing inspired her to create fantasy worlds of her own, which set her on the path to writing in various sub-genres of fantasy. If you want to keep up with her writing ventures, feel free to follow Jordan on: instagram.com/jordandugdaleauthor

ROMANCING THE REALMS
JADE CHURCH

COURTING THE TIGER KING

COURTING THE TIGER KING

"Fucking fuck!" He shook out his hand to ease the sting, squinting against the dusty darkness in the tunnels that had them all stumbling around like blind idiots. If the witch would hold still for just two seconds, then maybe she'd know that they weren't there to harm her.

It was difficult to communicate that while being struck with her sparks of silver lightning though.

They'd hunted her down over the course of weeks until his men had received word that the witch had been spotted in the forest that precluded the shore. If she left his kingdom now there was no telling when they'd be able to find her again, and he didn't have time to waste. Not with the curse breathing down his neck.

"I don't have time for this," he muttered, following the sound of the witch up ahead around the curve in the tunnel. How she'd known the tunnels were here, he wasn't sure. There were not many secrets that his kingdom held that he did not know about and yet she'd managed to evade them for an impressive amount of time. Louder, he called, "For the last time, Sonnet. We're here to—*Ouch!*" The pain sparked his anger, the beast within snapping at the reins and Wren decided he had no reason to hold it back.

The change was a warm cascade over his skin. Heavy paws hit the dirt floor as his senses sharpened, the tunnel no longer appearing pitch black. A metallic scent tickled his nose and he chuffed, suddenly understanding why the witch hadn't utilised anything more than sparks to dissuade them from following. She was injured, which meant she likely didn't have much more magic in her reserves since it depended on the life energy of the user.

He moved quickly, his stride long between his paws, and he caught up to the witch easily. She spun, silver eyes widening as she lifted her hands between them and only the faintest flicker of magic answered her call. Blood coated her side and the pallor of her face was chalky, panic overtaking any logic she may have had until Wren knocked her to the ground with the press of one large paw.

Perhaps it was the pain that jolted her out of the panic, or maybe being face-to-face with a tiger knocked the sense back into her, because she stopped trying to fight and instead breathed a sigh of relief. "Your Majesty."

Sensing it was safe and that the witch was at last in her right mind, Wren let his beast fade away in favour of the man. With barely a thought, the magic of the change reproduced his clothes and he offered the witch a hand, frowning when she grasped it weakly. She couldn't die. Not when he needed her. She was the only known lunar witch left of her line and, consequently, the only one who could perform the spell he needed.

"Sonnet," he acknowledged. "What trouble have you got yourself into now?"

The infirmary was largely empty, affording the witch privacy as his team of healers worked to cleanse and erase the wound that stretched from her hip to her ribcage. Sonnet had fallen unconscious on the journey back to the palace and Wren could only pray to the goddess that the witch pulled through.

"Thank Selene you found her when you did. The worst is over now." Gabe clapped a hand on Wren's shoulder, making him grunt. He wished he could believe that his friend was right, but the ceremony he needed Sonnet to perform was only the first step in thwarting his curse. Gabe sighed, like he could see the doubt churning in Wren's mind behind his eyes. "Come, let her rest. There's nothing you can do here while the healers work."

That much was true at least.

Wren accepted Gabe's hand up as he stood from the uncomfortable wooden bench that lined the outside wall of the infirmary. He'd been out on the hunt for weeks and was desperate for a bath, whiskey, and bed. Not necessarily in that order. He didn't like to spend so much time away from court, but needs-must and this wasn't a task he could let fall to anyone else. Only his most trusted soldiers had accompanied him in an effort to keep their task under wraps.

He followed Gabe out of the room and into the stone corridor, their footsteps muffled by the green runner that wound through the halls. Wren must have looked worse than he'd thought if the unusual tightness of Gabe's jaw was anything to go by.

"Tell me," he said quietly and Gabe nodded, scrubbing a hand over the blond stubble on his jaw before heaving a sigh. His amber eyes were weary when they met Wren's.

"More of the same. Whispers mostly, that the king would

rather be out fucking and hunting than looking after his court."

Wren snorted. If only that were true.

The hour was early, most of the castle hadn't yet stirred as the sun began to stream weakly in through the windows that lined the corridor. But still, he was careful to guard his words lest someone be lurking unseen. In a kingdom full of shifters, you couldn't trust anything you saw—sometimes the fly on the wall was a grown man in disguise.

"Someone is going to a lot of trouble to sow discord," Gabe continued, the early morning light washing over him and dyeing his white skin momentarily gold. "But whoever it is, they're being careful."

"Well, hopefully this should be the last hunt I'll have to go on for a while." Then they would have no reason to complain or spread rumours.

The entrance to his chambers was a welcome sight and he nodded in greeting to the two guards who stood sentry before he turned to clasp Gabe's shoulder.

"I need to rest, will you and Skye—"

"We'll keep an eye on your witch," Gabe confirmed, voice pitched low enough that the human guards wouldn't have picked up the words. "Rest, brother."

Wren smiled, the look fleeting as Gabe nodded and walked back the way they'd come. Gabe wasn't a brother by blood, but he had grown up with him and Skye and the three of them were close. The doors opened quietly beneath Wren's palm and the familiar scent of his rooms tickled his nose and relaxed his body automatically.

The hearth was cold but Wren couldn't be bothered to heat it, instead he wandered to the small golden cart in one corner of the room and poured a healthy measure of the amber liquid into a crystal glass. He sat down heavily into one of the plush armchairs arranged around the low, large oak table as he sipped.

He had his witch and had collected all but one of the ingredients Sonnet would need for her spellwork. This curse had been in his family for generations, so he was well versed in what it would entail. Lunar witches like Sonnet were beyond rare, they specialised in matters of the soul—a magic that many felt was too powerful to be allowed to exist. As a result, they had been hunted. His family had done what they could to protect the witches, but they were a stubborn lot and Wren was forced into secrecy; any hint of his curse could be perceived as a weakness that the court and their adversaries may pounce upon.

Worse, Wren wasn't sure that he could blame them for questioning his fitness for the throne if they discovered the truth. He'd only learned of the curse himself that same year. The ceremony Sonnet would perform could only be done during the cursed's twenty-fifth year. Now he had less than a year to find and bond with his mate, or the curse would take effect.

The only comfort was that Wren wouldn't know that he'd failed if that happened. Trapped in his animal form, Wren wouldn't know much of anything. He couldn't say the same for the kingdom and the throne. The chaos would leave them weak, scrambling for his replacement, perfectly poised for their enemies to close in.

He swallowed back the last of the drink, frowning in the darkness at the morbid turn his thoughts had taken. The glass thunked as he set it on the table, the sound loud in the quiet of the room as he stood and walked to the drapes and tugged them open until a small slither of light cut through the gloom.

His parlour space was where he did his best thinking, aside from when he was in the bath, it was also where he spent the most time with Gabe and Skye. Normally accompanied by drink and cards as they worked to clean out his coffers.

Dust motes swirled in the small beam of light, returning some warmth and brightness to the room as he turned and walked into his adjoining bedroom. A balcony waited to his left, the drapes shut to keep the sun out while he slept, but despite the security risk he often liked to sleep with the doors open, enjoying the smell of fresh air that carried the scents of the forest below up to his room. He pulled open one drape, leaving the one closest to the bed closed to keep it in shadow, and opened the door, breathing deeply and enjoying the hint of earth on the air.

The bed took up most of the room, carved wooden posts forming the vague shape of trees and birds guarding the bed below like a woodland canopy. A copper tub sat in front of the empty hearth, steam curling up from the water within and he hesitated, gaze flitting between the promise of the bed and the heat of the bath calling to him.

His simple tunic and trousers hit the ground, discarded next to his boots and the small horde of weapons he'd had hidden on his person. The need to be clean was too strong to be ignored and he slipped into the water with a groan. After the rough sleeping of the hunt, endless days spent in the underbrush of the forest and the odd tavern, the opportunity to soak in the bath was heavenly. One of his attendants had even added his favourite jasmine oil to the water and the scent had his eyes falling closed.

Water slipped over his nose and he spluttered, jerking upright and blinking the moisture out of his eyes. Fuck. He'd spent all this time trying to break the curse, only to nearly drown in his bath.

Wren dunked his head and reached for a bar of soap, lathering his hair and body and rinsing quickly in the rapidly cooling water. How long had he been asleep for? He wasn't too pruney yet so he had to assume it hadn't been a long time.

A large towel had been placed onto the fabric seat of the wooden chair beside the hearth and he reached for it as he stood, toweling off roughly and pushing the dark fabric over his hair so the semi-long strands wouldn't drip down his back. There was also a small pot of cream on the chair, scented similarly to his favored jasmine, and he scooped up a portion with two fingers before working it across his face and hands. Spending so much time outside would leave him with weathered skin as thick as a bore's hide if he wasn't careful.

Mostly dry, he stumbled over to the bed and promptly collapsed atop the sheets face first. He was asleep before the sun finished rising.

Continue reading now on Kindle Unlimited: https://books2read.com/u/4EjdZl?store=amazon&format=EBOOK

ROMANCING THE REALMS

MICHELLE MORAS

COURTING THE SWAN PRINCE

COURTING THE SWAN PRINCE

The air is heavy with the Autumn Realm's constant amber haze, sunlight filtering through the oak trees' branches. I close my eyes, relishing in the warmth as it seeps into my skin. It's a perfect day for archery practice with my best friends. Best friends who are the princes of the kingdom.

"Ready to lose, Odette?" Odin asks, taunting me with his playful voice. He knows just how to provoke me. Ever since our earlier years in primary school, he was always teasing and toying with me, relentless in his pursuit to make me laugh or get a rise out of me. Ever the troublemaker, but I love him for it.

I open my eyes and shoot him a glance. "You only wish," I say, pressing my shoulders back and adjusting my bow. The target stands across the clearing, bark chipped where we've already missed a few times. "Besides, we all know Siegfried is the best shot," I say, looking over my shoulder at Odin's twin. Siegfried's cheeks flush after I wink at him. If Odin is the jester, Siegfried is like the royal librarian, wise and quiet.

Odin's smirk deepens, his gaze flicking between Siegfried

and me. "Well, then let's make it interesting," he says. "Whoever lands a bullseye first gets to marry Odette someday."

Freezing in my spot with heat rising in my cheeks, I glance toward Siegfried. His face is turning red too, but he tries to laugh it off, rubbing the back of his neck. I know it's just a silly game, but I'm baffled he'd wager such a bet. We're just friends, and to suggest we'd be more someday makes my stomach flutter with a thousand butterflies. Neither prince has ever dared to even hold my hand, let alone kiss me. Although, I've daydreamed of Seigfried doing those very things.

"Odin, that's…" Siegfried says, rubbing his temples. "Odette's too good for either of us."

"That may be true, but one of us will be king someday, so maybe she'll want to be queen. Besides, it's just a bit of fun, right?" Odin asks, flashing that charming, dangerous, gorgeous smile of his.

The twins couldn't be more different in personality or looks. Odin, with his dark, curly locks, wide jaw, and dimples, and Siegfried with blonde hair, a long nose, and high cheekbones. Their only similarity is in their stunning blue eyes that are now staring each other down. "Or are you too afraid to compete?"

Siegfried stiffens, the flicker of rivalry between them sparking as it always does when we do anything competitive. Neither wanting ever to appear weak, especially not in front of me. I'm not sure when things became this tense between them, this shift in their relationship to prove themselves. It's hard sometimes, balancing between them. Odin and Siegfried—they're like fire and water, and I'm caught right in the middle, tugged between their differences. But I don't want to choose. I prefer things to remain unchanged.

It infuriates me, especially when they should know they

have nothing to prove. I'll always be their friend and refuse to be something that comes between them.

Siegfried squares his shoulders, staring at me for a moment before nodding. "Fine," he says, tightening his grip on his bow.

My heart stutters at that, and my face burns at the idea that they would bet on me. This is silly, and we all know it's not serious. They could never marry me anyway. I'm just a simple elven villager and not future queen material, I remind myself. It's expected that their future partners will hail from the royal families from the other kingdoms.

"Hey!" I say, my voice rising to match their intensity. "And if I win? What then?"

Odin cocks his head, a glint in his eye. "If you win, Odette, both of us will give you a kiss."

"A kiss?"

My voice comes out in a squeak, and Odin grins wider, pleased with himself. Siegfried's face goes pale. We've always been close friends, but never outright flirted. My stomach twists and the sun feels too hot. If I'm being honest, I've daydreamed of what it would be like to mean more to Sig, but Odin? We might kill each other with how we argue about the silliest things. Besides, it's inevitable we won't see one another once they turn eighteen and go off to the royal college. I want to enjoy their friendship while I can and not complicate things.

"Well?" Odin asks, gesturing to the target. "Ladies first."

I shake off the nerves, focus my eyes, and raise my bow. It's just a game, I tell myself again as I steady my breathing and let the arrow fly. It sails through the air, swift and true, and lands…just outside the bullseye.

"Close, but not close enough!" Odin taunts, chuckling to himself, before setting up his own shot.

I roll my eyes and step back, pretending I don't care, but I feel my pulse quicken. Odin pulls the string back, his eyes narrowing as he lines up his shot. There's a confidence in his stance that makes me flustered, as if he already knows he'll win.

He lets the arrow fly, and with a dull thud, it sinks into the bullseye, dead center.

"Woo!" Odin shouts, throwing his hands up in victory. "Looks like I've won myself a bride."

"Just a lucky shot," Siegfried says, muttering under his breath.

"Luck?" Odin asks with a scoff. "Maybe you're just jealous because you're not as good as I am."

Siegfried's jaw clenches as he stares at the target. I see the way his hands grip his bow, his knuckles turning white as he lets go and his arrow soars towards the target. It misses its mark, just outside the center circle. He glares at Odin, and for a moment, it's as if there's nothing playful left in their rivalry. His eyes flick toward me, but he doesn't meet my gaze.

Siegfried's face darkens, and before I can say anything, he breaks his bow in half, turning and walking away, his steps quick and tense.

"Siegfried!" I yell, calling after him, but he doesn't slow down.

I round on Odin, fists clenched. "Why did you have to say that?"

Odin shrugs, unfazed. "It's just a bit of fun, Odette."

"Fun?" I glare at him, heart pounding with frustration. "You're being a jerk."

Odin raises an eyebrow, crossing his arms. "He'll get over it."

"You'd better hope so," I say, shaking my head. "I'm going to go find him." Without waiting for his response, I turn and hurry off in the direction Siegfried went, leaving Odin alone in the clearing. The sun dips lower, casting long shadows as I follow the path toward Siegfried's favorite spot—a tranquil lake where he goes whenever he wants to be alone.

I find him there, tossing stones into the water, each one making a ripple that spreads out across the glassy surface. His back is to me, shoulders hunched, his posture radiating frustration.

"Hey," I say as I approach him. He doesn't look at me, but I can tell he knows I'm here. "You shouldn't let him get to you."

He's silent for a moment, watching the ripples fade, and then he sighs, picking up another stone and hurling it into the pond. "Odin always wins, Odette. Always."

I step closer, reaching out but stopping just short of touching his shoulder. "It doesn't matter. It was just a joke. Besides, I'm not some prize to be won. And we both know I'm no one's future queen."

Siegfried's jaw tightens, and he stares down at his hands, as if the stone he holds contains all the words he can't seem to say out loud.

After chucking it into the lake, he meets my eyes. "You don't realize how special you are, do you?" he asks, shaking his head. "Odin always gets what he wants, Odette, especially if he thinks it's something I want."

I'm surprised by his omission. Does that mean Seigfried likes me more than a friend? I feel warm all over and bite my lip, searching for the right words. "Odin wasn't being serious. We all know neither of you can marry me," I say firmly. "We will be lucky to be able to stay friends. You both will move on to bigger and better things without me."

Siegfried glances at me, his eyes dark and full of something I can't quite place. "It won't be long before everything changes, and I dread it."

I shake my head, trying to brush off his words, but a small part of me feels unsettled knowing that they'll leave for the Royal College when they turn eighteen in a couple of years. "I don't want things to be different, but I know you're right."

He almost smiles at that, but it fades. "I wish... I wish I weren't a prince."

"How can you say that?"

Siegfried glances back at the pond, silent again. He tosses the last stone into the water, and I watch it skip once, twice, before sinking beneath the surface. "Compared to Odin, I just don't feel cut out for royal life. I'd much rather live in the village, like you. Enjoy a simple existence."

"That's why you'd make a great king. You understand your people and our way of life, and I know you'd fight to protect it."

He looks me in the eye as he takes my hand in his. "Thank you, Odette. You always know the words to say to make me feel better." He squeezes my hand before releasing it.

"Come on," I say, tugging his sleeve. "Let's go back. We can make Odin charm Madame Fallow for cookies as punishment for being an arse."

That earns me a genuine smile, and he follows me away from the lake, leaving the ripples to settle in our wake.

Two Years Later

"I wish you were coming with me," Siegfried says as he packs the last of his favorite books into his trunk. "You could fit in here and I'll sneak you into the college."

I let out a sad laugh at the visual of that. "Tempting, but

what would I do once we've arrived? Hide in your room all day while you're attending your courses?"

Sig lets out a frustrated grunt, grumbling under his breath about stupid royal rules. "I should have pushed my mother harder about convincing your uncle to let you enroll."

"It would have been no use. My uncle tested my abilities, and I'm not powerful enough to study further. Besides, I'm content with making teas and elixirs with my flora magic. You are meant for more. You'll have an amazing time, even if I'm not there."

"Doubtful," he says as he latches the trunk closed and turns to face me. His eyes are full of sorrow, and it breaks the false bravado I've been mustering up today. Despite trying to be happy for him, I'm hating this. I don't want him to leave; I want us to stay in our happy little bubble that we've been in the past year. Somewhere along the way, our friendship evolved into something more. Something deeper. Something I think might be love. But alas, all royals and nobles' elflings must go away to the Royal College at eighteen.

"You know this is hard for me too. I'm going to miss you so much, but it would be selfish of me not to want you to learn to harness your moon magic." Siegfried's powers emerged a couple of years ago, but it's been difficult for him to learn to wield them due to how strong they are. The moon's energy can flow into him, which he says will allow him to use it as a weapon and a shield. So far, he's only been able to use it to create light orbs and small beams. He needs to go to college.

"It's going to be the worst four years of my life. Every moment away from you will be absolute torture," he says as he steps closer, reaching a hand out to cup my face. I lean into the warmth, savoring his touch while I can. "But, I vow I will write to you every day, so expect a hawk delivery daily."

I smile up at him, bringing my hand up and resting it on

his chest. "And I'll write back just as often, but I don't want you to feel pressure to keep in touch. You need to focus on your studies and advance your magic. Don't worry about me." We've known this day was always coming, and sometimes I wish I hadn't let myself fall for him. Everyone knows there's an expectation that the royals find a suitable match while at the college. As deeply as I care for Sig, I know it's futile to hope he'd wait for me.

He drops his hand and frowns down at me. I'm much shorter than him, my head coming up to his chest. He's gotten so tall over the past couple of years, and so handsome, even when he looks at me in dismay.

"You really think I could forget you?"

"I'm just trying to be realistic, Sig. Our paths are going in different directions, and I don't want to hold you back. Our kingdom needs you — you could be the future king someday, and I'll just be making tea."

"But, I need *you*," he says with a hint of desperation in his voice. "Odette, maybe I haven't made this clear, but I... I love you. I always have. Going away to college will not change my feelings. You're what I want. All I want."

I gasp at the words I've been longing to hear, but a little voice deep inside me reminds me he's leaving and we're too young to be making such claims.

I reach out and clasp his hands in my own. "Sig, you know I love you too, but it may not be enough. You must make the kingdom a priority, and I won't ever blame you for that. Promise me you'll focus on yourself while you're there."

He looks away from me, his jaw ticking. "I don't agree, but I will promise you that, if you promise me one thing before I leave?"

"Okay... what?"

"Just tonight, let us be enough. Stay with me. Let me love you fully, wholly."

"Okay."

"Are you sure? You want me as much as I want you, right?" he asks, and I can't help but blush. We've come close so many times to letting ourselves go all the way, but something has always made it nearly impossible to get enough alone time. If this is our chance, I'm taking it.

"Of course I do, Sig, you know that. I'd regret it if we didn't, but I'm also scared it'll make telling you goodbye that much harder," I admit, looking down, trying to hold back the tears that threaten to spill out.

He lifts my chin with his fingers, forcing me to meet his beautiful icy blue eyes. I think they might be what I'll miss the most.

"I know, and you may be right, but I can't leave without showing you just how much you mean to me. My heart, my body, my soul — they all burn for you," he says before crashing his lips to mine. I let him pour all his love and angst into me as I kiss him back with everything I have. He may not be mine forever, but he's mine in this perfect moment, and I'm going to savor it.

We kiss. And kiss. And kiss some more, before he lifts me into his arms, my legs wrapping around his waist as he carries me over to his bed. He lays me down so gently that my chest aches. I try to steady my breath so that I can commit every touch, every kiss to memory.

"You are the loveliest elf in all the realm, Odette," Siegfried says, standing over me. "I'm the luckiest elf in all the realm to be loved by you. I'll never take your love for granted." A tear falls from the corner of my eye and slides down into my hair. He wipes it away with his thumb and then takes his time undressing me. First, taking off my leather slippers, then rolling down my stockings and tossing them on the floor. He kisses his way up my legs, teasing me with one quick press of his lips to that magic spot above my entrance before pulling my pantaloons off. I can't help but groan in both frustration and need. My middle feels like it's burning up in anticipation, and I'm sure he can see the evidence of my desire.

Just when I'm about to demand he hurry, he leans over me, our bodies perfectly aligned. I moan at the delicious feel of the weight of him against me. He hikes up my chemise and dress, teasing my core with his fingers. We've done this part so many times that he knows how to make me explode, playing me like an instrument.

"That's my girl, soak my hand so that you're ready for me," he croons over me, making my toes curl.

"Oh stars, Sig. I'm so close, don't stop," I say, my breathing turning ragged as I lose myself to his touch. It doesn't take long before I'm shaking and coming undone beneath him. He bends lower, kissing me hard to cover my cries as waves of pleasure flow through me, eventually ebbing away into mere ripples. And yet, I'm ready for more. Craving it. Craving him.

Siegfried rolls onto his back, pulling me with him. Sitting, straddling his hips, I lean down to kiss him while holding his face in my hands before trailing kisses down his neck. I push myself up, sitting atop him, so I can unbutton his trousers and slide them off. He sits up to take off his shirt, and I help pull it off. Then he does the same to my dress, loosening the tie in the back and lifting it over my head. There's nothing left, just our burning bodies, begging for each other.

"Are you sure you're ready?" he asks as he brushes my wild red curls back behind my shoulders.

"I've been ready. Make me yours," I tell him.

"You've always been mine, and you always will be," he says right before he lines himself up and nudges my entrance. I'm still so wet and warm that he slides in easily. There's a pinch of pain as he stretches me wider than I've ever felt before, but it dissipates into pleasure as Sigfried moves slowly in and out of me.

"You feel better than I could have ever imagined," he groans above me, as he pinches his eyes closed and bites his bottom lip.

It feels so good that I can't form words, so all I do is nod in agreement. Chasing the friction I'm craving, I lose all sense of time getting lost in the electric feel of him. Our bodies collide over and over as I ride him. When Sigfried brings his lips to my breasts, zings of lightning zap through my body. His teeth pull at my hard peak, and I come undone once again. "Yes, yes, yes," is all I can say as I get lost in the pleasure flowing through me.

Next thing I know, Siegfried flips us over and pulls my hips up, pressing into me from behind. "You have the most perfect body," he says as he caresses my backside before holding onto my waist. He feels so deep at this angle that I think for a moment maybe I can't take it. I grip the sheets beneath me and hold on for dear life as Siegfried enters me faster and harder.

Nothing has ever felt this good and this right. I squeeze around him, eliciting moans from his mouth before his movements get erratic. "Odette," he whispers like a prayer over and over, except it's me he's worshipping instead of the woodland spirits. Turning my head to look over my shoulder, I watch in fascination as he stills inside of me, only feeling a slight twitching before he wraps an arm around my middle and collapses against me.

We both roll onto our sides, facing each other with heaving chests, trying to catch our breath. Siegfried interlaces my fingers with his and kisses the back of my hand.

"Thank you," he says and kisses me. He stares into my eyes so reverently, like I'm the most precious thing in the world. I've never felt so cherished, so adored, so worshipped. "Do you feel okay? I didn't hurt you, did I?"

"I'm perfect. I'm sure I'll be sore, but that's to be expected, I think. Don't worry," I tell him and I mean it wholeheartedly.

"I hate that I'm leaving in the morning. I want to stay here with you and love you over and over and over again."

"I hate it too," I whisper, my voice beginning to shake with all the emotions I've been holding in. I've never felt so happy and sorrowful at once. Burying my head in the crook of his neck, I try to breathe him in and fight back the tears. But as he pulls me into his embrace and runs his hand down my locks, I can't hold them back.

"I know, I know," he says into my ear, consoling me. "It will be pure torture being apart from you. I swear to you that when I return, we will be together again."

"I hate their stupid rules. How can they keep you secluded for four years and not let anyone visit? It seems cruel to keep everyone away from their family and friends."

"I'll see if I can get my mother to get them to allow me visits, but it may not happen. That has been the rule for centuries upon centuries, unfortunately. Are you sure you don't want to hide in my trunk?"

"Wishful thinking won't get us anywhere. I'm just not ready to say goodbye," I tell him, wiping my eyes.

"Stay the night then. Let me show you the depth of my love until the sun rises."

"I'd like that," I say, as we crash our lips together once again. This time, our movements are not slow and sweet, but frantic and full of the desperation we feel to cling to each other.

We stay tangled up together, loving each other with

everything we have until we are both too spent for more. When the first rays of sunlight stream through the cracks of the drapes, I can't bear the thought of saying goodbye. So, I kiss him one last time before slipping out of his arms. Out of the castle. Out of his life for the unforeseeable future.

Every step away from him feels like wading through mud. I know he'll be upset that I left, but I refuse to say goodbye. My heart already feels like it's shattering, and I don't want him to feel any worse about leaving than he already does. He needs to focus on honing his power and not have me as a distraction.

So, I'll do the same. I'll build my life here, contributing what I can to our kingdom. And I'll hope that the next four years go by like a flash of lightning and pray he'll come back to me.

Continue reading now on Kindle Unlimited: https://mybook.to/NKPMHD

ROMANCING THE REALMS
CHLOE HODGE
COURTING THE FAE CAPTAIN

COURTING THE FAE CAPTAIN

'The Mithrian Fae are among the most ruthless species recorded. Unlike their elemental brethren across the seas, theirs is a race that reveres bloodshed and darker power. If you cross them on a bad day, don't expect to see another.'
-*The Trials and Traditions of a Mithrian Fae*

I had always known I'd never outrun fate ... that didn't mean I couldn't try.

Lightning forked through the sky as I made my way inch by careful inch down the rain-slick slate beneath my bedroom balcony. Thunder roiled; a large crack making me flinch so violently I nearly lost my grip and tumbled to the precarious drop below.

My heart bashed against my ribs. I'd done the climb many times before and was no stranger to the risk, but my fingers were so cold, it was an effort to curl them into the narrow ridges of stone. One wrong move and this foolhardy endeavour would all be for nothing.

But I had to go. My father would ship me off to Domeratt

tomorrow to join a host of other would-be-wives hellbent on marrying the city lord's son—a captain of the Shadow Court's vast naval army, or so I had heard.

Frankly, I couldn't care less what the male's titles and achievements were. I had no desire to vie for his attention. Stories of how highborn fae treated their wives in the Shadow Court had often floated past my ears. The servants in my home liked to gossip over juicy scandals or female misfortune. And, seemingly, there was a lot of that in my homeland. When one was born into a world of immortal necromancers and dark magic wielders, one was bound to get a little more comfortable with death or other ill-fated fortunes.

There were four courts in the fae land of Mithria, each with their own class of magic wielders–Spell Weavers, Soul Speakers, Bone Cleavers or Blood Mages. I belonged to the Shadow Court, though my magic had yet to reveal itself.

I frowned, pressing myself flat against the stone as one of the castle servants reached out to tackle the banging shutters of a bedroom window beside me.

Halfway there. Just a few more balconies to navigate and castle guards to avoid. I'd prepared for this, though. This was a climb I'd timed more than once, considering patrols, guard rotations, and any other disturbances one might find when scaling a damn building as tall as this one.

Ironic, that I was the damsel locked atop my father's tallest tower. Only, he had no idea of the kind of extracurricular activities I got up to when he wasn't looking. Take rock climbing, for example. Not very demure. Not very ladylike.

A slow smile spread across my face. The conditions were less than favourable, but I'd trained enough times in hazardous weather to know the grooves and footholds as well as the back of my hand. Besides, this was just the kind of challenge that made me feel *alive*. The only other time I felt like this was when tinkering with potions and brews.

Alchemy. *That* was my true passion. Something I had done under my father's nose since I was a little girl, and something I had no plans of stopping. Which was exactly why marrying some pompous noble who thought of females only as breeding vessels was not on my list of things to do.

I was nearing the lower levels now. My fingers were turning blue with the cold, but I'd have time to lament the stiffness later. Just a little further and—I froze. Because just below me, bundled up in furs and staring out from the balcony edge, was one of the ladies of court. Melania, judging by the ginger hair wisping out of her braid. And that female? The only thing she loved more than herself was money and power. Or any means in which to get it. If she spotted me ...

I sucked down a breath and forced my teeth to stop chattering as I waited. All she had to do was look up. Why in hells was she outside anyway? The winds were bitter and howling, the cold sinking deep beneath my bones. No one in their right mind would be out here unless ... oh.

A male strode onto the balcony, gathering Melania in his arms as he turned her and claimed her lips. My body went taut. It wouldn't be any real scandal or surprise to see a noble getting cosy with another member of the court, but this was not a male any female had a right to covet.

That was Declan James, Blood Sword of my father's and, more importantly, a married male. Scandal, indeed. If word got out about this affair Melania would be finished. Declan would receive no real punishment, but that's the way it always went with the male fae in Mithria. Bastards.

My muscles were screaming as I held onto the wall for dear life. Sweat bubbled over my back, forming little rivulets that dribbled down my spine. *Please, please just go inside and go back to bed.*

He whispered something in her ear that made her laugh and blush prettily, then he was pulling her back towards his chambers. She protested coyishly, and it took everything in me not to roll my eyes. I'd bet my left tit she was already naked beneath those furs.

Five steps.

Four.

hree.

Two.

I almost heaved a sigh of relief when they took one last step, their heads nearly disappearing beneath the threshold.

Maybe I'd done something to piss off the gods. Maybe it was the boot that slipped ever so slightly out of the groove it was jammed in, but right before that last step, Melania fucking Harron raised those pretty blue eyes and gasped as she found me staring right back at her.

She took in my clothes, the braid, the gaiter pulled up over my face before her eyes slowly moved to my own. Recognition set in before the bitch smiled like it was the best day in her miserable little life.

Melania whispered to Declan, who looked up with piercing blue eyes of his own. He'd always given me the creeps. That male was colder than the deepest frost or the most bitter of winds. And I knew when he looked at me that I was as good as dead.

He swore and stepped indoors briskly, though his face remained a mask of calm. I fucking moved, hightailing it across the wall as fast as I could go. My shot at escaping this hellhole just dropped by half, and the odds were never great to begin with. Declan was not a forgiving male, nor would he forget. Even if I made it safely back to my rooms, I knew he'd eventually come for me and make it look like an accident. Maybe even pay some lowlifes to do the job for him.

My heart thumped; my palms slick and clammy. I could either continue down the wall and run, or find a public place to lay low in. There was no way he could harm me in plain sight of the castle patrons.

I looked longingly at the ground. My future was at stake. My freedom. But what chance did I have of making it out now? My father would be furious with me if I returned and Declan informed him what had happened, but he wouldn't do much more. Not when the Rite was coming up tomorrow. Everything would be swept under a rug and kept hushed. I'd have my life, yes, but what was that really worth if I was never free?

Fuck it. I bypassed the closest balcony and kept descending. The heavens opened, and rain poured down in a sudden torrent of rage. My hair was sodden within seconds, my visibility drastically decreased.

I blinked back the water in my eyes just as Declan reappeared and nocked an arrow to a bow. My heart dropped into my stomach. He wouldn't take me out on the wall, surely? His arrow could be traced back to him, and then where would he be? That evil male looked down at me, took aim, and *smiled*. Terrible and cold, and joyful with the hunt. Oh yes, he fucking would. Perhaps he was a greater asset to my father than I'd realised. Perhaps my father would turn a blind eye for his precious Bloodhound. Declan had never liked me. Maybe covering the affair was just an excuse to shoot me down.

The arrow flew, speeding through the air towards me. And as a scream tore from my lungs, thunder cracked in answer, swallowing any sound. I took one look at that arrow, prayed to any god who might be listening ... then jumped.

Continue reading now on Kindle Unlimited: https://mybook.to/EunI

ROMANCING THE REALMS
MIRANDA JOY
COURTING THE MOON PRIEST

COURTING THE MOON PRIEST

SORAYA

Everyone on the island holds their breath, eyes locked on the night sky. We wait patiently for the twin moons to overlap, forming a single supermoon as they do one night every thirty days.

"Almost," Mariel whispers, gripping my hand tightly in both of hers.

The moons overlap, almost entirely consumed by one another. The moment the second moon is gone from sight—fully nestled into the other—a roar of appreciation rises from the beach. The conjoined moons' glow intensifies, sending radiant waves of iridescent light streaking through the dark sky.

In response, the jungle brightens, glimmering with the gifted power of our goddesses.

"Praise the moons," I whisper, excitement bubbling up in my chest.

The bright silver light casts an ethereal glow across the

island. The rivers shimmer, running down the single verdant mountain and through the jungle like narrow arteries. They all feed into the ocean around us. The currents pulse softly, as if alive. Along the banks, all through the island, the plants harbor the same magical light. Their usually vibrant green coloring mirrors the ribbons of blue-green streaking through the sky beside the newly formed supermoon.

A smile overtakes my face, and my shoulders soften. Mariel drops my hands, throwing her arms around me.

"Blessed Union, Soraya," she squeals in my ear. I squeeze her back, and she pulls free. Music starts playing, and the gratitude of the villagers is palpable. "I'm going to snag us some nectar. I'll be right back."

She bounds off toward the hut at the edge of the sand, waving animatedly at everyone she passes. Most of us were born and raised on the Isle de Lunith, and we're a fairly tight-knit community.

Strong arms snake around my waist, startling me. The scent of salt and earth, mixed with a familiar musk, invades my nose, and I chuckle.

"This dress does things to me," Joss murmurs into my neck, invading my personal space.

Swatting his arms away, I turn to face him. Moonlight dances on the droplets lining his deeply tanned chest. He runs a hand through his short brown hair, slicking it back. It glistens from his dip in the ocean. His lips raise into a teasing grin, and my expression softens, mirroring his.

I playfully roll my eyes. "We're all wearing the same thing."

Gesturing around the beach, I take in the various celestial servants scattered on the beach, mingling with the rest of the island's population. Everyone drinks, dances, and feasts tonight, celebrating the moons' union.

The priests and priestesses are easy to pick out, all dressed in similar wispy, lightweight garments in the color of the moons—pale silvers and off-whites. Some don cascading gossamer gowns with thin straps, others have flowy pants with billowing arms, but they're all variations of the same look with cascading layers.

"No," he says, arching a light-brown brow. "You certainly are not." His fingers trail up my covered collarbone until his hand lands on my exposed shoulder. "I like *yours* best."

Planting my hands on his bare chest, I gently push him back. "We talked about this!"

"I thought we were friends." He fake pouts, running his fingers through his wet hair.

"Exactly—*friends*."

He gives me a broad, charming grin. "And I'm honoring your wishes… by being very friendly."

I can't help but laugh and roll my eyes, amused by his quick quip. "You know damn well what I mean, Joss Thalor!"

"It's impossible to keep my hands off you." He groans. "I miss you already."

It's my own fault for blurring the boundaries between us. I might've ended our official relationship, but I haven't kept him out of my bed.

I shake my head, scanning the beach for Mariel. She's out of sight, likely having made her way into the hut for our drinks. As much fun as Joss is, I ended things for a reason. No matter how handsome, kind, and funny he is, I just don't want *more*.

Not the same way he does.

My eyes flit to the moons. I want a love like *theirs*. Lore says the two moons were previously goddesses who sacrificed their mortal forms and cursed themselves, all to spend eternity together, hung in the skies side-by-side, only kissing once per month.

They're forever suspended overhead, only shifting to touch on Union Night and separating by morning.

I don't necessarily want their fate, but the thought of a passionate, all-consuming, eternal love lingers in the back of my mind. With Joss, things are comfortable, but the thought of being without him doesn't steal my breath.

When I glance over at him, he's staring out at the dark ocean, all the previous humor gone. My heart spasms violently. We've been there for each other our whole lives, including when he lost his mother to the very sea he loves.

The guilt gnaws at me, and I step beside him. I nudge him with my elbow. "Wanna go find some silverdew?"

The flower, indigenous to the Isle de Lunith, only opens at night. Though it sprouts in abundance, it's a cherished flower, mainly because it's our primary export and the source of our island's income.

It can be tapped for nectar—the delightful, fruity brew we enjoy for a buzz. It also provides a more intense, euphoric high when the petals unfurl and the pollen is snorted.

Joss shoots me a crooked smile. "Later? I'm going to catch another quick dip with the other tideborn—before they get too nectared."

Squeezing his hand in understanding, I nod. When he leaves, I dig my feet into the cool, packed sand, watching the water gently lick the shore. With my back to the revelry, I take this moment to myself to just *be*.

My lungs fill with fresh, salty air with a fruity tinge. It smells like home—like *everything*.

I love Union Night. Not only for the obvious—the energetically charged revelry, the merriment, the magic—but because I feel as if I'm truly one with the island. Fingering a strand of teal hair, I smile down at the color, feeling less like an outcast because of its unnatural hue and more like I'm an integral part of the ecosystem.

Shoving my hair over my shoulder, I squint, catching the faint ring of the smaller moon as it nestles in front of its larger counterpart. One night a month, when the moons align, the Isle de Lunith comes alive with magic. Even though I've experienced it twelve times a year for twenty-six years, it never ceases to fill me with awe.

Amazement tickles my insides, and my heart pulses in time with the flickering fireflies lighting up the beach.

Familiar faces play the shell horns, blowing merrily into the seashells as they sway to the music. Drums and stringed instruments accompany them, blending into a tune that instills a need to move. It's melodic and hypnotic. A group of celestial servants throw their limbs around as they release pent-up energy in dance. Others chant in groups, leaning into gratitude mantras to thank the goddess moons for their protection.

Every soul dances barefoot on the sand, connecting intimately with the land, and celebrating another night—another month—of life-sustaining magic.

Every soul except for one.

I gaze toward the temple atop the tallest hill, which settles into the trees far beyond the village. It's where the celestial servants live and work—the point of the island closest to the moons. Even from this distance, I glimpse a hint of light sparkling from the top where the moonstone lives, absorbing the energy on this powerful night as it does during every Union.

Sparkling waters crest over the stony side, feeding into our rivers.

"You'd think out of everyone, *he* would be down here celebrating," Mariel yells, thrusting a drink at me.

"Where have you been?" I graciously accept the beverage, wrapping my lips around the bamboo straw peeking out of the coconut shell. The fruity, slightly sour tang of nectar washes over my tongue, and I close my eyes to revel in it for a moment.

"Maybe one day he'll stop thinking he's too good for us," she says bitterly.

A soft sigh escapes my lips as I open my eyes and face my best friend. "You know how he is, Mariel."

"*Reclusive*," she says sarcastically.

My lips press into a thin line as my head swivels toward her. "Hush." I glance around to ensure no one's eavesdropping on her talking poorly about High Priest Raziel Kasper. Granted, I've heard enough whispers to know many of the villagers think the same way. "He's our Moon Priest."

"Exactly." She lowers her voice, but the way she slurs tells me she's already had a little too much fun during tonight's celebration. "With how up the moons' butts he is, you'd expect him to show face during the most sacred night of the month."

"I'm sure he celebrates in his own way." I squint at the temple, unable to understand why he'd choose to skip the Union. The High Priests before him were known for flashing their magic on this sacred night. He's an enigma for hiding his powers from the islanders.

She snorts. "I'm not the only one who notices his attitude."

Mariel isn't wrong about him being a bit of a recluse, but he's our island's Highest Keeper. *The* Moon Priest. The Goddesses' Anointed. The moons chose him to oversee the magic and, thus, the life of our island.

Yet, he snubs every ceremony.

Mariel raises her drink to the moon, and her bracelets clink together noisily overhead. She throws her head back, closes her eyes, and lets out a *whoop*.

"To the moons!" she yells.

"Praise the moons," I say with a soft laugh.

"Hey, there's your man." Mariel nudges me with her elbow.

I turn to catch Joss heading toward us. He charges the last few steps toward me, and despite his bare feet sinking into the soft sand, it barely slows him down. His muscular arms wrap around me, squeezing me as he playfully nibbles on my neck.

"Joss," I chastise, swatting at him. "You're getting me wet!"

"I wish," he murmurs.

He spins me around, and some of my nectar splashes over the side. The sheer, wispy bottom half of my gown floats around me, the slits parting to reveal my bronzed legs, toned from my daily treks up and down the temple's archive stairwells. The delicate silver chains crisscrossing my midsection hold the dress in place with effortless grace. The tiny star and moon charms tinkle with the movement.

I laugh. "Put me down!"

He obliges, placing me back on my feet. I stumble, quickly reorienting myself and adjusting my neckline to ensure my chest is fully covered.

"What are you two talking about?" Joss's green eyes twinkle with jest.

I'm glad to see he's swum his previous sorrows away. The grief hits him from time to time, and though I can't relate in the same way, I know what it's like to miss a mother. Unlike him, I never knew mine, though. Where he misses a person, I miss the idea of one.

Mariel, having refocused her attention on us, smirks with amusement. Her dress matches mine, but where mine is high in the front and plunging in the back, hers is the opposite, showcasing her glorious cleavage. The pale coloring contrasts beautifully with her brown skin and dark curls.

The outfits are symbolic, marking us as priestesses of the moon—a reminder of who we are and who we serve.

The Moon Priest.

My eyes flick back in the temple's direction. I find it rather blasphemous to talk poorly of him or the moons he protects. That *we* protect. Mariel, on the other hand, loves instigating and stirring up the 'monotony of our island'—her words, not mine.

"We're not talking about anything," I tell a waiting Joss. "Hey, would you mind grabbing me another nectar? Please?"

Joss gives me a broad smile and then glances at Mariel.

"Make that two?" Mariel says, twisting a curl of dark hair around her finger.

Joss thumbs us up, then jogs off toward the Nectar Hut— our beach tavern.

His muscles flex with power, only the tiny fabric of his hemp water shorts covering his ass.

"Your boyfriend is a delight," Mariel says. She grabs my hand, tugging me through the sand, closer to where the band plays their live instruments.

"You know we broke up." I raise my voice so she can hear me over the melody.

She whirls toward me, rolling her hips to the tempo as she raises a brow. "I saw him sneaking out of your bed this morning."

"Yeah, but we're not—"

"You *always* find your way back to each other." She spins, arms overhead, and her face tilted to the sky with glee.

"This is different, Mar." Shaking my head, I give up and let the music sink into my bones. I move naturally, matching Mariel's steps.

"He would've bonded with you in a heartbeat."

I flush at the thought of completing the Union ceremony

with Joss—on a night like tonight, when such bonding events occur. I'd be lying if I said I hadn't imagined it a thousand times over.

I shake my head, and a few tendrils of hair fall into my face. "I don't want that—we're better as friends."

"No," she says sternly, gesturing from me to her as she dances. "*We* are better as just friends. That man is better as a husband, and you know it, Soraya."

"It was never serious." I stop moving to the music and dig my toes into the sand instead.

She snorts. "He loves you something fierce."

I kick a hearty amount of sand at her legs. She squeals, kicking sand back at me.

Joss appears with our drinks, cutting the conversation short. Mariel teases him about something, but his eyes stay locked on me. I flush under his attention, hating that I'm letting both of my best friends down with my decision.

Not wanting to think about it, I fiddle mindlessly with my straw and return my attention to the temple, catching the light refracting from the moonstone atop.

Everyone around me is focused on the music, the moon, or the drinks, socializing and dancing in spades. Though the source of the magic comes from the sky, the moonstone nestled in the temple's summit is the heart of our island. It absorbs the pulsating magic sent down from the goddess moons, after all. Without it, there would be no magic. No island.

Suddenly, the gleaming light flickers out, and the top of the temple goes dark. My heart trips over itself, and I nearly drop my nectar.

"Joss," I yell, grasping his arm tightly with my free hand.

He stops mid-conversation, turning to me with concern etched into his features. "What is it?"

"The moonstone." I turn back to the temple, raising my hand to point, but the soft glow has returned, wavering hazily above the temple.

"What about it?" The worry leaves his voice, and he gives me a curious look.

"She's obsessed with that thing," Mariel says, giggling. "Overcome by its sheer beauty from time to time."

"I can understand what that's like," he says wistfully, his gaze boring into me.

Mariel giggles.

Sighing, I glance down at my drink, shaking my head. I take a long pull, finishing it off in one go while my friends cheer.

"Nevermind," I whisper, blinking stupidly in the direction it sits. It flickered for a moment—I swear it. Or maybe I had too much nectar, and my eyes are playing tricks. My lips stay sealed, not wanting to rouse unnecessary fear on a sacred night, but sweat beads on my spine.

My hand rises to the center of my chest, mindlessly hovering there.

Joss and Mariel laugh at something, talking animatedly. None of their words stick in my brain. Instead, my eyes stay glued to the temple as if I might catch the moonstone winking again.

"I should check on the High Priest," I say in a rush, interrupting their conversation.

Mariel looks at me as if I've lost my mind.

"Is he sick?" Joss asks with a frown. "We have our island assembly tomorrow."

I shake my head. "Something just feels *off*." The words are weak—strange—even to my own ears.

"Ooookay." Mariel takes the coconut out of my hand, tossing it onto the beach. "No more nectar for you. Let's dance it off." She grips my hand and tugs me closer toward the shore, where waves gently caress the packed sand. "Come on, Joss!"

We navigate the merriment, smiling and nodding at everyone we pass.

A pit of dread builds in my stomach, but I don't fight my friends. I can't make sense of my feelings on my own, let alone verbalize them. Instead, I allow Mariel and Joss to sandwich me as we sway our hips in rhythm to the drumbeat.

We drink more nectar, and later, when Joss's hands snake around my waist, threatening to steal me away to the bushes, I let him.

My eyes continue to flick toward the temple, and the unsettled feeling lingers, even though I try my best to let Joss *distract* me.

Continue reading now on Kindle Unlimited: https://mybook.to/lmxJAj